AF260538

THE LEAPER

Lorn Macintyre was born in Taynuilt, Argyll, and spent formative years on the Isle of Mull, both places being the inspiration for his poetry and prose and his exposure to Gaelic culture. His doctorate on Sir Walter Scott and the Highlands shows how that area of Scotland was romanticised and misrepresented in literature by 'the Wizard of the North,' with lasting detriment. Lorn is the author of the *Chronicles of Invernevis*, about a Highland landed family, of which four in the series of novels have been published. He has published two acclaimed collections of short stories based on his years on Mull and its characters, including his own legendary father Angus, poet, bank manager and obsessed Gael. Lorn's poetry, like his fiction, records and laments the disappearance of a traditional way of life, with accompanying decline in the Gaelic language, and the exploitation of the environment, with some wildlife under threat of extinction through the use of chemicals. Lorn's website is at <www.lornmacintyre. co.uk>

THE LEAPER

LORN MACINTYRE

GRACE NOTE PUBLICATIONS

The Leaper
© Lorn Macintyre 2017

ISBN 978-1-907676-91-8

The right of Lorn Macintyre to be identified as the proprietor of this work has been asserted
by him in accordance with the Copyright, Designs and Patents Act 1988

Front cover photo Calgary Bay, Isle of Mull
© Margaret Bennett Collection 2005

www.gracenotepublications.co.uk

Grateful Thanks

To Mary, devoted spouse and supporter,
to Ian MacDonald, friend and Gael,
and to Erica Hollis, skilled proofreader

Èiridh tonn air uisge balbh
A wave will rise on quiet water.
(Gaelic proverb)

One

'Buntàta 's sgadan.'

The old man had requested potatoes and herring for supper as if the Gaelic feast were already in his mouth that May day in 1983. Seumas had dug up the big potatoes he had planted, washing them under the tap in the chipped stone sink in the scullery. He filled a pot from the sea to cook the herring he had been given off a boat in the town because you couldn't catch them any more with feathered hooks off Rubha nan Ròn. While supper was cooking on the open flames of the range he spread the local paper out on the table, then carried the two pots through to the scullery to drain them, returning to tumble out their contents into two heaps on the paper before helping the old man to the table.

After his stroke the old man's right arm was like a useless flipper across his chest. Once the most sure-footed of men, especially in a pitching boat, he now lurched to the table as if he had a cargo of whisky in him. They sat opposite each other, using only their hands. The old man picked up a potato, imprinted with ink from the death notices, breaking it in his fingers and when the steam had escaped he put a piece into his mouth before peeling the silver skin from the fish and breaking off a portion.

'Tha seo blasta,' this is tasty, he pronounced.

The old man was wearing an open shirt and trousers with braces, sagging at the waist, like a clown's outfit, completed by his bulbous red nose. He had sandshoes without laces on his feet for the comfort of his corns. He wasn't tall but he had wide shoulders and had been a ferocious fighter in his time, on one memorable occasion, stripped to the waist in a blizzard, taking on two big men off a Fleetwood trawler and thrashing them. As his son fondly watched him eating he smiled at the thought that the old man looked like a seal, with his bald head, his whiskers, and no neck on the powerful physique. He was eating potatoes and herring, representing the two toils of his life, the earth and the sea. There was a little pile of fish skins by his left hand, but he ate the potato skins, with the dark soil in their crevices. He was laying the fish bones at the edge of the paper as if engaged in creating an intricate puzzle.

'*Tha mi dol don taigh-bheag,*' I'm going to the little house, the old man announced suddenly, hobbling towards the door.

Dìleas, faithful, the collie dog, came back alone ten minutes later, whining and pawing Seumas's foot. He ran round the corner of the house. The old man had fallen asleep in the stifling *taigh-beag,* on the plank with the hole in it, his head on his chest, trousers round his sandshoes, a bluebottle sounding mournfully in the enamel pail under him.

'*Tiugainn,*' come along, the son coaxed gently, catching the old man's hand.

The old man pitched forward, his face among the *buidheagan an t-samhraidh,* the buttercup, little yellow one of the summer, on the bank of Allt a' Ghobha-Uisge, the burn of the water ouzel, as it swung behind the house on its way down to the bay. Seumas knelt, turning the old man over and opening his shirt before putting his mouth to the old man's white moustache and trying to pump life back into his chest. Seventy three years of the scent of peat fires were ingrained in his skin. But the old man was getting cold, and his eyes had rolled up into his head as if to show that he was finished with the world. The doctor would have to walk over the hill to tell the son something he already knew, that his *athair* had gone, and the undertaker would have to come to measure him, then take the coffin over the moor on a hired tractor. He couldn't afford it.

He wiped the old man's *tòn* with torn-up newspaper from the rusty nail in the *taigh-beag* and carried him on his back, grasping him by the wrists, the sandshoes slithering through the grass in which the ticking of the grasshopper sounded like a lost watch. He removed the old man's clothes and sat him naked on the plain wooden chair in front of the fire, holding him in place with a length of rope wound round his chest and secured to the chair back. He used the hot water in the kettle to wash the old man tenderly, as though he were an infant, taking a wet cloth to the moustache to get the pieces of his last feast of herring out of it. He thought about shaving him, but it would be difficult, the way his head kept slumping forward.

Seumas went upstairs and brought down the only suit the old man had possessed and the white shirt last worn for his wife's funeral, but leaving off the black tie. He dressed the old man, putting the sandshoes back on his bare feet. He pulled in the dinghy on the rope and waded out to it with the old man on his back. He had to take the dog on this final journey because she had been the old man's and because she adored her dead master, which was why Dìleas, whom the old man claimed understood Gaelic like a human, was whimpering and licking the old man's ankles.

He transferred the corpse to the launch and laid out the old man between the seats with one of his creels as a pillow. The old man whose name was Murchadh, Murdo, had made the creel on the shore in a long-ago summer, bending the steamed hazel wands over the flat stone for ballast on the board, then plying the big wooden needle to make the lattice pattern with the twine before brushing on the pungent pitch from the pot.

Seumas lifted the cover off the engine and jerked the cord, standing at the tiller as he headed across the bay, round Rubha nan Ròn, the Promontory of the Seals, where the old man had always shot his creels because he said that an iron ship had gone down there in his grandfather's time and that the holds gave the lobsters shelter to grow big. The old man and he had worked side by side pulling up the slimed ropes, talking in Gaelic about other things because it was a rarity then for a creel not to contain a lobster. Seumas had seen two lobsters in the one creel, their claws so tangled in combat that the old man couldn't separate them and had to sacrifice the smaller one.

But the lobsters were small now, and some had dark mottling on their shells which the buyer wouldn't touch because he said that the top people in the London restaurants wouldn't pay for blemishes on shellfish delivered whole to their tables.

The launch with his father's corpse stiffening across the seats, his moustache dripping with spray, the dog lying beside her master as if her body heat could bring him back to life, passed the fish farm on the port side, Sgeir nan Eun, the Skerry of the Birds, to starboard. The town (though it hardly merited the status, because there were only six hundred inhabitants) was two miles round the treacherous coast and when the launch puttered to the steps beside the pier he left the body in it and went into the telephone box, but there was no book to give him the doctor's number, so he had to phone directory enquiries. The doctor's receptionist said that he was out on a call.

'Can I take a message?'

'It's Seumas Macdonald here. My father's just died and I brought him round in the boat.'

The receptionist asked him to repeat what he had just said.

'He's lying in your boat at the pier?' she reiterated incredulously.

'Yes. I brought him round because there's no road to the house for the undertaker.'

'I think you should phone the police,' the receptionist advised.

'I haven't murdered him.'

'I'm not suggesting that, but there are procedures.'

He put down the receiver and went into the shipping office on the pier, asking if he could borrow a bogie.

'What's it for, Seumas?' the bemused clerk, who had been in school with him, wanted to know.

'To move something. I'll bring it back soon.'

He was given the key to the building where the goods that used to come on the cargo boat from Glasgow had been stored when he was a boy in the 1950s, but everything came by road now, on the big vehicular and passenger ferry at the other end of the island, and the bogies hadn't been used in years. He trundled one to the top of the steps, lifted his athair behind the knees and round the shoulders from the launch like a sleeping infant and laid him on the bogie. He removed his own jacket, covering the old man's face and chest before pulling the bogie behind him along Main Street, its wheels a mournful groan. People leaning out of windows and spectating on the pavement were laughing, assuming that the man on the bogie with the dog lying snugly beside him was drunk and incapable, and someone even hurried for a camera. He wheeled the bogie along to Caldwell the undertaker's shop at the far end of Main Street.

'My father's dead,' Seumas informed him.

Caldwell looked up from his work at the bench in the corrugated shed, a wood shaving curled like a question mark in the plane.

'I'm sorry to hear that. What do you want me to do?'

'I need a coffin for him.'

'I'll come to the house tonight to measure him.'

'You don't need to. I've brought him.'

'Jesus Christ, man, have you no respect for the dead?' the undertaker challenged him when he saw the corpse on the bogie outside his shed.

'See that you measure him right,' Seumas cautioned him.

'What's that supposed to mean?' the undertaker asked truculently.

Caldwell no longer made the coffins for the island because it was cheaper and easier to order one from the mainland. It was said that he had made a mistake in measuring a corpse after he had one too many whiskies, and when the coffin arrived, Caldwell didn't want to hold on to it for the next corpse that would fit it, nor did he want to pay for the coffin's shipment back to Glasgow, so he snapped the neck, forcing down the lid. Others insisted that the story was a calumny, and that Caldwell treated the deceased with care and respect.

'How much will the coffin cost?' Seumas enquired after he had held the tape at his father's feet so that Caldwell could measure him.

'It's not only the coffin. The remains have to be stored, the grave dug – assuming you have a lair.'

'He's going in beside my mother.'

'Do you want me to order flowers?'

'No flowers.'

'In total, then, let's say two hundred and fifty.'

'You'll get your money,' Seumas promised him.

As they were talking the police car arrived because the doctor's receptionist had phoned.

'What's going on here?' the sergeant demanded, seeing the corpse on the bogie.

'My father died an hour or so ago and I brought him round to the undertaker,' the son informed the officer of the law.

'I've never seen anything like this, not even in the years I spent in one of the worst parts of Glasgow among the gangs,' the sergeant, who belonged to the mainland, judged, pushing back his cap, as if scratching his forehead would bring clarity to his brain. 'There's going to have to be a post mortem.'

'I didn't kill him, and I don't want him taken to the mainland, to be cut up like a pig,' Seumas reacted angrily. 'He was old and he had a strained heart from lifting creels.'

'I'm going to have to sort this out with Dr Murray,' the sergeant concluded, perplexed. 'Meantime I'll phone for the ambulance and get the deceased taken to the mortuary at the old folks' home. I'll let you know the outcome,' he said, turning to Seumas.

He went along the street to the bank, an imposing building. He had been in it with his father, when the old man had a cheque from the sale of lobsters which he needed cashed. They would be standing, waiting to be served at the sloping wooden counter when Alan Maclachan the manager came through from his office. This wasn't a chance meeting. It was the day that the manager wrote his weekly reports for head office on the overdrafts he had granted. He sat at the large manual machine, typing with two fingers, two keys colliding in mid-air and having to be clawed down, the wide carriage slammed back for the new line, the ribbon becoming more and more ragged with the force of his strikes as he underlined (using the red part of the ribbon) his assertion that the security of the loan was undoubted, though no repayments had been made for months. Round his shoes were scattered spoiled sheets of paper. The faceless man in head office who read these reports shook his head in sympathy at the lyrical account of the fictitious storm that had prevented the farmer from getting decent prices at the mainland sales, and therefore funds (a head office word), to repay some of the alarming interest accruing on the customer's unsecured loan.

Alan Maclachan rose from the typewriter and stood at the window for an inspirational cigarette before introducing the avid reader in an unprepossessing office in Glasgow to the next character in the saga. The clerkess had strict instructions not to disturb him on the day of the reports, but when he saw the fisherman and his son coming up the steps into the bank he went through to the counter. He knew the fishing family who lived along the coast and kept to themselves. He also knew that they were among the few remaining Gaelic speakers on the island, and since he was obsessed with his native language, there was always a seat for a speaker in his office, even though the occupant of the chair didn't have a penny in the bank.

He greeted the two Macdonalds in Gaelic.

'What can I do for you?' he asked in the same fluent tongue.

When the old man explained that he needed a cheque cashed, though he didn't have an account in the bank, the manager did something he never did with any other customers: he went behind the counter and took charge of the transaction, counting the notes in his hand with a red pimpled sheath on his thumb with a speed Seumas marvelled at, the notes blurred, like the whirring wing of a bird taking off in flight.

'Come on through,' he invited them, holding the door open to the empty office and patting the dog.

He kept a bottle of whisky and glasses in the bottom drawer of his desk for favoured customers, meaning Gaelic speakers with a *sgeulachd*, a tale, or even *fothal*, gossip, to tell, but without hurrying, even though a Colonel was waiting at the counter for an audience in which to ask for an increase to his already massive overdraft, having discovered yet more leaks in the roof of his dilapidated mansion.

But Alan Maclachan had died in 1979. The new manager was called Smythe. He was from the south, without a word of Gaelic, and in contrast to Alan Maclachan's untidy tweed suits, he wore sharp pinstripes.

'The manager's busy,' the female assistant, her bank's logo on the cravat, repeated.

'I'll not bother,' Seumas told her.

He went along to the hotel. His best friend Donnie Morrison had left school even before the legal age. He had become an apprentice in the garage because he was obsessed with engines. He had been driving his father's tractor since he was ten, sometimes taking it out on to the main road and putting it through its paces as if it were a car. Donnie could get engines started that Nicholson the boss of the garage had given up on. But when oil had started to be extracted from the North Sea Donnie had gone out to the rigs as a fitter, sticking it out through storms and brawls. On a weekend's leave to Glasgow he had met a woman from a well-off family. Her father had added a dowry to Donnie's savings so that he could buy the local hotel from the couple who had been letting it run down for years. Donnie had received considerable grants to do up the hotel to attract tourists, putting in private bathrooms and a cocktail bar with recessed lights and high stools, tapes playing Sinatra songs to put the drinkers in the mood for more.

Donnie came through, his gut spilling out over the waistband of his trousers.

'What can I do for you, my friend?'

'The old man's died, and I need to arrange the funeral.'

'I'm sorry to hear about your father. He was the last of the characters in this town.'

Every month for years the man from the Pearl had tramped over the moor to collect the premium, marking the books of the insurance policies in the old man and Màthair's names because Seumas's parents couldn't bear the shame of the parish having to bury them.

'How do I get the money for this?' Seumas asked, placing the old man's policy on the reception desk in front of Donnie, who unfolded the ragged document.

'It's for £100. How much is the funeral going to cost?'

'Caldwell wants two hundred and fifty.'

'That man's a robber of the living and the dead. You can get a death grant from the Government, but it's very small. When I buried my father two years ago we got £15. So you're a hundred and fifty short, which I don't suppose you have. I'll lend it to you, and I'll phone up Neil Matheson the Pearl man and tell him to come and pick up this policy and arrange for you to get the money for it.'

'They'll take him to the mainland for a post mortem,' Seumas informed his friend anxiously.

'I'll have a word with Dr Murray and tell him it would be a travesty if they took your father to the mainland, when he died of natural causes. When Caldwell has the funeral notice printed, tell him to bring me a copy and I'll put it up in the bar.'

Two

After leaving Donnie Seumas went to the undertaker to assure him that he would get his money for burying the old man. He returned the bogie to the pier and went along to the shop. Dogs weren't allowed, so Dìleas sat patiently on the pavement. When Seumas was a boy a local couple had run the shop and all the business was done in Gaelic. Macphail had worn a white apron wrapped round his lean frame from his chest to his boots, with a pencil behind his ear as if it were an additional visible bone. The tin of Carrs Biscuits was tilted on a stand and Seumas had pressed his face to its glass top, salivating over the dark chocolate. Once Macphail had opened the top and given him a biscuit, and the taste had lingered in his mouth into his sleep, when he dreamed that the lid was off the box and he was consuming the entire contents, his fingers and mouth covered in dark chocolate. Màthair always went to the lidless box at the end, plain biscuits broken in transit and sold cheaply by the handful.

Macphail cut the cheese with a wire with the precision of a surgeon making an incision. The streaky bacon fell away from the slithering wheel into his palm, slice by slice, to be slapped on to the paper, the brass weights moved on the scales as if he were playing a swift game of chess with himself. The pencil was detached from the ear and did the sum heavily on a paper bag, all the time talking in Gaelic to Màthair.

It was a Spar shop now, with steel shelves, run by an English couple. The biscuits came in packets with easy open strips and the cheese was sealed in plastic, with a sell-by date. Seumas took a box of tea bags because there were no packets of leaf and asked the surly girl at the till for an ounce of cigarette tobacco and a packet of papers.

He went out on to Main Street with his plastic bag. The town had been founded as a fishing station because of its sheltered bay. The old man claimed that he could have walked across the decks of the boats from one side of the harbour to the other when he was a boy, and that everyone spoke Gaelic in those days. Young women had come from other islands and from round the Scottish coast to gut the herring landed from the groaning derricks off the fleet of boats. The gutters stood from dawn until darkness with their sure blades, but the ice and preserving salt in the barrels they packed the herring into opened up hacks on their hands which, even bound with rags, were agony. Màthair had been one of the herring girls, but instead of following the boats round the coast she had married the old man.

There were only a couple of small fishing boats in the bay now, and the few old people who had Gaelic scarcely used it because there was hardly anyone to speak it with. Seumas recalled with affection the bank manager, at his habitual stance at the window, on the lookout for native speakers, knocking the pane to call them in for a dram or cup of tea and a lengthy conversation, though there were impatient impecunious customers waiting to see him.

Seumas was passing a row of fishermen's cottages where the old man had had many ceilidhs with *sgeulachdan*, stories, and songs when he was a young man in the 1930s, but now they had security locks on the doors and double glazing to keep out the sounds of the sea. They were owned by English speaking incomers who used them for holiday homes, which meant that local young couples couldn't get accommodation. It made Seumas angry, and he wanted to kick in the gate with the name Seaview. Gaelic was the language he had first learned, the only language spoken in the home. The old man had had very little English, and when he was forced to go into it he became confused and breathless, as though about to suffer a heart attack, as if *Beurla*, the English tongue, was causing an arterial blockage.

Seumas went back down to the launch and started the engine. It was getting dark and the flocks were returning to Sgeir nan Eun for the night, its splintered precipice white with their shit. The dog was sitting upright in the bow, vigilant as if she were the navigator. The man at the tiller knew the exact distance to keep from the coast to avoid the rocks and use the least fuel because he had been handling the launch since he was a boy and the tiller was like an extra arm as he swept into their bay. There had always been a light in the window, but Màthair was gone four years, and now the old man too, who would have been waiting for his supper in the chair with the burst webbing trailing on the flagstoned floor by his sandshoes, a hole cut at one big toe to give relief to the corn, carved at with his open razor, but always growing again, hard as stone, though steeped in a basin filled with the sea.

He moored the launch, lashing the tiller. Dìleas leapt into the dinghy before he stepped in to row himself ashore with powerful even strokes. The house was always cold now. Màthair had kept a peat fire burning in the grate, a kettle near to the boil. He struck a flame as he went to the sideboard, lifting the globe of the paraffin lamp carefully. The flame wavered, but filled the fragile mantle. The worst thing that could happen on a winter night was the mantle suddenly collapsing on its wire frame, the membrane flaking to a white powder and no spare in the house, when they had to make do with a candle.

There was enough fire left in the grate to boil the kettle. Having fed Dìleas, the metal dish containing rabbit, a habitual meal but always appreciated, clattering under her snout on the flagstoned floor, Seumas sat in the chair that had been the old man's. The former occupant's pipe was lying on the grate where he had put it down that afternoon when he hadn't come back from the *taigh-beag*. He picked up the pipe and opened the punctured metal cap on its hinge. The last fill of tobacco was still in the bowl narrowed by carbon, the stem bitten through where it had been clenched between the old man's false teeth. One day Seumas would smoke this pipe, but it wasn't time yet, so he put it back where the old man had laid it down for his last feast of *buntàta 's sgadan*. The bereft son made himself a cigarette in tapered paper.

The house was two up, two down, with a slated roof. The pine on the dovetailed walls was under layers of yellow paint which Màthair had applied every five years, leaving the door and window open so that the sea breeze would dry her interior decoration before he and the old man came home for their supper.

There had never been enough money to do up the house in the lifetimes of his parents and besides, it would have been too much disturbance. There was no question of electricity: to bring a cable two miles over the moor would have cost a fortune which the estate wouldn't pay. Her son had once shown Màthair a magazine with a picture of a blue coloured Aga cooker, with insulated lids to retain the heat of the four cooking plates, and the promise that it would stay on all night, burning the minimum of fuel, but she looked at it fearfully as if she were in danger of losing the range she knew inside out, finely adjusting the vents to catch the breeze, trimming it as if it were a sailboat.

'It would take us a hundred years to pay that off,' màthair told her son, putting the illustration of the blue stove in the grate installed by his grandfather.

Màthair had lost half her body weight in a month and had to be taken to hospital. They offered to send two men across the moor with a stretcher, but it was easier on her for her son to take her by boat. When he carried her down to the shore, her frail arms round his neck, she weighed no more than a small sack of the whelks which he and the old man gathered at low tide. The dog had come with them on that final journey, and as he came into the bay and saw the ambulance backed down on the pier, its doors open, Seumas started to weep. He would have gone with her to the old folks' home twenty miles away, but he had to go back to look after the old man, who was bewildered and distressed at the disappearance of his wife after so many years. The old man had felt the lump the size and hardness of a small turnip under her nightdress, but believed that it was a benign growth like the type he had found on his cow and cut away with his open razor without any ill-effects. His people had always been good with animals, and men had walked horses and cows miles to the dwelling by the sea to have their animals treated by the surgeon whose gifts came not from books but from God, leeches and *lusan*, medicines prepared from plants and herbs on bog and shore.

The lid of the kettle was lifting now and Seumas made tea with a tasteless bag, spooning it out and throwing it among the ashes. He punctured the can of condensed milk with the dagger of the tin opener and switched on the radio. It was a Gaelic request programme, and as he drank his tea he listened to the song about a drowned lover. The wireless (the name by which the old man and Màthair called it) had been the most precious item in their house, apart from the Gaelic Bible, because it linked them with Gaelic elsewhere. He had sat by himself on the school bus in the 1950s, the recharged glass accumulator between his boots, terrified that a fight would break out and that the accumulator would be knocked over, its power spilt over the floor. The track passed through a bog, but he could have walked it blindfolded, his boots swishing through the wet heather as he carried the accumulator so carefully, never ceasing to marvel that its acidic interior contained a week of sweet Gaelic choirs and soloists, like the tiny people Màthair claimed lived under mounds on the moor. The old man buffed the terminals with a matchbox and then the wireless came alive.

The old man sat smiling, the nape of his neck against the chair, his pipe with the punctured tin cap going, as if he were relishing a symphony orchestra in a concert hall, not listening to a woman from Harris singing a lament about the treacherous sea on a windy night which made the wireless crackle and hiss as if contact was going to be lost any second.

His parents would applaud at the end of a song, and sometimes they sang together in time to the wireless. One New Year they had danced a waltz to Bobby MacLeod's accordion band on the flagged floor, Màthair's head on the old man's shoulder, with that beatific smile on his face as he steered her round the table to the Gaelic tunes, with the same sureness as he took the boat through skerries.

When the accumulator was flat or a lightning storm interfered with reception, they talked in Gaelic. Seumas would sit at the table covered in the oilcloth, doing his homework by the light of the lamp, hoping that the mantle would collapse and he could put away his jotter. The old man would begin telling a story which he had heard from his own father sitting in the same chair and which the old man had narrated so many times that he had it word perfect. He told it slowly, his fingers locked together, hands away from his chest as if he were praying, a smile on his lips.

Sometimes the old man would pause, not because he had forgotten what was coming, but because he was struck by the mellifluous sound of the word he had just said, waiting for its music to fade in his head before going on. He looked regal, in that chair, like a high king with his white head and locked knuckles. He told the classic tale of Deirdre and Naoise. She was due to marry King Conor of Ulster, but fell in love with Naoise, one of the sons of Uisneach, a champion of the Red Branch of Ulster. The two lovers fled to Scotland, and the old man's evocative Gaelic described how they had lived in bliss in a bower on Loch Etive-side in Argyll. The old man whistled the three-note call of the *trìlleachan*, the sandpiper that had wakened the lovers in the dawn, and he blew between his thumbs to make the hoot of the *cailleach-oidhche*, the old woman of the night, the owl, that sent them to sleep in each other's arms. The old man's voice slowed and lowered in caution as he told how King Conor had enticed the lovers home to Erin with a promise of safety, with Deirdre warning against a return. However, she followed Naoise to Ulster, where he was murdered through the King's treachery.

The old man's voice rose in anger as he narrated how Conor had taken Deirdre by force, then dropped to a whisper as he told how the heartbroken beauty had thrown herself under the wheels of a chariot. Some of the old man's words were Irish Gaelic because he said a Macdonald forebear had been an oarsman on the Clanranald *birlinn*, the galley that had braved the waters between South Uist and Carrickfergus in Antrim.

Màthair listened attentively. The tale took several nights, and would be resumed as soon as the supper dishes were done and peats piled on the fire, the tobacco alight under the metal cover of the old man's pipe. His voice had a sonorous quality and Màthair fell asleep with a smiling mouth, with the lovers safe in each other's arms in their leafy bower. The old man continued his narration as much for himself as for his son as the paraffin level fell in the lamp, the wick in its glass container in the graceful shape of an erect sea horse. But she woke and had tears in her eyes at Deirdre's violent death, though she had heard the story before from the same narrator.

Seumas made himself another cigarette in the chair while the tin dish, which had travelled across the flagstones under the dog's snout, came to a halt by her new master's chair. She gave Seumas a paw with love and loyalty. As he held the paw he regretted that he hadn't taken in the old man's stories, though he had heard them so many times. He couldn't even repeat the first instalment, but he could remember most of Màthair's stories, perhaps because she was from North Uist, her Gaelic different from the old man's, softer, richer, and when she used a word that he didn't know the old man would stop her politely, requesting the meaning with the same courtesy as when he had asked for her hand at the barrel of herring she was filling on the pier, her aching fingers bound, but her heart soaring at the proposal in such attractive Gaelic from the good looking fisherman in the cheesecutter cap. For all of Seumas's conscious life they had exchanged Gaelic words as some couples exchange kisses or gifts.

When Màthair was telling a story on a windy night Seumas would close his jotter without rebuke from the old man, turn down the flame of the lamp, and go to his place at the fire, on the stool between his parents, to listen and learn. It might be a story about men on a fishing trip, shouting to their friends standing by a fire on the shore, warning them away because there was an extra person who had drowned the previous year standing by the fire. She told the story so well that the old man's knuckles whitened as he gripped the arms of his chair. The tragedy was, his parents couldn't read or write Gaelic because they hadn't been taught it in school, where English was the preferred language, and speaking their native tongue, even in the playground, brought corporal punishment. They could only speak it and all that wealth of stories and songs in two dialects of Gaelic had died with them.

The old man had kept a dozen sheep and a cow on the ten acre hill and moor croft. Màthair had milked the cow in the byre, pulling the udders as if they were some kind of musical instrument, manual bagpipes accompanying her Gaelic songs, the milk hissing into the pail between her wellingtons. But after the arthritis had seized her knuckles the old man had sold the cow. Their own milk hadn't been pasteurized, though it hadn't done them any harm. Seumas bought the sterilized version from the chilled cabinet in the Spar store, in the absence of a fridge using a bucket of sea water to keep it from turning.

The old man had divided his time between the land and the sea. Even a dozen sheep took a lot of looking after in that unfenced landscape, since they could stray over the moor and be swallowed by the bogs. It was too expensive to ask the vet to come the two miles from the main road, since he charged walking time as well, so the old man had dug out the maggots from their *tòns* himself and treated their other afflictions with the cures of his Gaelic tradition, freely available from the moor without a prescription.

Màthair gathered *lusan* to heal the ailments of the household. She gathered *Trì-Bhile*, the three-leaved bogbean, from a clear lochan on the moor, boiling it into a bitter tonic to cure the old man's indigestion when he had eaten too many mackerel. She also used the plant for her own arthritis. She picked *Chù Chulainn*, Cuchullin's Belt, meadowsweet, to relieve Seumas's headache after doing his homework by the weak light of the lamp, and when his younger sister Eilidh was upset she was given the *lus* to soothe her nerves. The old man wore *rideag*, bog myrtle, behind his ears to repel the midges, making him look like a Roman emperor, and Màthair placed it among her scant, often repaired, amount of bedlinen in the drawer to scent it.

She also collected short curly seaweed from the shore and boiled from it the pudding called *carraigean* which, she told her son, would put strength into his bones. Seumas always took a second plate, and the old man, as he spooned it up, pronounced that the blancmange-like dish tasted as good as its Gaelic name sounded.

One acre was always given over to hay each year for the cow's feed, and in the summer Seumas would be kept awake by the sound like a rusty screw coming out of sea-soaked wood as the corncrake kept up its monotonous call all night. It was *treòna* in the old man's Gaelic, but màthair had it as *trèan-ri-trèan*, Seumas preferring her version because it caught the repetitive sound.

The old man cut the hay with a scythe and Seumas bundled its fragrance in his arms, the thistles pricking as he carried it to where Màthair was building the stack round three slanted posts like a wigwam. One evening in August 1955, when Seumas was nine, when they were finishing the hay before the weather broke, Niall Coinneach MacCallum the schoolmaster landed from his boat. He had brought his collie dog called Sona, Gaelic for happy.

MacCallum had come to help with the harvest and he stood on the stack, telling them from his elevated position that it reminded him of his young days on the croft above the Sound of Mull. The schoolmaster had placed the perfumed hay on the stack until the light went, singing Gaelic songs along with the old man and Màthair as the scythe tinkled like an orchestral triangle against stones and the two dogs raced along the shore, splashing in the shallows. But the big curved blade had stopped close to the nest where the *trèan-ri-trèan* sat on its eggs. Seumas wanted to see and MacCallum had jumped down from the stack, parting the stalks to show the boy the speckled bird he had never managed to see before, though the *trèan-ri-trèan* had been calling since he was born. The bird's indignant eye confronted the intruders, and its island home of hay was left in the stubble field. Màthair had come with the can of milk, four cups from her wedding china, and a plate of oatcakes with her own cheese which MacCallum pronounced *air leth grinn*, exceptionally exquisite.

Three

The old man was an inveterate beachcomber, and when a storm was blowing he would lie awake, eager to get out at first light to the shore to see what gifts the sea had deposited. He had an impressive collection of fish boxes, some with the names of Irish dealers on their sides, and stacked in the rafters of the byre were many lengths of timber and boards, some that had been in the sea so long that they had barnacles embedded. Once, before Seumas was born, a body had been thrown up by the onshore blast, a naked man, as Christ must have looked when He was taken down from the Cross, Màthair said as she washed the corpse reverently on the flagstones in front of the fire while the old man went in the launch for the police.

Once every five years the old man would make repairs to the *taigh-beag*, closing the lichened boards the wind had splayed, creosoting them with the brush that went backwards and forwards like the swish of the tide. The laird who owned the house hadn't offered to make any interior improvements and the old man hadn't asked.

Seumas took the net out of the bag and spread it on the shore. The old man had taught him never to put away a net with a tear in it because you never knew when a run of fish would appear in the bay. He could remember one time when the water was churning with sea trout, while he and the old man stood up to their thighs in the shoal.

He crunched along the shore to the house, sitting on the step, spooning beans from a can, a meal Màthair would never have allowed, since she believed in fresh food and said once that there would never be a tin opener in her house. As he ate, her son, who hadn't been passed her cooking skills, was surveying Camas na Cille: the Bay of the Cell. MacCallum the schoolmaster had thought that a holy man, probably a saint from Ireland, must have come into this bay and built himself a cell of stones from the shore, but there were no remains. Maybe the stones had been taken to build the house behind him. Camas na Cille: the peace was in the name, in the small flock of birds scurrying on the shoreline in autumn, having fled the frozen north: *pollaran*, the dunlin.

He was up on the hill one evening, playing with a shinty stick when he saw the rowing boat coming into the bay. As the rower came closer he saw that it was the schoolmaster. The day before Seumas had left to go to school but instead had wandered over the moor, looking for birds' nests, and had come home as usual in the summer afternoon. MacCallum must be coming to tell his parents, and the old man would thrash him with the willow stick kept in the corner for chastisement. When it was swung at his *tòn* it made the sound of approaching wind. He wanted to run away, but MacCallum had laid the oars in the boat and had one seaboot in the shallows.

The old man went down to shake hands and help him haul the boat up. MacCallum was carrying a bottle of Old Mull whisky as he came up the track to the house. Seumas was so ashamed that the schoolmaster would see the way he lived, because when he had come to help stack the hay he had declined an invitation to come up to the house for a dram. What if he needed the toilet and had to be shown round to the *taigh-beag*? He ran inside and hid at the top of the stairs as MacCallum's bald pate came in.

'Come into the good room,' màthair invited the visitor. 'I'll light the fire.'

'I'd rather go into the kitchen,' the schoolmaster said.

Seumas sat on the stairs, trembling with fear, but they weren't talking about the truant. This was a social visit and the conversation was in Gaelic. That was what MacCallum the Mull man had come for, to hear Gaelic again because hardly anyone spoke it in the town.

'Come down, Seumas, it's Mr. MacCallum,' màthair called up to him.

The schoolmaster was in the old man's chair, but he wasn't looking around at the shabbiness of the room. He was in animated conversation in Gaelic with the householder opposite. MacCallum seemed to be relishing the Gaelic more than the big glass of whisky in his hand. He had taken a black notebook with a thick rubber band round it from his pocket, and when there was a word he didn't know he stopped the old man and wrote it down.

They were talking about birds, and when the old man referred to the *asaileag*, MacCallum said that he hadn't come across the name before. 'I don't know what the bird is called in English, but that's the Gaelic name I heard from my father,' the old man explained. 'I used to see it, out at sea, when I was on the minesweeper. It's the small black bird that seems to climb up a wave. I'll tell you a story about it and the old village of Socrachadh along the coast. A man in the town told me that the village was haunted. He said that when his son was camping at Socrachadh he couldn't sleep for the sound of crying. The man said that it was the *tannasgan*, the ghosts of the dead crying because they no longer recognized the village they had been brought up in and had been happy in. I left him with his belief, though I knew the truth. You see, once the village was cleared the *asaileagan* moved in. Every night they came in from the sea to their nests among the stones. And the crying the young fellow in the tent heard was the birds. Now what name do you have for these birds?' he asked the visitor.

'I know these birds as *luaireagan*, storm petrels,' MacCallum spoke.

By the end of the evening four pages of the book were filled, and the whisky bottle had lost a quarter of its contents. MacCallum asked if he could come again as they helped him to push out the boat, watching him disappearing into the dusk with his Gaelic glossary in his pocket, the oar blades rising and falling expertly, cormorants following to their roost on the Sgeir. That night an immense wave swept up in Seumas's dream, with a little bird walking up it, without fear, it seemed.

On the schoolmaster's next visit he had a big book in the kitbag he had carried in North Africa, and which now contained a half bottle of whisky and box of chocolates.

'This is Dwelly's dictionary,' he announced to the company. 'Isn't it a wonderful thing that an Englishman should learn Gaelic so well that he spent years going round, collecting words?' He opened the book on the oilcloth by the lamp, as if it were a Bible he was about to read from. 'You get different names in different places for the same birds and the same plants.' He turned to address the old man by the fire, whose pipe was aiding concentration, because he was receiving lessons in Gaelic as well as his son. 'You have the word *asaileag* and I have *luaireag* for the petrel. Dwelly gives other names for the bird: *lucha-fairge*; *luch-fhairge*; *amhlag mhara*; *ceann biorach na stoirm*. He notes that the word they use in Lewis is *pàraidh*. That's because they're said to walk on the water, as St Peter did, which is how they came by their name.'

MacCallum turned to Seumas. 'That's the rich wonder of Gaelic, boy, with different places having different names for birds and plants, and other things too. You're always learning. There never was born – and never will be born now – a person who can claim to know all of Gaelic in all its variations. I'm constantly learning from your father and mother.'

MacCallum was keen on birds and had a collection of eggs in the glass case at the back of his classroom. There were holes at the ends of the eggs where the life had been blown out of them with a reed. MacCallum was collecting the names of birds now instead of their eggs, writing them down as if they were fragile and could crack at any second, the life leaking from their Gaelic shells.

Seumas sat smoking on the stony shore. Everything in the landscape was named in Gaelic. The burn whose estuary was now flooding in the rising tide fifty yards from his boots was called Allt a' Ghobha-Uisge, after the water ouzels that bobbed gracefully on stones in its flow. Where it entered the bay otter pups with their mother could be seen cavorting in the dawn.

He smoked another cigarette in his contentment as birds with Gaelic names called from moor and shore. As he plucked a strand of tobacco from his bottom lip he saw the grey pate of a seal surfacing, its whiskered face watching him with human interest, as if the old man, who would never shoot a seal, had been reincarnated swiftly as his favourite creature in the element that he had loved and respected, but never feared, all his life. Màthair had a belief from her island that seals were seals by day and women by night when they emerged from the sea to charm men. The old man had nodded solemnly, the little fire crackling in his capped pipe. He said that there was plenty of fish for the seals as well as for themselves.

Allt a' Ghobha-Uisge came spilling down from the moor. One night the old man had taken a torch in one hand, his son's hand in his other, leading him up the energetic water in the November night which made their breaths visible in the yellow beam, like the spectres màthair had seen on her island. The old man had shone the torch on a pool and pointed out grey shapes nudging the gravel: sea trout, going up the burn to spawn.

It wasn't only Seumas's eyes and ears that were attuned to landscape and seascape. When he walked through the aromatic heather on the moor, the old man was beside him, in search of a lost sheep, bleating in the briars binding it. The steam rising from

Dilèas's wet coat by the fire after a swim in the lochan brought back màthair's shining face as she scolded the dog for pursuing a duck. Rotting seaweed recalled the decomposing whale. Peat smoke brought back MacCallum to the table, with his Gaelic dictionary.

The hazel sticks were like a little grove in the corner, growing up through the flagstone. The old man wouldn't go in search of wood for a stick until after October, when the sap had gone down. He remembered the night that the old man had found the long straight branch, with the natural curve for the handle, intertwined with ivy in the wood up the coast which he had been going to since a boy and which didn't even have a Gaelic name, as if no one else knew about it. Seumas imagined that the scented secluded place was like the bower of the lovers Naoise and Deirdre in the old man's protracted tale.

The branch had gone home in the launch, lying across the old man's knees. That was another thing about the old man: he had patience. The sticks had to stand in the corner for a year to dry out. Then on a winter's night he had taken the ivy-bound hazel stick to the fire and stood it between his knees. He put on the spectacles with one leg missing which he had found on the shore after a storm. He used a pencil to draw the outline of the handle base, which he cut out with a small saw, as if he were a surgeon performing an operation perilously near a vital artery.

'It's going to be a beautiful *cromag*,' the old man predicted. 'Now, the handle.'

The old man had asked farmers on the island to collect the shed horns of rams for him. For this exceptional stick, the *cromag* of a lifetime, the old man took a long time choosing a handle from the selection of horns spread out on the table by the lamp. He hesitated, he touched, then moved on to the next, lifting the whorled object. This was the part of the creation of the *cromag* which màthair didn't like, because the chosen horn had to be boiled in a pot to soften it, the front door having to be left open because of the stink.

Flattening out of the handle, shaping it and fixing it to the stick took several more nights. The old man liked to put decoration on the end of the curled handle. It was always a thistle, carved with the knife blade and the thumb, the same way as he pared tobacco from the black block. When he created the decoration his pipe was out of his mouth because it required total concentration. The wireless hadn't even been switched on for the Gaelic request programme.

But this time for the exceptional stick it wasn't a thistle. What was taking shape was a face. At first it wasn't possible to say if the face belonged to a human or an animal, but after four nights it was becoming the face of an eagle with fierce eyes and a hooked bill.

The old man didn't suddenly announce: 'This stick's finished.' He walked it about the room, round the table as if even the resonance of the tap on the flagstones was a sign of its quality. This exceptional stick was across Seumas's knees in the launch on an August morning in 1976 when they went as a family to the agricultural show. Màthair put her jam into the competition and the old man showed his sticks in the handicrafts tent, sitting in the glade of them stuck in the turf, puffing his pipe.

The year when the ivy-bound hazel stick was shown the tent was crowded, with everyone wanting to touch it as if it were a Druidical wand with healing powers. But the old man sat guard over it and it was viewed from a distance.

They began to offer him money for the stick.

'One pound!'

'Two!'

'Three!'

The bids were being shouted but the old man sat impassively smoking his pipe.

'Five pounds!'

Everyone turned to look. It was the laird in a tweed suit of plus-fours and a two-way hat. Five pounds would have bought paint for inside and outside the house, but the old man sat impassively, though some of the others had taken off their hats in the presence of the laird. The old man was facing his feudal superior through the glade of sticks, but shook his head at the exceptional offer. Instead he gave the unique stick away for nothing to an old man who had expressed its beauty in equally beautiful Gaelic that bound the old man's heart and moistened his eye.

There had been another stick in the corner that the old man had been working on when he took the stroke. After he lost the power of his right arm Seumas had made him try to use the knife in the other, but the old man hadn't the strength to hold the stick between his knees, and the blade cut in and ruined it. He had taken up the stick in his left hand and thrust the tip between the bars of the grate, feeding it to the flames inch by inch until it was consumed.

The mouth of the burn was flooded by the tide now, so Seumas fixed the end of the net to the stake driven into the shore and piled the rest on the platform at the stern of the dinghy, pushing it off with his boot as he rowed round in an arc. It really needed a man on the shore, at the other end of the net to do it properly, another reason for missing the old man, who couldn't read a page but, as MacCallum the schoolmaster had said, could read the water when there was a shoal in the bay. When all the net was immersed Seumas started to take it in, pulling up more mesh till he came to the next fish, this time a rock cod which he would eat himself. When all the net was back on board he had a dozen sea trout in the box which he transferred to the launch before going round to the town, carrying his catch along the pier to the hotel with its lit-up sun lounge.

'How's the fishing?' Donnie asked.

'I've got some for you,' Seumas told him, lifting the box up on to the counter.

'They're beauties,' the hotel proprietor enthused. 'The guests go for fresh trout, especially the English ones. I'll take the box round to the kitchen and put them on the scales.' When he came back he took £8 from the till and gave them to Seumas, always more money than the market value as a subsidy to his friend.

'I told you years ago, if you'd come out to the rigs with me you could have set yourself up instead of trying to scrape a living from the fishing. They just aren't there any more. The sea's been over-fished by these bloody big trawlers with their miles of nets, hauling up everything.'

'I'll manage,' Seumas said defensively.

'Listen: some of my guests want to see the birds on the rock. You can take them out in the launch, three pounds a head, say. It's easy money.'

He was getting angry with his only friend from school. He didn't want to take English people with binoculars and woolly hats out to see birds that had Gaelic names.

'Have a drink?' Donnie suggested, turning to the gantry.

But he had never been a drinker because he had never had the money or the inclination. The old man had been, for a time. When war broke out he had volunteered for the navy. He had wanted to go on a battleship, but they had put him on to a coastal patrol vessel because of his knowledge of the local area. For six years he had gone up and down the west coast looking for mines and periscopes because the convoys came that way. He had shown the crew how to use a splash net in a quiet bay, and they had lived on fresh salmon and trout while the nation was on war rations.

By the time he was demobbed in late 1945 the old man had a serious drink problem. Most of the money he made from lobster fishing was spent in the pub, and the launch had seemed to steer itself home some nights as he splashed ashore, stumbling up to the house, confronting his frightened wife who had been sure that he had had an accident, and that the infant Seumas in her arms was fatherless.

One summer afternoon in 1955, when Seumas was nine, a man had come over the hill. It was a stifling day, the tenth in a heatwave, but the stranger was striding purposefully. He was powerfully built, wearing a black reefer jacket and a cheesecutter cap.

'This is your uncle Dòmhnall,' màthair introduced him.

But it wasn't a social visit for a dram and a scone with cheese. The old man had been drinking in the town and had just managed to get the launch home. He was sleeping in his chair when he was lifted out of it by the lapels by his brother-in-law. Before màthair ushered Seumas out of the house she carried the lamp through to the scullery so that the mantle would survive. She stood on the shore, hugging her son as they heard the smack of fists and furniture being overturned. The fighters rolled out of the door, locked in a wrestle. They rolled down the shingle, feeding plover taking off, whistling out to sea in alarm. Then both men got up, facing each other. The old man was weak at the knees, and when the fist caught him under the chin he seemed to rise into the sky before he fell backwards with his arms out. Màthair was crying as she hid her face in her apron, but Seumas was watching, horrified yet fascinated, not knowing which battler he wanted to win.

The uncle dragged his brother-in-law over the shingle and washed his bloody face in the sea, then carried him back up to the house, asking Seumas to put the chairs the right way up again. After he had kissed his sister and ruffled his nephew's hair the stranger went back over the hill with the same purposeful stride, back to the island he had come from. The old man was badly cut but he never got drunk again. He would take a glass of whisky at New Year, and a modest one with the schoolmaster, but he never again caused màthair a moment's anxiety through drink, and they never again saw her brother. The stranger might have been a spectre striding over the hill that summer day, except he had left with blood on his fists.

Four

'Do you remember the Macgregor sisters?' Donnie asked.

'Of course I do.'

'Myrtle's staying here.'

'Staying here?'

'She booked in last night. She came in that nifty little sports car that's at the front of the hotel. We were talking about you and she said she would like to see you again. I told her you would probably be in with fish. She's finished dinner now; I'll go and get her.'

'No,' Seumas pled, panicking.

He wasn't dressed for a meeting like this, and anyway they would both be embarrassed.

But Donnie had left. A minute later he appeared with her.

Seumas saw a more mature, even more attractive version of the schoolgirl. The pigtails had gone and this time he could see the curves of her body in the slacks and blouse. He was awkward, holding out a hand. She kissed him on the cheek.

'After all those years, Seumas! You've hardly changed.'

He had never been very good at making conversation.

'And you too,' he managed to say.

'I went to the school today, down into the sheds,' she said wistfully. 'I was in the boys' side for the first time.'

He took this as a reference to what had happened between them in the girls' shed, feeling his face getting hot under the neon tube of the bar.

'It's wonderful to see you,' she enthused, putting her arm through his. 'You must come through to the sun lounge and have coffee.'

'I have to get home, before the light goes,' he excused himself.

'Tomorrow?'

'How is your sister?' he asked, evading the invitation.

She was looking down at the backs of her hands as if there were blemishes.

'Heather had breast cancer. Losing your sister is like no other loss, especially when we were so close.'

He didn't know what to say, it was such a shock.

'Come tomorrow around eleven for coffee,' she urged. 'It'll be good to have someone from the past to talk to.'

Next morning he lifted the creels and found six lobsters in them, a good omen. He went ashore to wash at the stone sink and put on a tie with his pullover, wiping his boots with the cloth from under the sink. He opened the engine full throttle as he sped towards the town, past Sgeir nan Eun, birds coming and going, many feeding young. He tied up the launch and did his business with the buyer, getting a good price for the lobsters. Myrtle was waiting for him in the sun lounge of the hotel, and this time he kissed her. A girl appeared with shortbread and coffee.

'It was a surprise to find Donnie Morrison running this hotel,' Myrtle said. 'I remember how the teacher had to spend half the day getting a simple answer out of him. Now he rings up figures on the till no bother. But tell me about yourself.'

There wasn't much to tell.

'Heather and I once went over the hill to see you.'

He sat up in the chair.

'We felt sorry for you, you seemed such a loner, so we baked a cake to take to you and set off. When we came over the hill and saw your father down on the shore we took fright.'

'I'm sorry you didn't make it,' he said with genuine feeling as she brought back his boyhood loneliness.

'Why don't you move into the town? There would be company for you.'

'I like being on my own.'

'Well, I don't.'

'I don't follow.'

'I'm divorced. It was made final last week and I got into my car and started driving. I didn't know where I was going at first; the road seemed to take me here.'

'That's sad,' he sympathized.

'He was a bastard, a glib talker with another woman on the side. The strange thing is, Heather warned me, don't marry him, Myrtle. It was the only time I didn't listen to her.'

'Do you have children?'

'Neither of us did, yet the gynaecologists could find nothing wrong with us. It makes it more lonely. The thing is, Tom never allowed me to develop my own interests. I started doing voluntary work but he made me stop it because he said I was neglecting him. He was making a lot of money as a lawyer, which is why I got such a big settlement in the divorce, to keep me in the style to which he's made me accustomed.'

'Are you thinking of coming back here?' he asked.

'The first night I drove into the place I thought, I'm home and I'm never going to leave. I even made enquiries to see if I could buy our old home, but it's become a holiday house, only occupied for a few weeks in the year. This place has changed so much, I know so few people.'

There were a lot of things he wanted to say. He wanted to tell her: *That bastard who betrayed you with another woman needs his head looking at. You're just as attractive as you were at school; no, more so.* But he didn't say anything. He was fumbling with a cigarette pack because he didn't want her to see him rolling his own.

'Did you see anything that day in the shed?'

'What?' His voice wavered, the match stalling on the abrasive strip on the box.

The sisters Heather and Myrtle had auburn hair which they wore in plaited tails down their chests, and pleated kilts of Macgregor tartan with buckles at the hips. They were both in MacCallum's classroom. He had primary five, six and seven, sitting together in their own age groups, and through the wall in the other classroom Miss Maclaren had primary one, two, three and four, again in their own classes.

Heather was the older by a year and was in Seumas's class. Myrtle was in the class below. The inseparable siblings came to school hand-in-hand, little matching satchels on their backs, wearing brown brogues with serrated tongues because their croft was two miles up a rough track, their Christian names derived from the landscape they travelled through. They played together in the shed that was segregated from the boys by a four feet high stone wall, at the end of which, between it and the school wall, was a gap of two feet. Some of the bigger boys went through the gap, coaxing girls into the boys' lavatories with the bait of sweeties while MacCallum was having a cup of tea and a smoke in his house.

This Friday morning Seumas and Donnie were the first boys to arrive at school, Heather and Myrtle Macgregor the first girls. The two boys went through the gap in the wall into the girls' playground and down into the shed, where the two sisters were skipping side by side.

'You're not supposed to be on our side,' Heather challenged the intruders.

'There's nobody else about,' Donnie pointed out. 'Mr. MacCallum's still in his house and Miss Maclaren hasn't arrived yet. Show us what you've got and we'll show you ours.'

The skipping ropes stopped and the sisters looked at each other.

'You show first,' Heather said.

'No, you,' Donnie insisted.

Dropping their pants to their white ankle-socks, the sisters raised their kilts and held the hems under their chins as they stood together.

Seumas peered at each of them but couldn't see anything. He was having another inspection when they saw the door of the school house opening. The two boys managed to get through the gap in the wall without being seen by MacCallum.

The boys in the schoolmaster's room were making fireside brushes out of foot-length pieces of thick rope, and the girls were sewing coloured strands of raffia into round hemp tablemats. Heather went out to get a yellow streamer of raffia, her hips swaying in the cute red and black kilt. Seumas was more confused than ever, wanting to lean over and whisper to Donnie: did you see anything? But MacCallum was watching the class with that warning habit he had of half closing his right eye when he sensed trouble.

Seumas couldn't understand it as he sat binding string round the floppy brush. He knew his own thing could go stiff – Donnie had demonstrated in the shed – but where did it go? He puzzled over it as he crossed the darkening moor, the finished brush sticking out of the schoolbag on his back like a leek. The first time màthair used it to sweep up the ash in front of the grate it turned black.

'Did you get an eyeful that day in the shed when you and Donnie came through the gap in the wall that morning to see what my sister and I had?' Myrtle repeated herself in the sun lounge of the hotel, a 37-year-old divorcee now.

'I'm ashamed,' Seumas told her earnestly.

'Don't be. It was a perfectly natural enquiry. But you never saw, did you, and you haven't seen one so far, have you?'

Did Myrtle know what had happened that day when the film van came to the school? The van usually came in the afternoon, unexpectedly, and Seumas was one of the boys detailed by MacCallum to carry in the equipment, the screen in the long black slim box, the shining projector and the circular metal canisters of educational films about the wonders of the world. Seumas sat on the wooden bench beside Heather. The windows had been blacked out for the show. Heather felt for his hand and put it under her kilt. When he touched it through her pants the yielding softness of the cleft made him feel weak. As the loin-clothed native tapped the sap from the tree on the screen Seumas's thing stiffened, and when MacCallum raised the blinds he had to hide his erection by pulling down his jersey.

'Did you enjoy it?' Heather asked sweetly, but he didn't know – and never worked out – if it was the film or the feel she was referring to, though he thought about it often in his bed under the sloped roof, the moon of desire in the skylight.

Myrtle's hand was covering his on the arm of the wicker chair in the sun lounge. He knew that he could go upstairs with her and that if she were satisfied she would stay.

'I have to go,' he said, rising.

'Will you come again tomorrow?' she pleaded. 'There's such a lot to talk about.'

'I should be in with more fish.'

As he was going out he looked back to where she was sitting, but she wasn't there. He saw the sisters together in the girls' shed, in the light of that long-ago early summer morning of 1958, standing together with their kilt hems held under their chins, the smooth whiteness of their stomachs narrowing to a great mystery he couldn't see.

Five

On his way home on the launch he was remembering a visit when he was thirteen. One day a man carrying a case and a backpack had appeared over the hill above the house. The only other person who came with a case was the Pakistani traveller who joked with màthair in Gaelic he had learned on other islands from lonely wives he tempted with skimpy nylon knickers with the maker's label cut out of them stretched between his dusky fingers as he offered them on hire purchase.

Seumas and the old man were varnishing the dinghy when the stranger came crunching down the shingle with a case, his tweed jacket over his arm, brown brogues discoloured through his unaccustomed journey across the bog. As the visitor spoke to them in Gaelic the old man dipped the brush in the tin and held it suspended against the sun, the globules of varnish shining, as if he had dipped the bristles in the burnished solar disk.

'Where did you learn your Gaelic?' the old man asked with his usual politeness.

'I studied it at university,' the stranger informed his questioner.

The old man nodded sagely as he applied the varnish to the curved timbers, working it well in.

'I thought it was book Gaelic. What brings you this way?'

The man knelt on the sand, laid the case flat and sprung the catches with his thumbs, lifting off the lid to expose two big reels.

'I'm collecting Gaelic songs and I heard that you knew a lot of songs.'

'Who told you that?' the old man asked in a tone almost of amusement.

'I heard it at the hotel.'

The old man held the paint brush up daintily, the way Miss Maclaren held her fountain pen when she was writing at the high desk in the infants' room. The old man looked down at the tape recorder.

'And what would you do with a song if I put it into that machine?' he enquired.

'Take it back to Edinburgh and put it in the library,' the collector explained, still on his knees on the wet sand.

'Put it in the library?' the old man repeated, brushing varnish again. 'What use is a song lying in a library? The songs I have were meant to be sung. I learned them at the fireside as a boy when friends came for a ceilidh.' He laid the brush across the mouth of the tin. 'It's quite a walk over the hill and you look in need of refreshment. Seumas, go to *màthair* and get this gentleman who learned his Gaelic from books a glass of milk and a scone – with plenty of her *càis*, cheese, on it.'

After he had the sustenance the disappointed collector clipped the lid back over his empty reels and departed. Seumas leapt up from the sand and ran after him, calling to him across the moor where an oystercatcher was wheeling crying, trying to lure the stranger away from its nest.

'What do you want?' the collector asked in Gaelic when the boy caught up with him. 'Has your father changed his mind?'

'What's in the pack on your back?'

'Batteries for the tape recorder.'

'What's the Gaelic for cock and fanny?' Seumas found the courage to ask.

The collector looked at the whippersnapper. Had he been put up to this by his father, to humiliate him even further?

'Ask your father. He's supposed to have plenty of Gaelic.'

'If I ask he'll take the stick to me.'

The collector now surmised that the query was sincere.

'The penis is *bod,* the vagina *faighean,*' the collector said, using the polite word for the female organ, the word the old man would use, though on the minesweeper men yearning for sex called it the *pit.*

'What's a penis, mister?'

He looked at the puzzled boy.

'The penis is what you have between your legs.'

'What's a vagina, mister?'

'It's what females have.'

'*Tapadh leibh*' (thank you), Seumas said, then went skipping home through the bog myrtle, repeating aloud '*bod! faighean!*' in case he forgot.

* * * * *

The old man had taught him to read water, but there was no sign of fish in the bay, and when he went out to lift the lobster creels they were empty. He didn't know what he was going to do, with no money in the tea caddy on the mantelpiece and no food in the cupboard. The potato sack in the shed was empty, and he hadn't shot a rabbit for several days. He went inside and ate the few slices of bread he had, scraping the golden paper for the last of the butter. The grate was full of ashes because he hadn't sawn driftwood, and he was hungry. He was also angry. When MacCallum spoke to Seumas in Gaelic the other children started to giggle.

'Let them laugh out of ignorance,' MacCallum switched to English. 'You have far more than they have: you have two languages, and the finer of them they don't have and never will.' Then he changed into Gaelic again. '*Chan eil i aca. Bha nàire cho mòr air am pàrantan 's nach biodh iad a' bruidhinn ann an cànain*

39

an athraichean nuair a bhiodh iad aig an taigh.' They don't have it because their parents were so ashamed of their native tongue that they wouldn't speak it in the house.

Seumas went up the narrow creaking steps to his bedroom with its coomed ceilings like a solid tent. He threw his trousers and jersey over the wicker chair and lay down on the horsehair mattress, looking up at the slanted skylight he had been seeing since he was a child, filled with stars, radiant moons, streaming with rain, and, on several magical mornings, piled with snow. He had seen skeins of geese crossing and the wings of a sea eagle darkening the glass, a fish in its talons for its raucous eyrie of young.

Tonight it was quiet, with the dog lying at the foot of the bed, lost in her own thoughts. He was thinking about the day in the shed.

When Seumas reached primary seven a boy brought a packet of postcards which his father had bought from a seaman on a foreign trawler which had sheltered from a storm in the harbour. The boy had borrowed them surreptitiously from his father for the day and showed them around the shed. Seumas now saw the extent of the mystery, the black-haired woman sitting on the chair with her knees up at her chin. That night he had his first wet dream. When he woke before dawn to find it drying against his skin he bundled up his pyjama trousers and went out, standing at the door, naked up to the waist in the wind, with the sea heaving up on to the shore. He washed the sticky patch on the trousers in Allt a' Ghobha-Uisge and pinned them to the line before going back up to bed, but staying awake so that he could retrieve the pyjama bottoms before the house was awake.

He had never been with a woman, though he was 37, late to be still a virgin. There were several words for virgin in the Gaelic dictionary, but they were all female. He was attractive to women, handsome in a rugged way, with a good physique, short and powerful like his father, the barrel chest an inherited gene. He lay having a last smoke under the skylight, the lamp on the floor beside him. The heat from the lamps of his boyhood had left black ovals on the sloped wall because at one time he had been scared of the dark and had fallen asleep with the lamp still on.

One afternoon after school Seumas had been tormenting the dog with a stick up behind the house.

'Fuck off!' he was shouting at it when the old man came along the shore.

'Where did you get that word?' the old man asked.

'In the playground,' Seumas answered fearfully.

He was expecting the old man to lay down the rabbits and gun he was carrying and go into the house for the willow stick. Instead the old man spoke in English, shaking his head: 'You won't hear words like that in Gaelic, son,' and then he had gone on into the house, leaving Seumas standing there, with tears in his eyes a blow wouldn't have left him with.

In the playground Donnie went through the gap in the wall into the girls' shed with a pocket of toffees, coaxing one of them back with him, enticing her down to the boys' lavatories. Seumas didn't understand what was happening. They had kept a single cow, but there would be no milk unless she had a calf. The first time Seumas had seen the bull coming over the hill he had run to hide, not only because of the ring through his nose, but because of the sack of his balls bouncing through the heather. He and the old man had gone with it to the cow. The bull had reared, its hooves up on the cow's back, and then a shaft had come out of its belly near the bag and begun thrusting.

'What are they doing?' he had asked the old man.

'*Tha iad a' pòsadh, a bhalaich*,' they're getting married, boy.

When Seumas told Donnie about what the bull had been doing to the cow, his friend had laughed, making Seumas even more confused. But he was angry now as he lay under the skylight. Since he had been born everything in his world had been named in Gaelic, from the fish in the sea to the meat on his plate. There were Gaelic words that they had never given him, but the man with the tape recorder and discoloured brogues had, and from that day on the moor Seumas had never used the English versions in conversation with Donnie, and since his friend wouldn't understand *bod* and *faighean*, he had kept these words within his head.

What had he been left by his parents? A language no one else could understand, a house, probably the most primitive on the island, where you did your shit into a pail outside. The houses in the town had modern amenities like electricity and inside toilets, and almost all of them would have television. In his frustration he wanted to get up and heave off the skylight, to go downstairs and lift the paraffin can from the scullery, to scatter its contents all over the furniture, the chair with the burst webbing that had been the old man's, the table at which he had sat trying to do his homework while the Gaelic stories were being told.

He has fumbled open the box, tossing the lighted match behind him. He has left the door open so that the wind can get in, the flames devouring the oilcloth on the table, eating the horsehair from the old man's chair, racing up the stairs to the beds, then finally climbing out of the cracked skylight. He hears the conflagration behind him as he goes down to the shore, the dog at his heels, the water in front of him bright with the fire. He wades out to the dinghy, the dog swimming beside him. He climbs into the launch, Dìleas lifted aboard, standing on a seat to shake the sea from her coat, delighted with the night's adventure. He knocks aside the peaked roof of the engine, turns the fuel cock, jerks the cord. As it splutters into action he pushes the throttle to maximum, standing at the tiller as he ploughs out of the bay, scattering the resting seabirds. He roars along under Sgeir nan Eun where the birds tumble shrieking from their ledges. He sees the pier light as he turns into the harbour. The launch bumps against the steps, because he hasn't put the old tyre as a fender over the side. He shuts off the engine but doesn't tie up. Let it drift aground on the rocks. He runs up the steps and will sleep on the slatted bench in the shelter until the bus for Glasgow in the morning.

He wasn't in the shelter waiting for the morning bus. He was still in bed and the intact house below him was peaceful, the dog soundless in sleep. All he knew was fishing, and the old man had taught him that. He knew how to make a creel and where to shoot it near the rocks at the entrance to the bay because that was where the lobsters were. He knew how to handle a boat, how to take the engine apart when it wouldn't go. He understood the wind and tides. He could anticipate the sea through the movement of the long smooth baton of the tiller in his fist. That was all he knew, though he could have known a lot more if he had paid attention to MacCallum. No, if his parents had paid attention to MacCallum, because on one of his visits in his boat, with his bottle of whisky, the schoolmaster had told them that their son was clever and that he could go to college.

The old man had nodded and looked at màthair.

'The sea's in his blood,' MacCallum said. 'He could go to college to study navigation and join the Merchant Navy. He would soon be an officer.'

It was an unconvincing argument to put to the old man, who couldn't read a chart, but could travel for miles close to the coast in a storm in bad light, without coming within ten yards of a reef. No one consulted MacCallum's pupil about his future ambitions as he sat at the table, listening. He was top of the class in arithmetic but he knew he wouldn't be going anywhere, there being no money to send him to college.

'I think I could get him a bursary,' MacCallum offered.

The old man didn't know this word bursary. Was it a Gaelic word exclusive to Mull? No, the schoolmaster explained, it was an English word, there being no Gaelic for the term that he knew. MacCallum poured whisky to stimulate his host's interest in higher education. The old man had a way of holding his strict ration of one glass, his pinkie raised, like a fop, as if he had a lace cuff. Higher education, when the old man hadn't gone back to school after the age of twelve because there were nine in the family? The old man knew all about the nature of inheritance. You got the boat but you had to keep your parents from the proceeds of the catch, and you had to look after them in the house because they wouldn't be going to an old folks' home, where there were wet chairs and not a word of Gaelic. Not that there was an old folks' home on the island at that time, so those who hadn't offspring to look after them were sent to the hospital in what had been the poorhouse in the ferry port on the mainland, and was still regarded as such.

'Do you know this song?' the old man asked his guest, and began to sing a song about the sea. It was an *iorram*, a rowing song, with a suitor crossing the sound to another island to claim his bride. Nothing was going to go wrong in the course of the song. He would get his bride, build a house overlooking the sea, and in due time make a cradle for the firstborn from timber gifted by the sea. As the old man sang the verses in his pleasing voice he pulled imaginary oars to his chest, and MacCallum sang the chorus in his impressive tenor, trimming his voice like a sail. College? There was nowhere to go, except back down to the launch at first light, to go out to the creels, to find four lobsters in them if you were lucky, when every creel used to be full and he would say to the old man: 'Why don't we put out another dozen?'

But the old man was prudent. Catch too many young and there won't be many adults left, he used to say.

* * * * *

It was the day of the old man's funeral. His son put on his only suit and debated whether to take the dog. She was sitting at his shoes, looking up expectantly at him, so he decided to take her for company because he knew that dogs had a sixth sense, like *an dà shealladh*, the second sight in humans, which màthair had had. The family hadn't been churchgoers, but on Sunday mornings the old man had said a Gaelic prayer and the three of them had sung a Gaelic psalm. Dìleas sat at the cemetery gate while he went in.

There were only six people – two of them old crofters – standing round the grave, not sufficient for the eight cords for the coffin, so one person on one side took two. Seumas had the head cord and gave number two, the foot one, to Donnie Morrison. After the minister said a prayer in English, having no Gaelic, and Seumas had thrown earth on the coffin, he declined Donnie's invitation to lunch at the hotel and instead wandered among the gravestones. He found the grave of Alan Maclachan. The bank manager had chosen the inscription, a Gaelic proverb, on his stone:

Mol an latha math mu oidhche
Praise the good day at the close of it

Six

Seumas was going to see his sister.

He was up at six, standing naked, washing at the cold tap at the scullery sink while the range heated a kettle of water. He shaved using the mug and the old man's open razor which he had stropped on a leather belt that had belonged to his father for the same purpose. He stirred the badger's head brush on the cake of soap and used slow careful strokes.

He put on the suit which he had bought for Donnie's wedding. He took money out of the tin on the mantelpiece and carried his polished shoes down to the dinghy, then transferred to the launch. The wind lifted his tie out of his jacket as he passed the line of lobster floats. The lights of the town were still on and the bus was sitting at the top of the pier. He bought a return and sat near the back.

Eilidh was three years younger than he was. He had sheltered her from the wind as they crossed the moor to the school bus, and on dark nights he brought her home on his back, the torch she was supposed to be holding to show them the way wavering in the sky as if she were signalling to someone in the constellations. She was sleeping when màthair lifted her off his aching back and carried her to the fire to revive her. But he never saw her being bathed in front of the fire because he was sent upstairs, and the old man also went up.

Eilidh was in Miss Maclaren's classroom. The wall between the two classrooms opened on rails for important occasions like prize-giving, when the local laird, born on his family's Somerset estate and spending most of his time there, came in his kilt of adopted tartan to give out the books he had bought. One afternoon there was a music lesson next door. Some of the pupils were singing and MacCallum looked up in irritation from correcting jotters, his eye half closing. They were waiting for him to go through to tell Miss Maclaren to keep it quieter when Eilidh started singing. It was a lullaby màthair had taught her, as she swayed her on her knee by the fire, about an infant taken away by the fairies.

'Dh'fhàg mi 'n seo na shìneadh e,
Na shìneadh e, na shìneadh e;
Gun d' dh'fhàg mi 'n seo na shìneadh e
Nuair dh'fhalbh mi bhuain nam braoileagan.

Fhuair mi lorg an dòbhrain duinn,
An dòbhrain duinn, an dòbhrain duinn;
Gun d' fhuair mi lorg an dòbhrain duinn,
's cha d' fhuair mi lorg mo chòineachain.'

I left my darling lying here,
Lying here, lying here;
I left my darling lying here,
To go and gather blaeberries.

I've found the wee brown otter's tracks,
The otter's tracks, the otter's tracks;
I've found the wee brown otter's tracks,
But ne'er a trace of baby O!

It was as if there was no wall between the two classrooms. MacCallum had raised his head and Seumas saw the tears in his eyes.

> *'Fhuair mi lorg a' cheò sa bheinn,*
> *A' cheò sa bheinn, a' cheò sa bheinn;*
> *Ged fhuair mi lorg a' cheò sa bheinn,*
> *Cha d' fhuair mi lorg mo chòineachain.'*

> I got to find the mountain mist,
> The mountain mist, the mountain mist;
> Though I got to find the mountain mist,
> I didn't find my baby O.

When she skipped with the other girls in the playground Eilidh's feet became fankled in the rope. The other children in her class proceeded into primary five in MacCallum's room, but she was kept back for a year in Miss Maclaren's room. When an educational psychologist came to the school and tried to talk to her she became agitated and wouldn't respond. At home, sitting at the table with her jotter, she would suddenly burst into tears. Seumas went and sat beside her to help her with her homework, but it wasn't the sums. She couldn't say what it was, not even in Gaelic, but she woke sobbing in the night and he heard màthair trying to hush her in the room across the landing where she slept with their parents.

She started playing truant from school in the year that her brother moved to the secondary school. No one knew where she went to, but the whipper-in came over the moor one day, still wearing his bicycle clips, his coat tails lifting in the wind.

'It's a very serious business, not attending the school,' he had warned the old man, who was varnishing the dinghy. 'You can get taken to the court for it.'

The old man's brush didn't stop. He didn't say: *But she sets off from here for school.* He said: 'She hasn't been herself lately. I'll make sure she goes to school.'

That night the old man asked her where she went instead of going to school, but she wouldn't answer him. He didn't threaten her; instead he sat, a beaten perplexed man, his cold pipe in his fist.

'It's your responsibility to take her to school,' he ordered his son.

'She goes on the bus with me, and gets off before me,' Seumas answered. 'If I take her to school I'll get into trouble at my own school for being late.'

One morning Seumas watched her getting off and crossing the road with her schoolbag on her back. When the bus was round the bend he asked the driver to let him off because he was feeling sick and was going home. He reached the primary school as Miss Maclaren was swinging the clattering bell in her fist at the door to her classroom, and he saw that his sister wasn't in the line. He wandered through the town looking for her, worried that a man might molest her.

He took the road home, leaving it to walk along the promontory towards Rubha nan Ròn because she liked to watch the seals there. He noticed her schoolbag lying on a rock, and followed her trampled trail down through the high bracken. The place was called Socrachadh, Gaelic for settlement. The word sounded so strong, so durable, fused into the rock. The old man said that eighty people had lived there, including his own relatives. You could still see the lazybeds they had made on the slope to grow their crops, but the Gaelic speaking laird of the time, whose family had owned the estate for four centuries, had decided to put sheep on the ground, and had offered the tenants assisted passages to Nova Scotia. The old man had the story in his expressive Gaelic, with all the pauses for dramatic effect. The factor and his henchmen had come on horseback to force the people down to the shore, to the sailing ship waiting in the bay, and when they refused to move they had come back with fire-brands.

Seumas clambered over the stones and looked through the ruined window. His sister was sitting in a corner, staring, as if she could see something that he couldn't see, the way a cat will watch the corner of a room.

He went in and crouched down beside her.

'Why do you come here?' he asked gently.

She showed no surprise or anger at seeing him, as if she had expected him to come eventually.

'The people here are nice to me,' she answered in Gaelic.

'There aren't any people here, Eilidh. They left long ago, for a place called Nova Scotia, long before Athair was born. You heard him talking about them. They were forced to leave. Mr. MacCallum told us about it in the class. He said that an old crippled woman had had her roof burned above her by the factor.'

'They *are* here. There's the girl I play with,' she insisted, pointing.

Though Seumas listened intently to màthair's stories about the dead coming back, he knew that he was squatting on his heels in a house that contained only earth and tumbled stone now. He also knew that his sister wasn't right in the head. But what was he going to do about it? Leave her to jink school, coming to this ruin to talk to herself every day until the whipper-in caught up with her? They would take her away. They had taken away a man in the town in a jacket with straps, and he had rolled along the ground to the ambulance, shouting swears in English until the doctor had given him a jag in the rump.

'We'll leave them in peace,' he told Eilidh, taking her hand.

* * * * *

A letter came, asking the old man to take nine-year-old Eilidh to Glasgow to be examined by a specialist.

'Glasgow?' màthair repeated, frightened.

'It's a mistake. I'll go round in the boat today to see Dr Urquhart,' the old man said.

Eilidh was sitting at the table by the lamp, staring with her big pupils as if there weren't a wall in front of her and she could see across to Socrachadh and its spectral inhabitants, long since in their graves in Nova Scotia.

'We have to take her to Glasgow,' the old man confirmed when he returned from the town.

'What for?' màthair asked fearfully.

'I don't know, but they'll send us word.'

A yellow card came with Eilidh's name on it, an address and a date. The four of them were going, and a friend of the old man's was coming to milk the cow. Seumas pored over train and bus timetables, like a voyager planning to travel to a distant problematic land. The big ferry that could carry buses and cars was still six years away from the island, so they had to get the bus to the pier half-way down the island, where they embarked on the small steamer for the mainland, to get the train for Glasgow. Seumas had worked out that they would get to the city in the late morning. The appointment at the Infirmary was at two, and the train for home left at five.

They were all up before five on the morning they were due to leave. Màthair stood Eilidh in the scullery sink to wash her and put on the dress she wore to the school Christmas party. The old man shaved more carefully than usual, putting on his sole suit. Seumas put on his first suit of long trousers, purchased with the proceeds from lobsters. They walked across the moor in the early morning, with Eilidh crying that she didn't want to go to Glasgow, and the old man having to carry her against his shoulder like a baby. They waited for half an hour in the cold morning for the bus to come. Eilidh slept on a bench on the ferry, her head on màthair's lap.

It was the first time Seumas had seen a train. He was fascinated as well as frightened by its size and strength as it hauled them out of the town. Eilidh fell asleep by the window, and when the old man lit his pipe one of the other travellers demanded that he put it out.

'We want to go to the Infirmary,' the old man appealed to a passer-by, and was pointed in the direction of a bus stop. Each time a bus came the old man climbed the step to ask if it was going to the Infirmary. When the correct bus came eventually the journey took about ten minutes, and when they walked up to the massive building Eilidh began crying again. The old man passed the card across at reception. The woman studied it, then told them they were at the wrong Infirmary. Màthair suddenly looked very old.

'Where are you from?' the woman asked, and the old man told her.

She must have seen the weariness in his wind-and-sea-etched face because she told him to wait while she went on the phone.

'There's an ambulance going over to the correct Infirmary in five minutes. They'll give you a lift. It's against the rules, but you've come a long way and I can see that the wee lassie's tired.'

As they sat in the back of the swaying ambulance with its darkened windows Seumas felt for his sister's hand and squeezed it. At the second Infirmary the receptionist showed them the way to the clinic. The old man nodded, but as they were wandering down another long corridor Seumas realized that the old man was confused by the signs, so he took over the navigation. A nurse in a starched cap sitting behind a desk asked the old man for the yellow appointment card.

'The clinic's running late,' she informed them.

'How long will it be?' the old man asked anxiously.

'I can't say. Take a seat over there,' she directed brusquely with her pen.

There were a lot of other people waiting, and they were called away slowly, one by one. It was four o' clock when it was Eilidh's turn. The whole family got up to go with her.

'Only by herself,' the nurse ordered, leading her away by the hand.

They could hear her crying in the distance, and then there was silence. Seumas was thinking that they had done something to his sister, and he was about to go down the corridor to look for her when the nurse came back.

'We're going to have to keep her in for more tests,' she told them.

'But we've got a train to catch in under the hour,' the old man protested.

'I'm sorry, but the consultant wants more tests run on her.'

They didn't have a suitcase with them. They had taken money to treat themselves to high tea somewhere before going on the train, but they didn't have enough for an overnight stay. Seumas was watching the old man, but the old man wasn't going to tell the nurse about their lack of clothes and funds.

'When will she be ready to come home with us?' the old man wanted to know.

'At lunchtime tomorrow,' the nurse stated.

'Where are we going to stay?' màthair asked as they went out of the Infirmary, distraught at leaving her daughter and worried because the man who was milking their cow didn't expect them to be away overnight.

'My cousin Cathy's in Partick,' the old man remembered.

'Yes, but do you know her address?' màthair asked.

The old man had to admit that he didn't.

'Then we'll be sleeping in the station,' màthair complained in a rare moment of despair. 'We should never have brought Eilidh to this awful place.'

Now they were lost and it was getting dark. The old man could navigate his way home in the launch even when he had been drinking heavily, but he had no sense of direction in the city, and they found themselves back at the place they had started their wandering from.

'Ask this policeman,' màthair urged him, complaining about her legs.

The old man was asking the way and the policeman was holding up his arm. Then suddenly he looked intently at the old man.

'*A bheil Gàidhlig agad?*' Do you speak Gaelic?

The old man looked as if he had just been propositioned by the most desirable woman in the world. That beatific smile came over his face as he and the policeman conversed. The old man told of their troubles and the policeman said that there was no way a man with such good Gaelic was going to sleep in a Glasgow station.

The whole family was coming home with him because there was plenty of food in the house, and they could make up beds.

It was the best evening Seumas had ever had. One of the policeman's sons had a train set laid out in the loft, and they went up there to play. He loved the rasp of the key as he wound up the red engine, slotting it into the silver rails before releasing the brake. There was a tunnel and a platform with a guard standing with a red flag.

They were called down to a big pot of broth which màthair pronounced was the best they had ever taken, and it was followed by *buntàta 's sgadan,* with eight pairs of hands round the table and four dialects of Gaelic, the fourth being the policeman's wife, who came from Barra. It was a culinary and linguistic feast MacCallum would have loved. But as he ate the potato skin stained with the earth Seumas was thinking of his sister alone in the Infirmary. A year after the Glasgow visit she was taken out of school because of her disruptive behaviour. She never went back.

* * * * *

He was thinking of his sister as he rubbed away the breaths of the other passengers with his sleeve from the window of the bus he was taking to the outskirts of the mainland town. When he went in the door of the big forbidding looking building he was accosted by a little hunched man who held up a leather purse to him.

'Can you give me change for the phone?'

Seumas was fumbling in his pocket when the receptionist called across: 'Don't give it to him. He's got plenty money in his account here, and nobody to phone.'

In the long corridor patients were walking up and down. They were all ages, some of them stooped, some propelling themselves in wheelchairs, some shuffling along in slippers from which their heels lifted. A woman in a nightdress with ribbons at her scraggy throat and floppy slippers with baubles on them appeared beside Seumas, slipping her arm through his.

'Are you married?'

He nodded as he looked at the furrowed skin between her breasts.

'Then you're no use to me,' she said, breaking away.

They had gone once a year to visit Eilidh after she had been committed at the age of fourteen, not because of her violent moods in which she would hit màthair, who would have endured the heaviest of blows, so long as she could have her daughter with her. But when Eilidh talked about the voice within her head urging her to end her life of misery, Dr Murray's predecessor Dr Urquhart advised that it would be safer to send her to the asylum, though the old man didn't call it that. When MacCallum visited to enquire after Eilidh, the old man wouldn't use *taigh-cuthaich*, the Gaelic for asylum, to describe where his daughter was because the word for a wildcat was *cat-cuthaich*. He had come across one once on the moor, and it had hissed and spat at him, crouching as if to launch itself at him with long claws unsheathed. *Cuthaich* had too many connotations of ferocity and rage, so the old man, in rare censorship of his beloved native tongue, referred to his daughter as being on *tìr-mòr*, the mainland.

On their visits to Eilidh the old man had always looked older in this corridor, his head bent as they approached the unit where Eilidh was. The nurses had tried to make it a home-from-home with carpets on the floor and pictures on the walls, though nobody knew whose faces they were in the frames. There was also an upright piano which nobody could play.

The nurses weren't expecting Seumas, and asked him to wait while they cleared the other inmates out of the room. They were watching him apprehensively, and one of them approached cautiously and touched him as if he belonged to a different species. At first Eilidh didn't recognize her brother. He hadn't seen her for nearly a year, a neglect that made him ashamed, but there had been the old man to look after since his mind had begun to wander. His 34-year-old sister's hair was grey, her looks gone. She had lost teeth at the front, but they hadn't been replaced by dentures. He embraced her and gave her the box of chocolates he had bought for her.

'How are you getting on?' he asked her in Gaelic.

She stared at him as if she didn't understand the language he had spoken. But though she had spent most of her life in the asylum, having wires put on her head to give her electric shocks, they hadn't jolted the Gaelic out of her disturbed brain, and as he sat with her in the corner, holding her hand and talking in their first language, he seemed to see her getting younger and younger until she was the girl again they had gone to fetch from the Infirmary in Glasgow the following day. They had expected to find her hysterical, but the nurses had given her a doll which she was allowed to take home.

All those years later, in the asylum, she asked Seumas in Gaelic how they were at home.

'Màthair and Athair are both fine,' he told her, because it had been so difficult explaining to her that màthair wouldn't be coming to visit her again, and now the old man had gone too.

She threw back her head and began to shriek with laughter as if she had just remembered a Gaelic joke. The nurses came and linked their arms through hers, walking her backwards to the unit which would be her home for the rest of her life. Seumas stood at the end of the corridor, watching her getting smaller, and saw her again with the schoolbag on her back as she went in front of him across the moor. At the road end she took from her schoolbag the white socks and sandals she loved so much, leaving her shoes under a flat stone in the unlikely event of rain. But that was before she began talking to the dead among strewn stones and threatening to put herself into the sea.

When he started to weep an arm of one of the patients went round him.

Seven

Seumas hooked up one of the glass floats off Rubha nan Ròn, but the creel underneath it was empty. He didn't bother to lift the last one, but slewed the launch back to the shore. The lobsters were finished. It couldn't be natural because they had been breeding for years in the rusty hold of the iron ship since the old man was a boy, but now their shells had black blotches.

He was so angry that he kicked at the empty box at his boots as the engine raced, ploughing water. He rowed ashore, taking his temper out on the strokes, making the water boil. It was all finished. There were only a few pounds left in the tin on the mantelpiece after his trip to see his sister. Where was he going to get money from to live on? Wait for the next tide to bring a few sea trout?

He threw stones at the sea as if it had betrayed him. Where was he going to get a job? There was nothing in the town. Seumas patted the dog sitting beside him, and that calmed him.

'We'll manage somehow, Dìleas,' he assured his faithful companion, and the dog licked his hand in support.

He heard feet swishing through the heather behind him, then crunching over the shore. He thought it was the postman, grumbling because he had had to walk over the moor with mailshots which Seumas tore up in front of him, advising him to do the same to save his legs. But it wasn't a letter; it was a folded document that was being handed to him over his shoulder. He turned and saw Sandy standing behind him.

Sandy had been in the same class as Seumas in primary school. He played with Dinky Toys on his desk when he should have been paying attention to what was on the blackboard. The wheels of the toys made a rumbling sound which annoyed Miss Maclaren. She took Sandy out to strap him but that made no impression on the boy's hand and he went back, grinning, to his desk to continue to trundle his toy.

One day when he was in primary five, in MacCallum's room, Sandy had brought a bulldozer to school. It was brand new, yellow, with rubber treads that moved as he pushed it across the desk. MacCallum didn't hear it, otherwise he would have confiscated it.

'That's nothing,' Seumas told Sandy at playtime. 'I've got a bulldozer this big at home,' he boasted, showing the dimensions with his hands. 'I'll bring it in tomorrow if you swap me for the one you've got, though it's a lot smaller than mine.'

'I'll need to see it first,' Sandy said cautiously.

'If you give me yours today I'll bring mine in tomorrow.'

Seumas went home with the bulldozer. It was the first quality toy he had ever had. He ran it over the oilcloth on the table and on the concrete floor in the scullery. He even ran it up the stairs to his bed. He told his parents that he had exchanged his best marbles for the toy.

Next morning Sandy was waiting by the bus.

'Where's the bulldozer?' he demanded.

'I forgot. I'll bring it tomorrow,' Seumas promised.

'I want mine back,' Sandy said, putting out his hand.

'I left it at home.'

Sandy would have fought him, but he had the disadvantage of too much weight, so he sat in the class, running an imaginary bulldozer over his desk while MacCallum wrote on the board.

Every morning Sandy was waiting at the bus stop, but there was no bulldozer, big or small. He warned Seumas: 'My daddy's coming to the school to see you about it.'

Seumas had seen Sandy's father. He was a big man who worked on the roads. But he had grown too attached to the bulldozer, and anyway, it was now lacking a tread.

'I'll swop you for it,' he told Sandy.

'What will you give me for it?'

'These two marbles,' Seumas offered, taking them from his pocket and laying them in the groove on Sandy's desk.

'I want more than these for it,' Sandy demanded, so Seumas put another big marble in the groove and when Sandy shook his head he took a fourth out of his pocket.

Sandy held his hand under where the inkwell should have been and caught the marbles on his palm, mesmerized by the swirling blue pattern within the fourth marble, as if this had been Seumas's intention. At dinner time Seumas played Sandy at marbles and won back two of his big ones, including the blue one.

Nearly thirty years later here was Sandy, standing over him.

'Are you still driving the ambulance, Sandy?' Seumas asked amicably.

'No. I'm the sheriff officer and I hereby serve you a summons for' – he hesitated as if consulting a piece of paper in his hand – 'for non-payment of Domestic Rates.'

'I don't know what you're talking about, Sandy, but of course I never did in school – neither did Miss Maclaren.'

'Rates have to be paid on domestic properties in Scotland,' Sandy said, as if he had memorized the legislation like a poem that appealed to him.

'Not on the kind of house we live in.'

'Oh yes,' the sheriff officer replied earnestly. 'Two years ago your father put the house into your name, so you're responsible for two years of arrears. You've had notices.'

'I probably put them into the fire with the other junk mail.'

'You're in serious trouble.'

'So will you be, you bastard, if you don't clear out of here!' Seumas shouted, scrambling to his feet. He picked up a stone and flung it after the fleeing sheriff officer. 'Away and play with your Dinky Toys!'

He sat fuming on the shore. Sandy had always been a sneak, running to Miss Maclaren with stories. He would run to the police, saying he had been assaulted, though he wished now he had kicked his fat arse.

It was all going to hell. No lobsters, no money, and now this. Seumas's temper was rising into rage as he noticed the floats like little fires marking the creels out in the bay which he and the old man had shot after bringing up polluted lobsters from the sunken iron ship off Rubha nan Ròn. He went up to the house for the rifle and the box of bullets. When the first flare was in the sights he pulled the trigger and heard the float exploding. The dog ran up to the house. He went along the line, the spent bullets tinkling between his knees on the shingle as he shattered all the floats. The little fires set by the old man that had been burning along that shore on so many sunny days were now out. The ropes would be sinking to the bottom, to lie until they rotted.

But destroying the floats still hadn't used up his anger. He roamed the shore with the rifle, and if any living thing had showed itself he would have shot it. He felt as if he were losing his mind.

The old man had had a brother, but he wouldn't talk about him. All he said was – and he only said it once: 'Erchie had to go away.' To where? Seumas had asked màthair, but she looked at him as if she were frightened to transmit information about her mysterious brother-in-law. But Seumas knew because a boy in the playground he had been fighting with shouted: 'Your uncle Erchie's off his fucking head!'

It had been worse than a blow to the stomach. The other boys crowded round, shoving him. 'Off his fucking head! Off his fucking head!' until they nearly had the jersey off Seumas's back.

Now he understood why the old man had been so reluctant to acknowledge his own brother. Eilidh had inherited her uncle's madness. The old man was frightened because he knew it was in the blood, and màthair was frightened because she knew she had married into it.

So he could have inherited it too, only it wasn't showing up until later in his life. What had happened to Erchie? Had he died in an asylum, probably the same asylum that Eilidh was in and where she too would end her days? Maybe Erchie had done himself in. He looked at the gun in his hands, then hurried with it up to the house. The dog was cowering on the step and he went down on his knees to hug her, apologizing for frightening her by the violence of his actions.

'We'll need to get a move on, the tide's coming in,' he told her, ruffling her coat, harmony restored between them.

He spooned out from the pot the rest of the rabbit he had cooked for himself and the dog, and the metal dish propelled by Dìleas's snout in it began its usual audible progress across the floor as the contents were consumed. He found a tin of beans with rust on the top in the cupboard. It wouldn't kill him, and he opened it, eating them cold with a fork as he stood at the door, looking across the bay whose landscape he had altered by smashing the old man's line of floats, brought as gifts by years of storms, sunk in a moment of tantrum.

He splashed with the oars, but there were only two small sea trout in the net, barely enough for his supper, never mind taking to the hotel to sell. Why was this happening to his livelihood? He had heard on the Gaelic radio an aquaculture expert warning against the growth of fish farms on the west coast. He claimed that poisonous chemicals that were being used to prevent sea lice in the farmed fish were going into open water, and that the waste of the fish dropped to the sea bed could pollute wild species.

It was these bastards round the headland who had emptied his net, so he was going to have to do something about that. He searched the tool box but there wasn't a wire cutter. He could still do damage, though. He fried the trout and made a careful cigarette. He couldn't leave till it was dark, so he sat on the doorstep listening to the Gaelic request programme. The songs went past him, out over the darkening bay where even the birds seemed to be listening. He understood now why the old man had brought a bride to this hard place where Gaelic was in the rock, running like glittering veins of quartz. It was in the bay, in the names of the birds that MacCallum had written down so carefully in his little notebook with the elastic band, the dipper going backwards and forwards on the stone in the burn by the *taigh-beag* where the old man had passed away doing a *cac*.

Runrig, the Celtic rock band, was performing *Cearcall a' Chuain*, about the circle of the sea, and Seumas listened as he smoked. There weren't many English words for the sea, but there were plenty in Gaelic. *Fèath nan eun*, the flat calm of the birds; *muir*, the brooding sea lying in the bay on a still day; *cuan*, the ocean that came rolling into the bay on a windy day. There was a word that the old man had used: *marannan*, the big billows racing into the bay, bringing the flotsam, the whirling fish boxes, the bobbing glass floats as gifts. *Garbh-thonn*, the wave with the sound of anger in its Gaelic, the treacherous wave the old man shouted a warning about as you stepped from the dinghy into the launch and even then you weren't safe because there was *thar-fhairge*, the wave that broke over the boat. *Cur na mara* was sea sickness. But there was no Gaelic word for the sick polluted sea that swirled round the fish farm except *eu-dòchas*, despair.

When it was dark he climbed into the dinghy. It was too dangerous to take the launch, though it was a long row, but he had all night. He went out of the bay with slow determined strokes across to where the floats had been, and felt guilt at the shattered glass lying on the bottom. He rounded the headland, past the cormorants silhouetted on Sgeir nan Eun, like dark bottles that had been badly blown. They were subdued and accepted the swish of his oars as he passed them.

During the day when he passed the cages he saw the farmed salmon leaping out of the water, but they were quiet now in the night with not much moon. He tied up the dinghy to the platform and walked round the gangway. The netting they had put over the fish to protect them from predators came away easily with the shears that the old man had used on the sheep. Below him he could hear restless fish. However hungry he was, he wouldn't eat them because of the chemicals they were being fed.

Half an hour later he was on his way home. He slept in his clothes, and at ten he went out to the launch and started the engine, opening it full throttle. The boat seemed to plane out of the bay. He felt elated. Ahead he could see the dense mass of birds round the fish farm, with men trying to scare them away with their arms.

'What's the trouble?' he shouted as he went close in.

'Some bastard's cut the netting to get at the fish!' the manager, a Sassenach, shouted back.

'Can I do anything?' Seumas asked.

'Thanks, but the police are coming.'

He went into the public bar of the hotel where Donnie was restocking the shelves.

'Sorry I don't have any fish for you.'

'I'm sorry for you,' Donnie said sincerely. 'And no lobsters either?'

'Nothing,' Seumas said bitterly.

Donnie put his big fists together on the counter.

'I hear someone's been at the fish farm.'

'So they told me when I passed it,' Seumas responded blandly.

Donnie was watching him, the way he had done when he was ready to pass him a sweetie in the class when MacCallum was writing at his desk.

'I prefer to serve my guests wild fish, and I don't approve of fish farms,' Donnie stated. 'But it's not the way to go about it.'

'How do you go about it?' Seumas asked, understanding the innuendo.

'Never mind that; you're not getting any fish, so you've got no money. I'm going to advance you some.'

They had been a team at school, sharing the little bag with the coloured marbles in them, small ones, big ones with beautiful designs, and between them they had augmented their collection in games in the playground, the glass balls colliding.

'You've already loaned me one hundred and fifty for the old man's funeral,' Seumas reminded him. 'I'll manage.'

'Only if you go and sign up for the dole.'

'That's what I'll do, Donnie.'

He went along the street to the office. The girl who answered the bell on the counter had been at school with him. She had a pronounced lisp which the boys had mocked.

Seumas explained that he had come to sign on because the fishing was bad.

Sheena was even uglier now with her thick spectacles and her lisp even thicker, a protracted *sss* sound.

'You'll have to go to the office on the mainland,' she told him in a tone that made plain she still didn't like him.

'I was on the mainland the other day, seeing my sister,' Seumas told her, drumming his fingers on the counter.

'You'll have to go to back,' Sheena repeated.

His sister was sitting in the ruined township, talking to people who had been sent overseas. The doctors in Glasgow said she was mad, a danger to herself, so she had been taken 'into care,' meaning the asylum. She had been a pretty girl, her pigtails bouncing on her shoulders as she skipped to *port-a-beul*, the mouth music she was making, until the rope fankled round her feet and she fell, the other children laughing as they continued skipping, the graceful arcs of their ropes going over their heads and under their coordinated shoes.

Seumas turned to Sheena, who was watching him through her thick lenses, her sibilant tongue ready.

'Did Donnie ever take you into the lavatories at school?'

She looked at him with incomprehension, her eyes, enlarged by the thick lenses, filling with tears of wishful thinking. The 37-year-old spinster threatened: 'I'm going to tell my mother what you just said.'

'Aye, you were always a clype, Sheena, running to Miss Maclaren and Mr. MacCallum.'

'I've told you, you've got to go to the mainland.'

'And what do I do when I get there?'

'You sign on and they'll try and get you a job.'

'Will they give me money?'

'They'll give you money but if they offer you a job you'll have to take it.'

'Where is this job likely to be?'

'It could be on the mainland, if there's nothing on the island.'

'What kind of job might it be?'

'I don't know, maybe working in a hotel on the mainland.'

'And if that doesn't suit me?'

'Look, this office doesn't deal with that,' she said, watching him with malice. 'I've got work to do.'

He let the door swing behind him. He was as well to go away to Glasgow rather than wash dishes for the tourists, even on the island. Maybe the policeman who had given them hospitality for the night when they had taken Eilidh to the hospital was still alive and would put him up until he found his feet.

Eight

He didn't go to the mainland to sign on the dole and he didn't go back to Donnie at the hotel. Instead he took the pile of local newspapers from the scullery, lifting out of the sideboard the tea set that màthair had got as a wedding present from the other herring girls and which had been used only when MacCallum visited.

He wrapped the pieces and stacked them carefully in the cardboard box he had brought from the Spar shop. He took the box out to the launch, stowing it under a seat before heading for the town. The local constable was on the gangway of the fish farm, notebook open, pen poised, as if about to charge the massing gulls with theft. As he puttered past Seumas didn't see one fish jumping.

He carried the box up the narrow street to the converted fisherman's cottage which had pieces of silver and a plain chair in the window. When he opened the door a bell was activated and a man with gold spectacles slid down his nose came through.

'Yes?' he said in a cultured English voice, as if he were being disturbed.

Seumas put the box on top of the glass case.

'I want to sell this.'

The man waited dispassionately while the prospective seller unpacked a piece. Then he held the cup up to the light as if there were a watermark in the china, turning it over and reading the bottom.

'How many pieces do you have?'

'It's all there,' Seumas told him.

'Yes, but how many?'

He had to unpack them piece by piece and stack them in their appropriate groups, cup, saucer, side plate. Three by six was eighteen, twenty with the milk and sugar.

'English bone china, the nineteen-thirties, made in thousands,' the man said wearily. 'I'll give you three pounds.'

Was he to take the money or wrap up all the pieces again? He took the coins and pulled the door hard behind him, leaving the bell clanging as the man put the pieces back into the box. He went to the Spar shop and bought tobacco, milk, bread, two tins of soup, a packet of frozen sausages. Donnie was outside the hotel, manhandling an aluminum keg as he passed down to the pier.

'Any more fish?' he asked.

Seumas shook his head.

'Pity, because I've got a party of Germans coming in tonight and that could have been the special dish. So what are you doing?'

He shrugged.

'I can give you a couple of days work here a week, shifting stuff for me.'

'Thanks all the same.'

He wanted to go home, but Donnie was detaining him.

'They haven't got anyone yet for damaging the fish farm.'

'I saw the constable there as I passed,' Seumas told him.

'You upset Sandy the sheriff officer.'

'He came with a summons about arrears of Rates,' Seumas said indignantly.

'You have to pay Rates on your house, Seumas.'

'It's a rented house.'

'That doesn't matter; you still have to pay Rates. When were they last paid?'

'Two years ago.'

'How has this happened?'

'The old man paid the rent, and I'll be paying it from now on. He must also have paid Rates. I didn't know that a house that doesn't have mains sewage and a road to it had to pay Rates, and I'm not paying when I don't have any of the services the people in the town here get.'

'Which is why Sandy served a notice on you. Look: you need to pay your arrears. I'll lend you the money.'

'Thanks all the same, Donnie, but I'm not paying. They can take me to court.'

'You'll regret it, my friend. What's the point on bringing trouble on your head? Now that your father's gone, you're alone in that remote house, Seumas. You need to apply for a council house in the town and mix more with people.'

'I like it where I am, Donnie, and I like my own company.'

He went along the pier with his Spar carrier bag. When he passed the fish farm the constable had gone. He fried the sausages in butter and ate them with the bread. The cigarette was the most important part to him as he sat on the shore. He was beginning to miss the old man's line of glass floats. Maybe he had been too quick with the gun.

It was funny, how you remembered things. He must have been about five years old when a rabbit came over the moor, jinking as if moving by clockwork. Then Seumas saw the shadow coming. He couldn't imagine what kind of creature could make such a huge shadow and he cowered behind the upturned dinghy in terror. As the rabbit veered down the hill the wings came into view. It was an *iolaire,* an eagle, and the spread of its wings was as majestic as its Gaelic name, echoing its fluid flight and its shadow, a dark plaid thrown down over its quarry.

The rabbit raced down the hill and the wings changed direction. And suddenly the eagle and its shadow merged. But Seumas didn't see it. He would look at the replay again and again in his memory, but would never see it. The eagle had the rabbit in its claws as it passed over the dinghy, so low that the old man could have touched the wings, and then it began to climb as it went towards the mountains, probably to feed its young in its inaccessible eyrie. The old man said nothing, pushing back his cap because even Gaelic words would have been inadequate.

Seumas made himself another cigarette to go with the memory of the wings as they came sweeping back. But this time it wasn't an eagle. The local constable had walked from the road end. He had a walkie-talkie on his chest.

'Hullo, Hughie, what brings you here?' Seumas asked.

Maybe Hughie had forgotten that they had been in the same class in primary school with Sandy the sheriff officer. But this wasn't about the visit of the sheriff officer with the Rates demand.

'The fish farm was vandalized,' the constable said.

'So I heard.'

'Someone cut the netting to let the birds in.'

'Is that a fact?' As he smoked Seumas kept his back to his visitor.

'Did you see anything suspicious when you were out in your boat?' the constable asked.

'I don't go out in my boat at night.'

'I didn't say it was at night.'

Only once did the old man put a foot wrong when he was moving from the dinghy to the launch, and he had corrected himself immediately.

'I assumed it was at night because this morning when I took the boat in they were trying to chase away the birds,' Seumas said.

'Where were you last night?' the constable demanded.

'Listen, Hughie –'

But the fact that he had shared his plasticine with Hughie in Miss Maclaren's room had nothing to do with this visit.

'I asked you a question.'

'I was here, last night.'

'Doing what?'

'Do I need to have been doing something? I was just here. I've been here all my life.'

The constable seemed to be writing all this down.

'I may be back,' he warned.

'And I may not be here,' Seumas told him. 'I may be out fishing. Ask yourself, Hughie, when you're sitting in a layby, waiting for drunk drivers: why would Seumas want to vandalize a fish farm?'

But the constable was going back up the slope, over the moor in his diced cap with his truncheon hanging from his side, his walkie-talkie cackling on his chest. He went up where the eagle had come stealthily, with its shadow bearing down on the ridiculous rabbit running as if it had a key up its *tòn*.

When the tide was right Seumas put the net out, but there was nothing in it, as if someone had cursed the bay and all that it contained. He went back into the house and opened the doors of the cluttered sideboard, lifting the things out on the flagstones because he had to find something else to sell. He shuffled through the packet of photographs showing his parents on their wedding day in 1938, the bridegroom with a flower in the lapel of his jacket; the bride in a white dress and matching headband; herring girls in attendance, in bright dresses instead of the aprons they had worn at the abrasive barrels of salt and ice. He found a snapshot of himself as a boy in a jersey knitted by màthair, standing, clutching his short trousers as if they were about to fall round his sandshoes; Eilidh standing with her hands clasped in front of her, the date on the back of the photograph 1954, staring as if the camera wasn't there, already in her own world with its voices of the departed.

But he couldn't spend all night looking at the photographs. He opened the other door of the sideboard and the grubby tea cosy fell out. He should clear out all this stuff and make a bonfire of it, but he was pushing it back into the cupboard.

'Excuse me!'

He turned on his knees to see who was rapping at the door. A blonde woman was on the step.

'Do you have any shellfish to sell?'

Seumas rose to his feet. She was wearing blue yachting oilskins with the trousers on braces up to her bust, the way the old man used to wear his when the weather was bad. Her blue boots had white tops.

'We were told to come here,' she said.

'Who told you?'

'Donnie at the hotel.'

He stepped past her and saw the white yacht in the bay, with a man standing by the boom, and a woman in dark glasses in the cockpit. He felt so angry that he could have struck the woman with the fancy voice and the expensive gear at his back.

'No, I don't have any shellfish,' Seumas said without turning round.

'But Donnie said –'.

'I don't care what Donnie said. I told you, I don't have any.'

He watched her lifting the rubber runabout into the water and pulling out with short red oars. There was a confab on the deck as she pointed to the house and its morose occupant. The sail was run up and the boat veered away. He stood, making sure it went out of the bay.

Every summer more and more boats were coming into the bay. One big white one had dropped its sails in the dusk, spilling its anchor. There was a lot of laughter coming from it. He and the old man were standing at the door, watching it. The people on board had taken off their clothes and were swimming naked in the bay. The old man had gone inside and come out with the gun which he fired into the sky. They watched the swimmers striking towards the yacht, shinning up the side, and then the anchor had been lifted and it motored at full power out of the bay.

Seumas went back to the sideboard to start on the drawers. He could hardly get them open, they were so crammed with things: pieces of string, scissors, sealing wax, a fountain pen, its nib splayed, the crushed box that had contained a mantle for the lamp. He opened the next drawer and in his temper tipped it out over the floor. The empty cotton reels, the old pennies, the single buttons rolled about the flagstones. There was paper spread in the bottom of the drawer.

He sat on the floor among the debris, turning the yellowed pages of the Canadian magazine. Màthair had relatives in Canada whose people had been cleared from her island a hundred years before and who kept in touch with her by sending magazines throughout the 1950s. The postman grumbled in Gaelic as he carried the bundle in his bag on mornings when the wind from the sea was trying to push him back over the moor.

Màthair had read the serials in these magazines avidly, though they were about a way of life she knew nothing about. She read about prairie families trapped in snowdrifts, when she had seen so little snow in her own lifetime. She read about fields of wheat the size of the moor beyond the house being harvested by huge machines. She read about men who came to propose on horseback, and she waited patiently for the next part of the story in the next bundle. Sometimes there would be a letter in the centre of the bundle, urging her to come out for a visit, but there would never be money for the fare, and she wouldn't have gone alone because her family came first, and the old man was hopeless in the house. When màthair was in hospital he had made Seumas a cup of tea, but hadn't boiled the water.

Seumas scooped the debris back into the drawer and went upstairs to another possibility. He hadn't touched his parents' room since the day he had pulled the old man's suit from the rail in order to dress him and take him to the town for the doctor to confirm the death. He opened the bottom drawer of the chest, releasing the naphthalene pungency of mothballs. He lifted aside Màthair's underwear reverently and found letters, written in a copperplate hand by her granduncle Fionnlagh. Two of her granduncles had gone out to work in the gold mines, and because they were intelligent and dedicated they had been made supervisors. When they knew as much about mining as those running it, they opened their own mine with a dozen black men. Within two months they had struck gold and were sending money home. But the other granduncle, Uilleam, was a gambler. *My dear niece,* Fionnlagh wrote to màthair's mother: *I am sorry to have to tell you that Uilleam lost our mine last Friday in a game of cards in Johannesburg ...*

Seumas found what he expected to find under the bundle of letters: Uilleam's Waltham watch, sent home as a memento after he was killed in a brawl over a disputed stake. It was a big pocket watch, made of gunmetal to withstand rough usage in a mine, and it had a thick silver chain with a silver threepence coin attached, sole survivor of the mining fortune.

'You'll get good money for that watch,' màthair had told her son, as if it were a substantial inheritance.

He wound the rasping wheel and the little gold second hand began to sweep round. Maybe it had never been wound since that night of the ruinous game of cards. He folded màthair's underwear back in the drawer as he had found it, and took the watch downstairs with him. By ten o' clock the next morning it was lying on the glass counter in the antique shop in the town, being examined by the proprietor with a black jeweller's glass screwed into his eye socket. He had the back open and was watching the miniature wheels going round.

'It's a nice watch of its type,' he conceded in his precise English accent. 'Good for the waistcoat pocket of a working man, but too heavy for today. I'll give you three pounds for it.'

'It's a good watch,' Seumas said, shocked, because he couldn't think of anything else to say.

'Three pounds,' the man repeated. 'And I'm taking a chance on it.'

Seumas took the money and went to the Spar shop. He bought the local paper and sat on a bollard on the pier to study the employment advertisements. An estate up north wanted a ghillie, but he didn't have any experience.

WANTED. EXPERIENCED BOATMAN TO RUN PLEASURE
BOAT ON LOCH LOMOND.

There wasn't anything else in the house to sell and there would be no fish in the net tonight. The three pounds hadn't gone far in the shop. No doubt he would be taken to court over the Rates arrears, and the constable would likely come back to ask more questions about the damage done to the fish farm.

It was finished, all finished. He made himself a smoke as he sat on the bollard. Once – and only once – the cousins in Canada had sent a present at Christmas, a silver box of sweeties. They were hard pink bonbons and they rattled round màthair's false teeth as she sat in her chair with her eyes closed, maybe imagining that the clatter she was making with her mouth was a horseman crossing the prairie at a gallop to propose.

The old man had received a present also, a bar of black tobacco which he shaved off in thin strips against his thumb with his knife before rubbing it between a palm and the ball of the other hand before tamping the strands into his pipe. When the aroma of the tobacco reached Seumas he recalled the film he had seen at school about the Canadian prairies, with a man smoking a pipe at the wheel of a massive combine harvester, three other machines moving in line in the vast field.

When MacCallum landed from his boat he sometimes had new Gaelic words, and the old man would roll them round and round in his mouth, getting the flavour of them as màthair had done with the bonbons from Canada, the cardboard box they had come in kept in the cupboard, as if it were sterling silver.

Gaelic was finished. He had nobody to speak it to now. It was a useless inheritance. They had made a fool of him in the playground after MacCallum had spoken to him in Gaelic in the class. He had been goaded into fights over Gaelic, and because no one else understood the language he was alone in the corner where two walls met. He had bled for Gaelic, limping home off the bus, his boot in his hand because of the kick on his ankle. He had cried for Gaelic in his bed under the skylight. Having Gaelic was like what he had once witnessed in the school shed, the humiliation of Eachann his classmate having his trousers forcibly removed to expose his small *bod* to much ridicule, with the girls leaning over the wall, sniggering when the sobbing victim was paraded round, arms pinned behind his back so that he couldn't cover his shame. The old man was dead and Eilidh would be in the asylum for the rest of her life. The language of his inheritance was like ashes in his mouth.

He went into the hotel for change for the phone box.

'I'm going to try this,' he said, showing the advert to Donnie.

'It's a pity,' his friend said. 'I can still give you work, but if that's the way you feel use this phone.'

Yes, the man on the other end of the line was looking for a boatman. What experience did the caller have? Seumas explained that he had been using the launch since he was a boy.

'I'll be glad to take a west coast man,' the owner said. 'I can give you a hundred pounds a week, for six days, and a caravan to live in.'

That kind of money was more than he and the old man used to make from the lobsters in three weeks.

'I can start next week,' Seumas told the man.

'Only one thing – no dogs,' the man stated.

Nine

He couldn't take Dìleas with him to Loch Lomond. She was the old man's last dog, and though she must be about fourteen, she had the energy of a dog half her age. No one in the town would take her, so he was going to have to put her down.

As Seumas was thinking this while drinking a mug of tea the animal was lying sleeping at his boots. It was a terrible betrayal, but there was no other option. But first he was going to have to decide what to do about the house. He couldn't see himself coming back once he got settled at his new job on the mainland. The idea of emptying the paraffin can inside, then tossing in a match, recurred because that would destroy all traces of the past. But he couldn't do it because it was the laird's house and because he knew that he couldn't burn his upbringing out of his brain. Besides, he would have to come back from time to time to see his sister.

He was going to have to search for the key to the door. The lock must have had a key at one time, though he had never seen it. Even when they had taken Eilidh to the Infirmary in Glasgow they had only pulled the door behind them. The postman knew to open it and leave the bundle of Canadian magazines on the chair, with the next eagerly awaited instalment of màthair's story about the suitors on horseback on the great prairies.

He tipped out the drawers again on to the floor, scrabbling through the contents, but there was no key, so he would have to nail up the door. He went into the scullery and pulled out the tool box from under the sink, taking a hammer and three rusty six inch nails the old man had extracted from a plank that had come ashore in a storm.

He left the hammer and the nails on the step and then went for the gun. The old man had been a crack shot and could roll a rabbit over at a hundred yards. Some nights they had gone poaching over the laird's land, dragging back a stag whose guts they pulled out and threw into the sea as if in offering to Manannan, the Celtic sea god. Màthair had known how long to give venison in an oven that had no thermostat or timer.

He put a bullet into the gun. The dog was lying on the floor by the old man's chair, as if he were still there, her belly rising and falling in sleep. He crunched along the shingle curve of the shore. The dog that was ahead of him now, snuffling among the seaweed, had been brought home under the old man's jacket on a stormy night. Màthair had stuck her pinkie in the bowl of milk and offered it as a substitute nipple to the puppy skidding on unsteady legs on the flagstones. Seumas had kept the puppy in bed with him for weeks, but it was the old man's dog and she had gone everywhere with him, on the hill and moor for the sheep, and in the launch for the fishing. In the evening she would be by the old man's boots as he talked in Gaelic to MacCallum. The dog knew Gaelic; it was the only language she would respond to.

Seumas was grateful that the dog was behind him as he walked back to the house. He was turning to raise the gun when he heard a big splash in the bay. If it were a fish jumping and not a seal it had to be a big one, likely a salmon. They had sometimes caught salmon in the net, which paid better than sea trout because the hotel could charge more for salmon fresh from the sea. But it could be an escaped fish from the damaged farm, revelling in the freedom of open water.

He fetched the net and lifted the dog into the dinghy. The mesh slid from the platform at the stern as he rowed in the area where he thought the splash had come from. He swung the oars in and stood up to pull in the net, seeing the commotion in the water caused by a fish, bigger than a sea trout, thrashing in the net. It was a grilse, *òigh a' chuain*, the virgin of the sea, a young salmon returning to its native river to spawn after only one winter at sea. The grilse, with its small mouth and narrow shoulders, lay between his hands, perfect in form, its scales flashing like tiny mirrors in the sunset. It seemed a violation, knocking its head against the gunwale instead of returning it to its element. As he hauled the rest of the net aboard it was heavy with sea trout.

He rowed jubilantly to the shore as the catch flapped round his boots with Dìleas sitting in the stern, watching them as if daring any of the fish to jump back over the side. He lifted his hand from an oar, leaned forward and fondled the dog's ears.

'And to think I nearly shot you, old friend,' he told his canine companion in Gaelic.

He fetched a box from the shed and knelt in the shallows, gutting the trout with a sure blade and rinsing out their bellies. He laid them carefully in the box, counting them. Forty-two. He would get good money for them from Donnie. As he stood up he noticed a fin. The old man and he had sometimes seen the fins of basking sharks like black sails from the launch, and once, out in the rowing boat, Seumas had noticed the massive dark shape alongside, beneath the surface. The shark could have risen with the boat on its back, overturning it, but somehow he knew that this was a docile creature despite its size, so he wasn't frightened. The shark whose fin was showing must have been attracted inshore by the guts from the fish he had chucked into the sea.

He carried the box of fish back into the house, removing the bullet from the gun in case of an accident. He left the box of fish on the floor while he started a fire, feeling excited, renewed. He wouldn't go away in the morning but would give the fishing another week.

He made himself tea and went out to the shed for a rabbit for himself and the dog. The sunset through the open door was turning the box of trout into a big block of silver. He rolled a cigarette, fish scales still on his fingers, and smoked deeply and appreciatively, watching Dìleas guzzling the rabbit on the step when the dog could have been getting buried by now. He speculated if the basking shark – if that was what it was – had chased the fish inshore, bringing him the bounty of the full box of fish. He went upstairs to bed, singing a Gaelic song, the dog following, bounding up in front of him, as if knowing she had been reprieved.

The fin kept thrusting up in his sleep. He swung his legs out of the bed and went downstairs, standing naked at the door in the starry night, looking across the bay, wondering if it were still out there, circling. When he went back up the dog lying on the blanket on the floor was whimpering in a dream, her nose lifting from her paws.

Next morning he shaved and put on a clean shirt before he took the box of fish and the dog out to the launch. The engine was singing sweetly in the clear balmy morning as he went round Rubha nan Ròn, the seals appearing to lift their flippers to wave to him. He waved back, ruffling the dog's head as if he had just acquired her. There was a new protective net over the fish farm, and he raised an arm to the workers on the floating cage.

'My God, I haven't seen one of these for ages,' Donnie said, lifting the grilse from the top of the full box of sea trout. 'Your luck seems to have turned.' He lugged the box through to the kitchen scales and gave him £20 from the till.

'Take it towards the money I owe you,' Seumas told him.

'No, no, we'll leave that till you get on your feet. So you're not going to the job at Loch Lomond?'

'I'll give the fishing another go,' Seumas told his friend.

'Good man. I'll take as much fish off you as you can get. Remember to pay your Rates arrears. If you're short I can make

up the sum. By the way, I think Myrtle sees you as a catch. She'll
be back.'

He didn't go to the Spar shop to buy groceries. Instead he went
up the narrow lane to the antique shop. Màthair's wedding china
which he had sold for £3, was in the window, but when he bent
down he saw that the little white ticket written in blue ink was for
£6. The bastard. He felt like bursting open the door and going into
the Englishman speaking on the phone at the counter. He had a
wad of money in his pocket and for a moment was tempted to go
back in and buy back màthair's wedding present, except that he
needed the money for living expenses. But he would come back
for the china.

Alice was behind the counter in the library, a well built, good
looking woman with black hair down to her shoulders. They
said in the town that she had Spanish blood in her veins from the
Armada wreck that had foundered further along the coast. She
was married to the driver of the local bus, but everyone knew that
Donnie had been riding her for years.

'Well, Seumas, I've never seen you in here before,' she said
brightly. 'Have you come to continue your education?'

'Do you have a book on sharks?'

'You're not thinking of taking up shark fishing?' she said, half
in earnest. 'That's what Gavin Maxwell did for a while on Soay.
I read an article, saying he has a tame otter in the Highlands he
treats like a chid.'

One afternoon MacCallum had looked up from the jotter he was
correcting.

'What are you reading under the desk?' he asked Heather.

She didn't look anxious as she brought out the book, because the
schoolmaster never belted girls.

'*The Wind in the Willows*,' MacCallum read the cover. 'A story
that turns animals into humans and makes them cute. Rat and
Mole ride in a rowing boat. Toad has crashed seven cars. Badger
wears a dressing gown and slippers. I'll give you something far

more instructive to read,' he told the girl standing beside his desk. He went to the cupboard where the raffia hung, taking out a book and holding it up to the class. '*The Wildlife of Mull* by Angus Maclennan. He was my mother's brother. There's a good chapter on watching wild otters at Ulva Ferry on Mull which Heather is going to read out to us.'

'All I'm wanting is a book on sharks,' Seumas told Alice.

She came over with him and went through the shelves.

'This is all we have.'

Seumas carried the book on marine creatures to the table and opened it at the plates. It couldn't have been a shark. Then what was it? A whale? It hadn't looked like the whale the storm had rolled up on to the shore when he was a boy, and whose stench filled the house until the seabirds had reduced it to a skeleton over a winter. He turned the page, but it hadn't been that big. A porpoise? He read: *Porpoises are shy creatures and most people only catch a glimpse of the rolling back.* No, the creature he had seen was bigger. He turned the page to another illustration: *The adult bottlenose dolphin has a sickle-shaped dorsal fin which curves backwards, and a beak.* He hadn't seen the beak, but he was sure that was the fin.

He sat studying the coloured illustration, then went back to Alice at the counter.

'Have you a Gaelic dictionary?'

'Oh, I forgot, you're one of the dying breed here with the language. I'm afraid we don't have a Gaelic dictionary. There's no demand for it.'

He left her stamping books and went down to the Spar shop, filling a big box, the first tins of meat the dog would have tasted; tins of creamed rice for himself; a frozen shepherd's pie; lemonade; three ounces of tobacco; three packets of cigarette papers. There was a satisfaction in unfolding the notes he had received for the fish and handing them to the uncommunicative girl at the till.

The dog hadn't moved from her vigilant position in the bow of the launch while he went about his business. They travelled home

as quickly as they had come and as soon as he was inside the door
he began raking again.

* * * * *

There had always been a pile of books on the table in Miss
Maclaren's room on the summer afternoon when the laird had
come to the school to present the prizes. Every year Seumas
received the prize for arithmetic, and even Donnie had been given
a prize, for perfect attendance, because he didn't want to miss a
day in the lavatories with the girls. But when Seumas was in the
last class, the 'Qualifying,' MacCallum had called one night. In
summer he rowed round to the bay, but when autumn came he
used his launch. As well as the half bottle of whisky and the box of
Black Magic for màthair, he was carrying a book.

'This is for you,' he said, giving it to Seumas.

It was an English-Gaelic dictionary, with an inscription in it in
MacCallum's lady-like handwriting.

*DON AON SGOILEAR EILE ANNS AN SGOIL AIG A BHEIL
CÀNAN GÀRRADH ÈDEIN*

◎

TO THE ONLY OTHER PUPIL IN THE SCHOOL WHO
SPEAKS THE LANGUAGE OF THE GARDEN OF EDEN.

Màthair had been so proud when her son read the inscription
to her, and the old man had nodded appreciatively. For the first
few weeks he had the book he looked up words in English and
shared their Gaelic equivalent with his parents. But the old man
was suspicious of books and preferred his conversations with the
schoolmaster as a way of acquiring new words.

He hadn't seen the dictionary for years and began a big search
for it. Was it in the wooden chest in his bedroom, with old bits of
toys; the battleship the old man had swapped for cigarettes with

the man who had carved it on the minesweeper; the jigsaw puzzles lacking decisive pieces? He found the dictionary at the bottom of the box and sat on the bed, looking up the Gaelic for dolphin.

An leumadair.

The leaper.

He now understood how MacCallum had loved Gaelic so much and was always saying what an exact language in was. *Lyame-uh-ter*, the leaper. When you said the word you could see the creature rising from the water, then falling back with a splash until the silence settled again. *Leumadair, leumadair.* He kept repeating the name all the way downstairs, as he had repeated *bod* and *faighean* as he skipped across the moor, having been given these intimate terms by the Gaelic learner with his obtrusive tape recorder.

'Come on, lassie, we're going to look for our new friend,' he told the dog.

He walked with big strides along the shore, watching the bay, but there was no sign of a fin. He wasn't perturbed and would wait until the tide was high. He sat on the shore with the net spread out over his knees, mending the tear that a big sea trout had made on its escape. A buzzard came over the hill, its shadow taking the sun from his face for a moment. He was glad that he wasn't on the bus to Loch Lomond. There was food in the house, cigarettes in his pocket and, best of all, Dìleas at his feet, scrutinizing the bay. And there was a new word in his head.

Leumadair.

By God, the old man would have liked this word. He would have rolled it around his mouth, and MacCallum would have liked it too. He could see the schoolmaster uncapping his fountain pen and committing the name to his black notebook, if he didn't know it already, since he had been raised on a croft overlooking the Sound of Mull and would likely have seen dolphins. But Seumas would have remembered if the name *leumadair* had come into the conversation between the old man and the schoolmaster. It hadn't because there was so much else to talk about, so many Gaelic names, of birds, of flowers, of wave formations, to exchange. There was so much to discuss, so many names to try to retrieve from the flotsam of time, to admire, to study before they were washed away again, to become extinct.

Seumas kept looking, but there was no sign of Leumadair, though the tide was coming in. He would give it another hour, so he went up to the house and scraped the defrosted shepherd's pie from its metal tray into a pot and put in on the fire. He fed the dog and had his smoke. He carried the net in his arms out to the boat, but there was still no sign of Leumadair. He paid out the net and splashed with the oars, but when he hauled the net in he knew by the feel that there was nothing in it.

The creature must have gone. It had chased the grilse and sea trout in towards the shore and had stayed for a couple of days out of curiosity. It could be out in the open Atlantic by now, maybe lying off the island màthair had come from. The mysterious appeal of the dolphin prompted the memory of the evening the old man, who had been round to the town in the launch, came into the house with a squawking sound coming from under the bag over his left hand. Màthair thought it was a hen, but when the old man whipped off the bag with the deftness of a conjurer, a green parrot was sitting on his wrist.

'What in God's name have you brought home now?' màthair asked in consternation.

'I got it for two pounds from a man on a trawler that came in because bad weather's coming.'

'Two pounds?' màthair almost squawked in indignation. 'There are a lot more useful things to spend two pounds on than a *pearraid*. That money could have got the boy a badly needed new pair of boots.'

But Seumas preferred to have the parrot. He was thrilled by the acquisition and went to stroke the magnificent burnished feathers, but when he tried to touch the head the bird let out a series of expletives in English. Màthair was shocked, but Seumas couldn't stop laughing.

'We'll have no bad language in this house,' the old man warned the parrot, shaking an indignant finger in front of its eyes, for which he received a peck and more swears.

'What's your name?' Seumas asked the bird.

'Freddie!' it squawked.

'We're going to have to change that,' the old man told it. 'From now on your name's Gilleasbaig.'

It took several repetitions by the old man and Seumas to get the parrot to utter its new name, after which its Gaelic lessons began in earnest, with *'S mise Gilleasbaig*, I'm Gilleasbaig. Next the old man taught it to greet them as they came in the door. The bird soon acquired an impressive Gaelic vocabulary. The trouble was, it delivered a monologue for most of the night from its perch in the kitchen, keeping them awake upstairs, until màthair told her spouse in desperation: 'I've to get up to milk the cow in the morning. Go and put that awful creature in the *taigh-beag* where it can't be heard.'

But the old man refused to degrade the clever bird by, as he said, putting it in among the *cac*. It stayed in the kitchen, and when MacCallum came to give Seumas Gaelic lessons, the bird also learned the new words, perching on the tutor's shoulder and sometimes tweaking MacCallum's ear, as if he had made a mistake in Gaelic. The old man sat with the bird on the arm of his chair, praising it: 'Well now, my feathered friend, you have more sense than most people in the town because you've made the effort to learn Gaelic.'

Seumas often wondered if it was màthair who had left the door open deliberately. But when the old man came in to find *Gilleasbaig a' phearraid* gone he was philosophical.

'It was such a clever creature, it must have sensed that the trawler it used to be on was passing and it flew out to sea to be with its old master. I hope it teaches him some Gaelic.'

Ten

Another tide, another big catch. Seumas was sitting on the shore gutting the sea trout, keeping an eye out for the rolling fin. He had the blade in the belly of a trout when Leumadair leapt fifty yards offshore, dazzling him by the whiteness of its underside before it slipped back in by the beak. He had the guts out of the fish when the dolphin came up again and this time it was playing with a salmon. He sat on the shore, roaring with laughter at its antics, remembering the games of shinty at school with the stick the old man had bent over the steaming kettle, the good feeling of getting the curve under the ball, whacking it skyward.

Leumadair seemed to be knocking the salmon high in the air with its beak, and almost before it came down it was sending it up again as it leapt and bucked across the bay. The dog beside him was an intent spectator, sitting with her ears forward, her head following the leaping animal.

He put the fish into the box and took them out to the launch. There was still time to get them on the dinner menu at the hotel. As he left the bay there was no sign of Leumadair, but passing Sgeir nan Eun the dolphin shot out of the water twenty yards in front of the boat, giving him such a fright that he jerked the tiller towards the rock, scattering the birds.

He opened the throttle as he followed the leaping body, but it went under and he thought the creature had veered away out into the open water. He eased the engine and, guiding the tiller with his elbow, made himself a cigarette, the frail paper fluttering in his fingers, when the grey shape came speeding along the side of the launch, rolling over as it passed. It was only a second's eye contact, but he saw in it intelligence, curiosity, mischief. He opened the throttle to its maximum, trying to anticipate where Leumadair would leap next, but it wasn't where he expected.

Leumadair appeared to be bouncing on its belly out to sea, as if trying to take him off course for a chase, but he had the fish to deliver before dinner at the hotel, so he pushed the tiller, bringing the launch round. He had to slow down the engine as the exhilaration of what had happened hit him. The creature which was disappearing into the distance, as if it had only discovered the joy of leaping, had chosen to honour him with its presence and its gifts because the box of fish at his boots was due to it.

He had never felt so at ease with himself and the world as he motored into the harbour in the peaceful afternoon, taking the catch up to the hotel to get his money. Then he went back up to the library.

'Have you a book on dolphins?' he asked Alice.

'You must have seen it.'

'Seen what?' he asked, mystified. He felt insecure in the presence of this good looking woman with the Celtic silver earrings who seemed to be thrusting out her breasts at him over the stack of books on the counter.

'The dolphin that's outside the harbour. The fishermen are talking about it.'

He was angry because he regarded Leumadair as being his.

The old man had been very careful and always liked to answer with a question.

'Is that what it was?' He used the past tense to imply that it had now disappeared.

She took him over to a shelf and pulled out a book.

'It may be a bit scientific,' she cautioned as she went back to the desk on her high heels, her hips moving provocatively. She must be good, the number of years Donnie had been with her.

'So this is the first time you've used the library? You've got a lot of catching up to do.'

He filled in a form, then watched her pushing down the rubber stamp with the date, taking the ticket from its little pocket.

'It's due back in a fortnight. There's a fine for overdue books.'

'Thanks.'

'You know, Seumas, I've always fancied you.'

He looked around, but there was nobody else in the library.

'You were always so quiet, so reserved. All the other boys wanted was to get the girls into the toilets to see what we have between our thighs, but you didn't do that kind of thing, did you?'

She was looking at him closely, head inclined as if she were considering him as her new lover.

'It was a long time ago,' he answered her.

'I'm not that old,' she said with some indignation. 'I remember seeing you in the boat with your father and thinking: he's not like the rest of us, going home to a house in a street in the town; he's going to a mysterious place none of us has seen. You didn't even have electric light, did you?'

'I still don't,' he said, embarrassed.

'I remember seeing you going on the bus, carrying the battery for the radio. It looked the most precious thing in your life to you.'

He didn't tell her that it was full of Gaelic songs for màthair and the old man.

'MacCallum the schoolmaster thought the world of you because you and he spoke in Gaelic, and no one else knew what the two of you were saying. That was strange too, a boy from along the coast from a place with no road to it, with a language most people couldn't understand. And your sister was so beautiful.' She shook her head sadly, then seemed to snap out of her reverie. 'Anyway, enjoy your book.'

There was no sign of Leumadair on the way home. After he had made his tea he opened the book and read that Leumadair was a bottlenose dolphin, a description that made him smile as he looked at the illustration.

> Bottlenose dolphins are distributed widely in warm and temperate waters throughout the world. However, they are relatively uncommon round the coast of the UK. The lifespan of a bottlenose dolphin is in general about 25 years, but animals as old as 50 have been recorded. These sociable animals usually live in groups of various sizes called pods.

So Leumadair was a loner. Or maybe there were more of them out there. That made him worried that it would desert him. He went to the door, but there was no sign of a fin in the bay. The last he had seen of it, it had been heading out to sea. Maybe he wouldn't see it again. That thought troubled him all evening and he couldn't sleep, but lay smoking, an arm under his head as he looked up at the skylight sprinkled with stars.

If he had stayed on at school he would have known more. One night when MacCallum was visiting and he was doing a jigsaw upstairs under the skylight, màthair had called up that the schoolmaster wanted to see him.

'Mr. MacCallum's going to teach you to write Gaelic, Seumas. He says it'll be useful for you,' she said respectfully.

'In what way will it be useful to the boy when the language is hardly spoken now in the place?' the old man asked his visitor for enlightenment.

'The Gaelic language is in our souls. Reading and writing it help to preserve it. To have two languages makes a person more interesting, more knowledgeable than someone who has only one.

And Gaelic, unlike English, hasn't been corrupted by slang or shoddy expression.'

MacCallum came once a week by sea in his oilskins, the line of sharpened pencils in the top pocket of his Harris Tweed jacket. They worked together on the oilcloth by the lamp, MacCallum asking him to speak the word. He tried to write it down, but it didn't come out as it had sounded. It was like learning a new language, but the schoolmaster was patient as he took a red pencil out of his pocket and corrected it.

'Now for the big test,' MacCallum said six months later, putting a new jotter in front of his pupil. 'I want you to write down what your father and I are saying to each other, Seumas. We'll speak slowly for you.'

It was as if the pencil were running away from him, as if he were writing the word even before its articulation was complete. He left gaps where the schoolmaster used a word heard only on Mull. After five minutes MacCallum came across, putting on his tortoiseshell glasses from the dented metal case and taking out the red pencil.

MacCallum always made noises at his desk at school as he corrected a jotter, with the pupil standing beside him. These were noises of protest at the use of grammar, at bad spelling, and he would slash at words with his red pencil as if he hated the English language. But tonight he wasn't making any noises and the red pencil was ticking the lines. He put 90/100 at the end of the exercise.

'You're a bright boy, Seumas. Go and show your father.'

The old man looked uncomprehendingly at the language MacCallum said he spoke better than himself, though the schoolmaster had studied it at the university.

'Seumas has done so well that I want to take him to a concert in the town,' MacCallum proposed to the old man and màthair. 'Bobby MacLeod from Mull is playing, and no finer accordionist has been born in the Gàidhealtachd, if not the whole of Scotland.'

Seumas waited behind after the school had been dismissed the following Friday afternoon. MacCallum took him next door into the school house where his sister Seònaid was preparing a supper for their guest. She had made him a pie of venison sent over from Mull by their sister, followed by a bowl of trifle, the first time he had tasted one, and would never forget. They went up to the crowded hall where the Mull accordion maestro was playing. Seumas sat between his schoolmaster and his sister, watching fascinated as the player's fingers moved so swiftly, so surely on the piano accordion keys, without even looking at them, without a sheet of music in front of him.

'I'm going to play a set of pipe marches,' MacLeod announced. 'There's space out there if you feel like getting up for a Canadian Barn Dance.'

MacCallum and his sister were first on the floor, and Seumas sat in wonder at the speed and grace of their footwork, as if they were young again at a ceilidh dance on Mull as they hopped round the floor. It was too late for MacCallum to take him home in his launch, so after the sister had given him his first ever glass of orange juice, with a plate of dark chocolate biscuits which he finished, he slept in the school house and was collected by the old man in the morning after a big breakfast of a *marag*, a black pudding, sausages and potato scones. Màthair wanted a full account of the evening's entertainment, and he told about the schoolmaster dancing with his sister.

'I heard he was a good dancer,' the old man stated, but without naming his informant.

A fortnight after the Mull accordionist's visit MacCallum placed a red coloured wooden box in front of his Gaelic pupil. Seumas opened the lid to reveal a mouth organ.

'I got it in the war from a German we took prisoner at El Alamein in North Africa in November 1942. It's a Hohner, a good one. I never mastered it, but you may do better, Seumas.'

He couldn't concentrate on that evening's Gaelic lesson for looking at the red box, and when MacCallum had gone he lifted out the elegant curved instrument. When he went up to his bedroom he tried to produce a tune by blowing and sucking, but it was difficult. However, màthair urged him to persevere, since there was music in the blood, a relative having been a well known piper who had won the Gold Medal at the Argyllshire Gathering at Oban, and the Clasp at the Northern Meeting at Inverness that same year.

On the Saturday night dance programme which they always listened to on the wireless, Seumas had heard the waltz *Fàgail Lios Mòr*, Leaving Lismore, being played. Màthair had sat beside him at the table, humming the tune to him night after night as he tried to play it along with her on the mouth organ. When he made a mistake she patted the hand of her frustrated son, telling him to persevere.

'Seumas has a surprise for you,' the old man told MacCallum a month later.

He lifted the hallowed mouth organ from its red box with German writing on it and played the tune note-perfect for his Gaelic tutor. Soon he had picked up other tunes from the wireless with màthair's help, and while MacCallum was having his supper of màthair's cheese and the bread she had baked herself, Seumas played their guest a medley of tunes, including some pipe marches from Mull, to MacCallum's delight.

* * * * *

Seumas had gone on to the junior secondary school in the town in 1958, promising MacCallum that he would take Gaelic, but most of the pupils in the class were learners and he was bored. Besides, he didn't like the teacher from Lewis, who was always boasting that the purest Gaelic came from his island. The Lewis man corrected his pronunciation and when he used the new form at home the old man asked him angrily what was happening to his Gaelic, so he had to tell.

'You'll speak the language as you learned it in this house and from Mr. MacCallum,' the old man warned.

Seumas also took science, but his mind wandered from the lesson why plants required light, because he didn't believe that you needed to know this to enjoy the *canach*, bog cotton; *bliochan*, asphodel; *mòthan*, butterwort; *lus na feàrnaich*, sundew; and the other plants in profusion on the moor he crossed on his way to and from school, all of which had Gaelic names pressed between the pages of MacCallum's notebooks like the plants themselves, which were also pressed within the schoolmaster's heart.

When out of boredom Seumas turned on a gas tap, Mackie the teacher with the spade beard belted him. He went home over the hill that night with hands that he had to hold in the sea to cool, but when màthair asked him what was wrong he wouldn't tell her because he would get the blame, not the brutal man with the strap.

He left school even before the legal age, and the old man hadn't sent him back. If he had stuck in at school he would be able to understand the book about dolphins downstairs and to appreciate more the creature that came into the bay. MacCallum had made a fuss about him learning to write Gaelic, but what good was it when he had no one to write to?

Next morning the fin was back in the bay, and he called to Leumadair as it leapt. But when he put the net out there was nothing in it, and nothing in the next tide either, though the fin was still rolling about, as if Leumadair were tormenting him.

* * * * *

One afternoon in Seumas's last year in primary school the schoolmaster had slung the map of the Dominion of Canada over the blackboard, explaining that many Highland people had been sent across to there in ships.

'It's what we call the Clearances,' MacCallum explained. 'The lairds wanted the land for sheep and the people had to go.' The stick in his hand was pointing at Seumas. 'You know the old village called Socrachadh near you where your father's people were cleared from.' The pointer was now back on the map, moving out into the Atlantic Ocean. 'The folks from Socrachadh were sent across here to Nova Scotia – *Alba Nuadh* in Gaelic,' he added, looking again at Seumas. 'All they had with them were the clothes they stood in and their Bible.' The pointer was now pressed against the floor. 'But they had much more: they had their Gaelic, and they were able to comfort each other in a strange land, singing their own songs. It was Gaelic that kept them alive.'

MacCallum removed the map from the board and began to write in straight lines in his feminine hand.

'Copy this neatly into your jotters.'

'Thousands of people were cleared from the Highlands –'

He stopped writing and turned from the board. His face had gone as white as the stick of chalk he was gripping, his eye half closed as if he had heard a boy misbehaving in the room, but even Donnie was writing quietly, since there was a strange, unique atmosphere of gloom in the room that day, though the sun was brightening the windows. Seumas was watching the stick of chalk in MacCallum's hand as he began to sway, as if to a Gaelic tune only the schoolmaster was hearing. The chalk began to move as he sank to his knees. Suddenly the stick burst into powder in his fingers as he keeled over. Myrtle Macgregor ran to the house next door for MacCallum's sister. The elderly woman with her grey hair in a bun transfixed with pins, an apron round her ample hips, knelt beside her sibling, taking his face in her hands as though he were her infant brother again. She was talking to him in Gaelic, and Seumas was the only one in the room who understood her anguished plea.

'*A Dhia, na leig leis dol a dhìth,*' Oh God, don't let him perish.

Then she laid his head on the floor and went to the school house to phone for an ambulance.

* * * * *

As he brought the launch into the bay Seumas saw the two policemen – the sergeant and the constable – standing at the door of his house. He and the dog climbed into the dinghy quickly. He pulled hard for the shore, dragging the keel up on the shingle and running up to the house.

'What do you want?' he confronted the sergeant.

'We're accompanying the sheriff officer in the execution of his business in case there's trouble. Stand back.'

Seumas pushed past them and went inside.

'What the hell do you think you're doing?' he demanded of Sandy.

'Poinding for a warrant sale for non-payment of Domestic Rates arrears,' Sandy sang as he went round sticking labels on the furniture, the same high voice with which he had repeated the multiplication tables in school. He pushed his hand down on the old man's chair to see how near the floor the springs went, then scribbled NO VALUE on the ticket he licked and stuck on the arm.

He crossed the narrow hallway to the other room. Màthair had kept it as the good room, with a carpet on the flagstones, a sofa in faded red velvet and two chairs from a sale at the manse, the furniture brought round on the launch. It had been Eilidh's bedroom when she had become too old to sleep with them upstairs, but their daughter had been taken to the asylum, and her bed had been dismantled and stored in the shed along with salvaged flotsam.

Sandy stuck a £2 ticket on the sofa, and £1 on each chair. When he went upstairs Seumas followed him.

'Don't touch that,' he warned as Sandy grasped the knobs of the bottom drawer of màthair's chest of drawers.

'Sergeant!'

The sergeant came up the stairs with a heavy tread and went with Sandy into the bedroom. The sheriff officer opened the squeaking wardrobe and saw, hanging there, the old man's one suit, retrieved from the undertaker for sentiment's sake. He hesitated before slapping on a 50 pence ticket. Then he opened the drawers of the chest and rummaged among the clothes.

'How does this sale work?' Seumas demanded.

'The place and date will be advertised in the local paper,' Sandy stated in his sing-song voice as he tested the parental bed with his fists. The springs had gone long ago, and the old man had tried to repair them with fencing wire, but the bed had sagged, as if he and màthair were lying in a stately barge with a brass prow, like a dead king and queen being conveyed to burial on the sacred Isle of Iona.

'Nobody will come. There's nothing worth buying here,' Seumas said scornfully.

'It's the law,' the sheriff officer sang as he wrote NO VALUE on the ticket, sticking it to the bedpost. 'Recovery of Rates arrears in the event of failure to pay.'

Seumas went to the little cabinet by the bed and pulled out the Gaelic Bible.

'How much is this going to go for?' he demanded to know.

'Who'll want a book they can't read?' Sandy asked. 'Keep it.'

Sandy crossed into Seumas's room, valuing the single bed with the iron frame at £1 (FOR SCRAP). He opened the wardrobe and put 50 pence on a ticket on Seumas's suit, and was leaving the room when he noticed the trunk behind the door. The sergeant helped him to tip out the contents. Pieces of jigsaw scattered with the few toys. Sandy picked up a Dinky Toy bulldozer with one of the tracks missing and looked at Seumas.

'It's yours,' Seumas told him. 'You may as well take it. What's this worth?' He demanded, tearing the shirt from his back and throwing it at Sandy.

'Watch it,' the sergeant cautioned.

'Fuck off out of it!' Seumas shouted, kicking out at the sergeant.

'You'll regret this, Macdonald,' the sergeant, who was from Glasgow and who had dealt with many hard men, warned him.

Eleven

After the two policemen and the sheriff officer had gone over the hill he snatched the shinty stick from behind the door and ran along the shore, striking at the shingle, sending stones flying in his rage, and by the time he reached the end of the bay the curve of the stick was splintered. He was so distraught that he wanted to wade into the sea and keep walking.

Then the fin approached: fifty yards, then twenty offshore.

'Come on, Leumadair,' he coaxed in Gaelic.

He walked out up to his knees in the chilling water, followed by Dìleas. The fin came closer and he went out up to his waist until the fin was only ten yards from him. He was up to his chest now, standing with his arms outstretched, feeling the creature brushing his fingertips as if his anger was running out through it into the sea, purifying him. The dog was swimming round the dolphin, out of curiosity, not aggression. Seumas remained standing until the fin moved away, and then he waded ashore again, Dìleas paddling behind him. He went into the house and removed his clothes, sitting naked in the old man's chair while he made himself a cigarette. He was in deep trouble now. If he didn't pay the Rates arrears they would come and sell the furniture so that he wouldn't even be able to sleep in the house. That bastard Sandy was doing it out of spite. Well, he wasn't going to win.

What would the old man have done? Seumas closed his eyes as he inhaled smoke, as if trying to contact his parent in the spirit world. The old man wouldn't have kicked out at the sergeant. He would have found the money somewhere to save their home. He had to save it because you couldn't put a price ticket on the memories, the old man, màthair and MacCallum exchanging the distinctive Gaelic of three different places with the joy of people sharing a box of chocolates of different centres, the flavour of the old man's Gaelic in MacCallum's mouth, the old man chewing over a Mull word, and màthair with the lingering sweetness of her own Outer Isles Gaelic.

Christ, they weren't going to win. He leapt out of the chair and ran upstairs, pulling off the 50 pence ticket from his suit. He put it on with the same white shirt he had worn to the old man's funeral. He took his shoes in his hand and rowed out to the launch, placing them carefully where they wouldn't get the spray. Then he opened up the throttle, his tie flapping out of his jacket as he motored past Sgeir nan Eun. He went to the hotel, but the receptionist told him that Donnie was out and wouldn't be back for a couple of hours.

'Have you any more books on dolphins?' he asked Alice in the library.

'My, but I've never seen you looking so smart,' she complimented him, eyeing him up and down. 'Do you have a date?'

'Not the kind you're thinking.'

'In which case maybe we should meet for lunch.'

He heard a serious proposition in her voice, but Donnie was his friend and he had been having a relationship with her even before the legal age.

'A book on dolphins,' he reminded her.

She took him to the same shelves and as she stretched to search he could see her nipples. She handed him down the illustrated book and he sat at the table, turning over the pages, looking at the photographs of dolphins under water. He felt soothed, after what had happened at the house.

'I hear you had a visit from Sandy,' Alice said as she came across again.

'Who told you that?' he asked in surprise.

'I have my informants,' she winked at him. 'But seriously, you must pay your Rates arrears, Seumas. Let me help you out. How much do you need?'

'I can't remember.'

'Yes you can, you independent bugger. I'll lend you the money. Why don't we go to the cafe for something to eat now?' she suggested.

He didn't want people seeing him with her because they would only talk. He had put on his suit because he had intended, overcoming his pride and independence, to go to the bank, to ask for a loan to pay the Rates arrears, against the security of the launch. But Alice had offered to lend him the money, so he read more about dolphins while he waited for her. She put on her raincoat and scarf, and they went down the street together, the collar of his jacket turned up against the rain.

The cafe was busy. They sat at the yellow formica table, sharing the menu in its grubby cellophane holder as they studied the three choices. The girl came up and he ordered a pie and a cup of coffee. Alice pulled off the head scarf and shook out her hair. She extracted two cigarettes from the packet with her red nails, putting one between his lips and offering him the light first. He was watching her face in the flame. In his third year at secondary school his class had gone to Glasgow to see a play, but he couldn't go because his parents didn't have the £5.

Alice came back with the first mini skirt seen in the town. It was black, pleated like a little kilt, and she wore it to the school hop. Seumas was sitting against the wall by himself. Donnie was in a

Strip the Willow set with Alice, and as they spun her skirt rode up round her hips, showing her silky knickers pulled into her curves. Miss Nicholson the geography teacher had rushed up to the platform, waving her arms to the ceilidh band to stop playing, but they pretended that they didn't see her because they were enjoying the show of Alice's thighs. Alice's skirt was now above her thighs as if a gale was blowing through the hall. The other dancers clapped them down the set in encouragement, and when the accordion finally squeezed shut and the cymbal above the drum shivered to a stop Miss Nicholson crossed the floor to give Alice a public row about her 'unsuitable attire.' The provocative dancer had tossed her head and walked away.

It was the ladies' choice now, and Alice was coming across to Seumas. He was making for the door, but she caught his hand and pulled him on to the floor. They had had a few lessons in dancing in the gym from Miss Begbie, the teacher whose tracksuit didn't conceal her curves, but Seumas couldn't remember the steps.

Alice had taken his right hand and put it behind her back above her buttocks for the waltz, holding his other hand as they went round. She kept stepping out of the way of his feet, but it wasn't that that was worrying him. She was pressing him close into the mini skirt and his *bod* was up. Miss Nicholson was glaring at them, but he couldn't pull back.

Alice held him closer and put her head on his shoulder. He was praying for the music to end, but it went on and on. He tried to walk naturally off the floor, pulling down his jacket, but it looked as though he had a wooden leg.

Donnie was waiting for him.

'I'm going out for a smoke,' he told Seumas.

They stood together at the back of the hall, looking across the harbour.

'That's some skirt Alice is wearing,' Donnie said.

'I don't think Miss Nicholson's very pleased,' Seumas pointed out.

'She needs a good ride herself, the old bitch. Look.' He opened his hand and showed Seumas something.

'What's that?' he asked out of curiosity.

'A French letter. Alice bought a packet in Glasgow and this is the last one.'

* * * * *

'It's finished between Donnie and me,' Alice announced as she dropped the flaming match into the metal tray in the cafe.

Seumas now understood why she was so willing to lend him the money.

'It's been going on a long time,' she said wistfully.

'What did Tommy say?'

'You know what Tommy was like in school. He spent most of the time rushing round the playground, being a bus. I know, why did I marry him? Well, Donnie went away to the rigs and I waited. When he didn't come back after a year I started going with Tommy. Then Donnie came back and we took up again. Donnie would bring up a bottle of whisky, and tell Tommy about drilling for oil. Then Tommy would go to bed. He knew fine what was going to happen when he left me with Donnie, but he didn't seem to care.'

Their food came and he hoped she would change the conversation because he didn't like this kind of talk, nor did he want to be confided in.

'Of course Donnie's wife knew, but she turned a blind eye because half the hotel is hers. Anyway, it's over, so I'm a respectable woman again.'

He was watching her as she ate. She was still attractive, though there were grey strands in her hair.

'I wish I'd left this place long ago,' Alice said wistfully, pushing her plate away. 'I could have been in a post in a library in the city and had promotion by now.'

'You can still go.'

'Tommy would never leave this place, and there are the children. No, Seumas, I'm afraid I'm trapped here.' She stubbed out her cigarette. 'Anyway, it's good to have someone to talk to.' She went to pay the bill and suggested that they went to the bank. When she came out Alice gave him the money for the Rates arrears.

'I'll pay you back as soon as I can,' he promised.

'No hurry. I know where to get you.'

He should have taken the money to the council office, but took it home with him in his pocket. There was no sign of Leumadair on the way back, and the fin wasn't in the bay either. He left the wad of money on the table and went upstairs, taking off his suit, going downstairs to sit smoking in the old man's chair, valued as worthless, yet he had been occupying it since his son had been born and had exchanged many Gaelic words with MacCallum from its sagging seat, his *tòn* inches from the flagstones, the dog's head between his knees.

There had never been much money, but as the old man said, there was plenty of fish in the sea and potatoes in the ground. When the caddy on the mantelpiece which served as their bank was empty he went fishing with the old man. Màthair would never have borrowed a penny. He looked at the wad of cash on the table and felt shame, as if she were still in the room. Once Donnie had loaned him a magazine with naked women. He had taken it up to his room and examined the spread thighs. He heard màthair moving about downstairs and was overcome with such shame at what he had done that he knew he couldn't keep the magazine in the house overnight, so he took it out and hid it in the shed at the back among the flotsam, to collect it on the way to school next morning.

But he had forgotten it, and when he ran back from the bus that evening it had gone. He would never know which parent had found it, but nothing had ever been said.

He put the money in his back pocket and rowed out to the launch. It was getting dark, but he knew his way and the beacon

on the pier guided him in. As he was walking up the brae he saw
the lights in the library. It was late opening night and Alice was
working at the desk. Several people were browsing. Seumas went
over to the shelf and took down the book on dolphins. He brought
it to the desk and when she opened it to stamp it she saw the
money inside it.

'Thanks all the same, but I got it.'

'Where?' she asked in surprise.

'I found some money in the house,' he told her. He was already
walking away, feeling cleansed.

She came after him and caught his arm.

'If you ever need anything –'

He went down to the hotel and asked to see Donnie.

'I saw the notice in the paper about the warrant sale. I warned
you, you should have paid your Rates arrears.'

Seumas shrugged.

'Tell me how much it is and I'll give it to you.'

Seumas revealed the sum and Donnie went into his office,
returning with an envelope.

'But I already owe you for the old man's funeral.'

His benefactor shrugged. 'What's a few hundred between
friends? Pay me back when you can.'

It was easier, less humiliating to take the money for the Rates
arrears from Donnie than from Alice. He went up to the council
office to pay it and to tell the clerkess to be sure to cancel the
warrant sale. He didn't want strangers in his house, raking through
the contents – especially when it still contained màthair's things.

* * * * *

He was putting away the net in the shed when he saw the sergeant
and the constable coming over the hill.

'You were aggressive to the sheriff officer when he came to
poind your furniture for non-payment of Rates arrears, and you
threatened me,' the sergeant said.

'I don't understand what you're saying,' Seumas informed him. 'It's a pity you can't say it in Gaelic, but of course you've not a word of Gaelic.'

'You know what I mean,' the sergeant said, duly goaded.

'It's a criminal offence, challenging a sheriff officer,' the constable by the sergeant's shoulder cautioned.

'So was what you used to do to the girls in the lavatories, Hughie,' Seumas reminded him.

'And you licked MacCallum's arse with your Gaelic,' the constable said. 'A dead language.'

'I'll show you if it's a dead language,' Seumas threatened, taking a swing at the constable, but missing.

'Assaulting a police officer,' the sergeant said, nodding to the constable.

The constable took off his radio and laid it carefully on a rock. Then he removed his cap and laid it on top of the radio. He drew his truncheon from under the flap of his tunic. There had been an argument in the playground over a big marble, a beauty with blue threads like peat smoke spiralling through it. Hughie claimed it, but Donnie had backed Seumas up, and he had fought and beaten the future constable.

The top half of the shore was called *cladach*. It was a hard but appropriate word because there were a lot of stones there, polished by the ocean over many thousands, perhaps millions of years, MacCallum had said in his geology lesson, with samples passed round the desks for inspection. The old man's glass floats had been deposited on the *cladach* where they had lain ready for him, miraculously unbroken with the spume still on them.

Once in the pub – in the days when Gaelic was still spoken in the town – three of the Irish navvies who were building the new pier had started to mock the old man's Gaelic, claiming that their Glens of Antrim version was superior. The old man had invited them out behind the pub, taking on the three of them at the same time, aiming at their abusive mouths. He had to be brought home in his own launch, but he had put one of them in hospital.

The old man had never brawled after that, and Seumas wasn't going to sully the place where he had been brought up. But his feet were losing purchase on the *cladach* as the constable laid into him with his truncheon. It felt as if the stones underfoot were running away from him. He was on his knees as the truncheon came down on his head, putting up his fists to resist when the heavy stick struck again, across his face. He was on the *tràigh* now, the lower part of the shore, a softer word and place because there was sand under his knees. He dug in his heels to fight back against the truncheon, succeeding in wrestling it from the constable's two hands.

Snarling, Dìleas leapt to his assistance, her teeth in the constable's trouser leg, but the sergeant used his truncheon to beat off the dog. Seumas was fighting back against the constable's truncheon because he didn't want Leumadair in the bay to witness his shame, his defeat. He fought back with his fists, but the two policemen were using their boots as well as their truncheons now, and his strength seemed to be leaking into the *tràigh*.

Seumas raised his head and saw the constable sitting on his heels, rinsing his truncheon in the sea. The dog was racing down to him, but Seumas called her back because he didn't want further damage inflicted on her. They weren't going to take him in; he knew by the blood running into his eye that they had made too much of a mess of his face to be able to explain it to their superior officers if Seumas went to the doctor to lay a complaint against police brutality. Their boots passed him, their cleaned truncheons under the flaps of their jackets again, and he heard the cackle of their radios as they fitted them on again before going back over the moor.

He lay on the sand, the dog licking his bloody face. Through his damaged eye he saw the fin circling, coming closer as if keeping him company. In the eerie silence he could hear the animal breathing, the sound of pity. He could see the back of the dolphin now, like looking through a big misshapen marble with a twisting grey thread through it.

The tide was coming in. When it was near his fingertips Seumas struggled to his feet and staggered back up to the house, the treacherous *cladach* sending him back down again. He put on the kettle so that he could have water to bathe his face, his left eye swollen, making the wall of the kitchen look curved.

He sat by the fire in the old man's chair, feeling the dog's body as she stood by his chair, asking her tenderly in Gaelic: 'Did that bastard hurt you with his truncheon, my love?' But there didn't seem to be any damage to the animal. The policeman they had stayed with when they had taken Eilidh to the infirmary in Glasgow wouldn't have done that to a man.

When he tried to roll a cigarette it came out with one end thicker than the other, the smoke making his swollen eye weep. The dog that had defended him with a rare show of aggression was lying calmly at his boots, and beyond the window the tide coming in over the *tràigh* was erasing all signs of the bloody assault.

When he went up to bed he kept bumping off the wall.

Twelve

There weren't any fish and Leumadair didn't come into the bay. He would soon have no money to live on, never mind paying Donnie back, and would have to get work on the mainland somewhere. On the way to the town he saw Leumadair's fin about a quarter of a mile off starboard, but he couldn't go over because he didn't have enough fuel. If he had to stop running the launch he would be stranded.

He bought the local paper, but there weren't any jobs he could do in it, so maybe he was going to have to take a chance and go down to Glasgow to look for work. He went home, climbed the stairs and emptied the contents of màthair's chest of drawers on to the bed, then carried the carcass of the chest carefully down the stairs before going up for the four drawers. He searched the shed and found some old sacks which storms had thrown up. He wrapped the chest in them, roping it securely before he carried it on his back out to the dinghy and rowed it out to the launch.

He lugged the chest up the steep flight of stone steps at the harbour, taking care not to scrape it on the stone. As he was passing the hotel with the burden on his back Donnie came out with an empty crate.

'Where the hell are you flitting to?'

'I'm taking the chest up to the antique shop to get a bit of money,' Seumas told him reluctantly.

'That man's a robber. He gives next to nothing, then sells the stuff on to a dealer from the south who comes with a big van. The wife will have a look at it; she's interested in furniture.'

Donnie helped him to carry the chest into the sun lounge and Dorothy came down to inspect it. The haughty blonde ran the hotel efficiently, but didn't mix with the locals.

'It's a nice piece,' she said, inspecting it like an expert. 'Turn it over,' she told Seumas.

'What are you looking for, a secret drawer?' Donnie asked her.

'No, woodworm.'

But there wasn't any woodworm.

'I'll give you seventeen pounds for it,' Dorothy offered.

Seumas hadn't expected to get so much from the dealer, and wondered if Donnie had made a sign to his wife to buy it.

'Take it up to our bedroom,' she ordered her husband before she went away.

'That'll keep you going for a bit,' Donnie said as he paid Seumas.

'I've decided to go to Glasgow. The fishing's no good and there isn't any work.'

'I could find odd jobs for you to do.'

'No, no, you've been very good to me already, helping me out with the money for the old man's funeral and the Rates arrears. I want you to take the launch towards the debt.'

'What do I want another boat for when I hardly have the time to get out in my own one?' Donnie said, trying to make it sound like a joke. 'Come on, man, you can't sell your father's boat.'

'I've made up my mind.'

Donnie was walking backwards and forwards, his trousers sliding down his big hips.

'The fisher boys were telling me there's a dolphin outside the harbour.'

'I've seen it,' Seumas admitted reluctantly.

'Some of the guests heard the boys talking about it in the bar and said they would like to see it. Why don't you take a few of them out in your boat? You could show them the rock where the seabirds nest, even if they didn't see the dolphin. You could take six of them out at a time.'

Seumas knew by the way he said it that he hadn't just thought of it.

'I'll need to think about it. Thank Dorothy.'

He bought his groceries and tobacco and filled up the launch with fuel. As he and the dog went out of the harbour he saw the fin, turning the tiller to go to it. When he was about a hundred yards away Leumadair leapt, as if acknowledging his presence, then disappeared.

He was preoccupied with his own thoughts. If he took people out to see Leumadair would that be a betrayal of a creature that had befriended him, driving fish inshore for him? He didn't know what to do and shut off the engine, making himself a smoke and switching on the radio he had brought with him because it was the Gaelic request programme. A listener asked to hear the Islay Gold Medallist Mary C. MacNiven singing *Fear a' Bhàta*.

> *'Fhir a' bhàta, na hò ro èile,*
> *Fhir a' bhàta, na hò ro èile;*
> *Fhir a' bhàta, na hò ro èile,*
> *Mo shoraidh slàn leat 's gach àit' an tèid thu.'*

> Boatman, ho ro eile,
> Boatman, ho ro eile;
> Boatman, ho ro eile,
> Farewell, and may you keep well in every place you go.

Seumas was sitting with his back to the gunwale, a hand trailing over the side, feeling the chill of the water as he listened to the song.

'An tig thu nochd no am bi mo dhùil riut,
No 'n dùin mi 'n doras le osna thùrsaich?'

Will you come tonight, or will I expect you
or will I close the door with a weary sigh?

He felt something brushing against his fingers, and turned to see Leumadair lying alongside. He hadn't heard it coming because of the radio and was so startled that he threw his cigarette into the sea. He knelt on the boards of the boat and put both hands over the side.

'Come on, Leumadair.'

The Gaelic song must have attracted the creature, but it was finishing. He took out his mouth organ he always carried with him and began to play a selection of Gaelic slow airs. The dolphin was lying beside the boat, as if listening to the recital. The dog had her paws up on the gunwale and, head cocked, was studying the strange creature lying beside the boat, puffing out through its blowhole. The next request on the radio was *port-a-beul*, mouth music, and he felt Leumadair rocking against his outstretched fingers.

He couldn't believe that this was happening to him, a Gaelic song going out over the water to attract this creature whose beak he was now feeling. Then, as the tempo of the song changed, the jaws caught him at the wrist. He panicked, trying to jerk his arm away, but the dolphin was clamping it gently. It was as if it were inviting him over the side into the sea to dance with it.

He began to sing along with the song, rocking the dolphin with his other hand while it held on to his wrist. The next request was an accordion selection of Gaelic tunes, including *Mo Mhàthair*, My Mother. As he rocked the creature beside the boat he thought of her rocking him to sleep in the house under the sloping slates as she crooned a Gaelic song. *Mo Mhàthair's* beautiful tribute had been written by a Mull man known to MacCallum, who used to sing it with the old man in that warm relaxed kitchen scented with peat smoke and whisky, with even the insolent parrot silent out of respect.

Leumadair stayed with him for the hour that the request programme lasted. It was getting dark and the tide was strengthening as he pushed the animal clear of the launch before starting the engine. But it wasn't going away. It leapt in front of him on the way home, as if exhilarated by the Gaelic song. At the entrance to the bay it veered, and he watched it splashing away into the dusk. He went ashore with the oars over his shoulders, fed the dog and lit the fire. He seemed to be in a state of heightened awareness as he moved about, lowering the globe on to the flame of the paraffin lamp, watching the way the yellow warmth spread over the walls. He moved about quietly in his contentment, tilting the kettle to the tea pot and making himself a cigarette as he waited for it to brew.

The old man had had a way with wild creatures, though he also shot them. He had seen a starving stag coming down off the hill to the house and the old man giving it an armful of the hay from the cow's dwindling heap of feed. He had watched the old man sitting on the shore repairing the net, a *feadag*, golden plover, perched on the toe of his boot, fluting as if giving the old man a private recital.

But what had happened to himself was different. This was a creature from the depths. Had it come to lie beside the launch because it liked the sound of the Gaelic singing, or had Leumadair been trying to tell him something? If he took visitors out and the dolphin came alongside like that, they would all want to touch it. No, their contact had been too intimate, like the contact with Heather Macgregor that afternoon in school during the educational film when she had guided his hand between her legs.

But if he didn't take visitors out to see Leumadair he would have to go away to look for work, and wouldn't see the dolphin again. He couldn't bear that. He would take them out, but he wouldn't let them touch the creature. That kind of contact would be for when he was alone in the boat.

He was excited that he had made the decision, and for the first time in months he began to put the house in order. He boiled up several kettles of water and washed his clothes in the sink in the scullery, using the ribbed board that màthair had used to get the dirt off the cuffs and collars of his shirts, singing as she scrubbed, as if the washboard were a type of musical instrument. When he had rinsed his clothes he took them out and pinned them to the line in the blowy night, his white shirt flapping up towards the moon, like one of the ghosts from màthair's eerie island. He stood outside, watching the bay, and though it was too dark to see a fin, he knew it was out there, and so he stayed, filled with wonder and delight. Where did Leumadair spend the night? Did it come close into the shallows and rest until dawn, or did it go out into deeper water, like the depth of some relaxing dreams?

He had read in the library book that because Leumadair was a mammal it needed air and had to rise to the surface. Did it drift up, still sleeping, to open its blowhole, sinking into the depths again? When he went into the house, still full of energy, he swept the floor and tidied up the place before sitting in the old man's chair, reading the library book about dolphins, making notes so that he could tell the visitors about it.

He learned that massive muscles in the rear half of its body moved the tail fluke to let a dolphin achieve speeds of over twenty five miles an hour, which meant that Leumadair could leave the launch behind. He read, but didn't write down, that their sexual organs were located in slits on their bellies, and he stared in wonder at the picture of copulating dolphins drifting together in blue water. He wrote down that they give birth to live young which feed on milk.

He hoped he could remember what he had written down, to tell the people he was going to take out on the launch. It was now one o' clock, but he still didn't feel like going to bed. He had let the fire die down and now did something that he had never done before: down on his knees on the local newspaper, he started to black-lead the grate, using the materials in the little wooden box màthair kept under the sink, including the old grimy glove. The stove began to glow in the light from the lamp. He took the piece of steel wool and ran it along the edging of the stove until he could see his own face.

He was pleased with his work, sitting back on his heels to admire it. Màthair had done it like that every Friday dawn, and he could remember his pleasure, coming down to go to school, to see it gleaming in the firelight, as if a new stove had arrived like a ship in the night. He was tired now, and went upstairs to bed. He had forgotten to wash his sheets, but would do them tomorrow.

He trailed his hand over the edge of the bed, as if he were still in the boat and Leumadair was coming alongside. When he shut his eyes he could still hear the Gaelic song going out over the sea. God, what would MacCallum have said about a dolphin that responded to Gaelic? And what would the old man have said about his launch being used as a pleasure boat?

He didn't dream about the dolphin: he dreamed about Heather. He wasn't in the school shed with her, peering between her legs. He was lying in the ruins of the village of Socrachadh with her as a woman, allowing him to remove her knickers and touch her. It was like fondling the mouth of a new-born lamb.

The morning was windy, with waves coming ashore, the launch tossing. If the weather didn't settle down he wouldn't be able to take visitors out today. He kindled the fire and made himself breakfast, the two eggs moving audibly in the boiling water as he listened to the forecast, hearing that it would quieten in the afternoon.

He put on his good jersey under the old man's oilskins. It was hard, rowing out to the launch, hard getting round Rubha nan Ròn. He stood with splayed legs, yielding with the swell as he worked the tiller, watching the precipices of Sgeir nan Eun tilting past. He didn't expect to see Leumadair but it came up, spectacularly, a hundred yards in front in a white explosion as it re-entered the sea.

'I'm going to take visitors out to see the dolphin,' he told Donnie.

'I knew you would, which is why I put up a notice on the board last night, asking for names. A dozen of them want to go out.'

'I can't take more than six, Donnie.'

'Do two trips. Take one lot out at two for an hour; give yourself half an hour's break before the next lot. How much were you thinking of charging?'

'Two pounds a head?'

'No way,' Donnie said emphatically, shaking his head. 'It's your boat; you're a skilled boatman; you know the place like the back of your hand. Three pounds per head for an hour's a bargain, even if you only show them the birds on the rock. Do you have lifejackets?'

Neither he nor the old man had ever used them, though one had been washed ashore after a storm.

'When you run a hotel you get queer things given to you for drink instead of money,' Donnie disclosed. 'I've got half a dozen lifejackets I've collected. That's them in the corner.'

They were almost new, and must be from his friend's own boat. Donnie brought him a plate of fish and chips for lunch. Seumas was getting nervous, not about the weather, but in case they didn't see Leumadair. What was he going to tell his passengers? But he had seen the dolphin on the way in; perhaps that was Leumadair's signal that it would be with the boat in the afternoon. Twelve times three: he saw the abacus of beads on rows of wires on the window ledge in Miss Maclaren's room as she taught them how to count, a finger pushing the beads in his mind. Thirty-six quid was a lot of money for an afternoon's work. No, not work, pleasure, watching a dolphin. It was as much as the old man had earned in a good week at the lobsters, more than he himself had earned in a week of good netting, with a shoal in the bay.

By half past one the white horses had disappeared from the harbour. He went down to tidy the launch, stowing anything loose out of the way and checking the fuel, the dog having to shift from her usual seat to make room for the tourists. They came along the pier in their coloured anoraks, the hoods up, cameras and binoculars round their necks. He shouted up to them to be careful on the steep stone steps. Stepping into the launch was awkward, so he inverted the box he used to bring his catch in, and when they were all seated he spoke to them nervously.

'We're going out to try to get a look at the dolphin outside the harbour. I've seen it myself quite a few times and so have the local fishermen. I hope we'll be lucky. I'll also give you a look at the seabird colony.'

As the launch ploughed out into open water he was watching anxiously ahead, hoping that Leumadair would show, but it was going to be hard to see a fin in the swell. He brought the boat as close as possible to Sgeir nan Eun, shouting out the names of the birds, including their Gaelic names, on the shit-spattered ledges while cameras clicked. At least they had something to take back with them.

He opened the throttle to take the launch along the coast, to the entrance to his bay, but didn't go into it. Half an hour had gone, and he turned the tiller. They were watching the sea quietly, but not wasting their time because one knowledgeable bird spotter was identifying out loud the flying birds. Some of the names Seumas didn't know, so he memorized them. But they were out to see the dolphin, and he feared that they were going to be disappointed. It was a dicey idea. Perhaps Leumadair was showing him that it didn't want other people about. It was raining hard now, and his passengers looked miserable, without shelter. But as he was turning to go back to the harbour one of them shouted. Instinctively he turned the launch round, thinking that someone had fallen overboard. He saw Leumadair leaping, higher out of the water than he had ever seen it go before. Its whole body was visible and it seemed to hang there, for the benefit of the cameras, before plunging back in by its beak.

It became a game. They were watching one side, and Leumadair breached on the other. Then one of the young ones was shrieking and pointing as the grey shape sped under the launch. It rose again, gracefully; it came alongside, rolling over to give them the eye. Then it was gone, quietly, into the depths.

The two teenage girls were hugging each other and crying, and Seumas saw the joy and wonder on the faces of the others as he brought the boat alongside the pier steps. He was self-conscious collecting the money.

'It's worth ten times that, to see what we've just seen,' one of the men enthused as Seumas took his elbow to help him ashore. 'Are you going out again tomorrow?'

Thirteen

Màthair's tea caddy on the mantelpiece was so crammed with money that Seumas had to leave the lid off, and he had already paid Donnie back what he owed him for the old man's funeral and Rates arrears loans. He was running four trips a day, taking six passengers at a time, making £72. Donnie was doing the bookings for him and tourists were phoning up from miles away, though he hadn't advertised the trips.

Each time Seumas went out Leumadair performed with a spectacular show, as if standing on its tail in the sky so that the cameras on board could catch it. It came close, crossing in front of the bow and often going under the launch. At the end of the trip the passengers were pushing extra money into his hands.

Some of them had asked for his address and had sent him copies of the photos they had taken. They were lined up on the mantelpiece beside the caddy, showing Leumadair out of the water or passing as a grey shape under the launch. Several children had written to Seumas, thanking him in their large awkward writing for the experience and enclosing drawings of Leumadair. He had pinned them to the wall beside the fire and given Donnie some of the photographs and drawings for the board advertising trips and local sights in the reception area of his hotel.

'Don't take any bookings for next Sunday,' he told Donnie. 'I want to go to see my sister.'

Donnie was connecting a beer cylinder under the bar and didn't look up.

'I never liked to ask. I thought she had died when I was out on the rigs.'

'She's been in the asylum on the mainland since she was fourteen. I want to take her out to see the dolphin.'

'Have you asked them if it's all right?' Donnie asked, tactfully leaving the word asylum out of the question.

'I'm going to phone them now.'

When Eilidh had first been taken into the asylum, màthair had gone by bus to the ferry terminal once a month to bring her home for the day. Seumas played with her on the shore, and she seemed so normal. But one afternoon she had disappeared. Màthair was frantic because the bus went in an hour, and if she didn't get her back in time for the last ferry she wouldn't get her out of the asylum again.

'I know where she'll be,' he told màthair.

She was sitting in the ruins of the house in Socrachadh that she had sat in before she was taken into the asylum. Seumas didn't like to disturb her, but could hear màthair calling in the distance.

'I don't want to go back to that place,' she wailed. 'I want to stay here and play with Flòraidh.'

If she became hysterical they wouldn't let her on the bus on the mainland, and màthair wouldn't know what to do.

'Flòraidh will come with you,' he assured her.

Her face brightened as he led her by the hand through the bracken.

'Where is Flòraidh?' she turned and asked anxiously.

'She's here with me. She's holding my other hand.'

Màthair hugged her instead of giving her a row.

'Flòraidh is coming with us to the end of the road,' he told màthair, giving her a warning look above his sister's head. 'Here, Eilidh, you take Flòraidh's hand and I'll take the other one.'

They went ahead together along the path, swinging the invisible girl between them. When the bus came round the bend with its headlights on he told her to say goodbye to Flòraidh. His sister kissed the air.

'You'll see her next time you come,' he promised as she went on the bus with màthair.

He went home and at ten o'clock took the torch along the track to meet màthair coming off the late bus. She looked tired and very old, and he held her hand as she walked slowly, her shoes swishing through the heather while moths fluttered against the glass of the torch.

'I won't be taking her out again,' màthair told him, close to tears, and he never knew if it was because Eilidh had misbehaved when they went into the asylum, or because it broke màthair's heart to have to put her into that depressing institution again.

But he was going to take her out again, after all those years. He went by bus and ferry to the mainland, two hours' journey in total. The same wee man, older now and more stooped, as if bowed down by the burden of his disturbed head, met him with the empty purse and a request for money for the phone, as if he had never left the front hall since Seumas's last visit. This time the receptionist's back was turned, so Seumas gave him fifty pence. The man looked at the coin in dismay, and, his fantasy shattered, began to weep.

As Seumas was going down the long corridor, past the slow wheelchair being propelled by a long thin pair of hands, the same old woman in the flimsy nightdress came up, slipping her arm through his as if he had never left on his last visit, shouting and crying coming from behind shut doors.

'Are you married?' the patient in search of sex asked.

'No.'

'Then we'll go in here for a cuddle,' she said, pulling Seumas by the arm into a doorway.

He disentangled himself gently and left her wailing. They had his sister dressed and waiting for him. She was standing in the middle of the lounge, surrounded by the other inmates who were staring at her as if they didn't recognize her, though they had been confined together for years. Eilidh was wearing a twin-set and tweed skirt, the clothes of another age for a young woman, clutching a handbag – one of màthair's jumble sale purchases – to her breast.

He took his sister's hand along the corridor. A wheelchair whispered past on pneumatic tyres, and the old woman, long past the menopause, who had propositioned him, shouted to him from the doorway: 'You'll get far more out of me than her!'

Donnie was waiting in his Land Rover at the ferry because there wasn't a bus until later. Seumas sat with his sister in the back, holding her hand. Her head was turned to the window, watching a world she hadn't seen for years. He leaned over to point out familiar places to her, but she showed no recognition.

'When do you want me to come back and take you to the ferry?' Donnie asked when he stopped at the road end.

'She's got to be back in by seven, and I've got to get the last ferry home.'

'I'll be here at a four-thirty,' Donnie promised.

He took his sister by the hand along the path they had taken together to and from school, but she walked like a person in a dream. He used to sit waiting for her patiently while she gathered flowers for màthair on the way home from school, but today he did the picking, giving her the little blue bunch of *currac-cuthaige*, the cuckoo's cap, the harebell. She held the delicate bouquet in her fist, then dropped them over her shoes. He was angry now. What were they doing to her in the asylum?

He tried to make conversation, but she grunted as if she had forgotten her Gaelic. He let her go first into the house, and she stepped over the threshold cautiously, as if there was potential danger. She didn't recognize the place where she had grown up in as he sat her in màthair's chair by the fire he had left burning, and whose embers he revived with the poker and driftwood.

'Where's Athair?' she asked.

'He went to the same place as màthair.'

She was staring into the flames, apparently without understanding what he had said as he prodded the potatoes with a fork to see if they were ready. Donnie's wife had given them a steak pie. He heated it in the oven and when he had set the table he called her across.

Even when he broke the pie crust with the spoon and let out the appetizing steam she didn't respond. The steak was tender but she showed no pleasure as she ate. There was a trifle to follow, also made by Donnie's wife, with cream on the top and red jelly, but she only ate half of what he spooned on to her plate.

He left the pots and dishes in the scullery sink and took her up to show her màthair's room. He sat her on the bed and put màthair's little woollen scarf round her neck, but there was no reaction, as if the asylum had turned his sister into a zombie.

'We'll go out in the boat,' he told her.

He took off her shoes and pulled màthair's wellingtons on to her feet, then put her arms through his anorak, zipping it up in case she became cold. She had loved going out in the launch with the old man and himself, taking the tiller round Rubha nan Ròn and waving to the seals, but when he helped her into the launch and sat her down it was as if she had never been in a boat before.

He started the engine and swept the launch out of the bay. He was praying that Leumadair would leap so that he could see some recognition in that expressionless face that seemed to be looking beyond the water into another land. In Gaelic it was called *Tìr nan Òg*, the land of the ever-young, but no one knew where it was, and his sister had aged prematurely.

There was no sign of Leumadair, though he cruised about for half an hour. His sister was sitting hunched up as if she were chilled, but he was going to make one last attempt. He had bought a cassette player for playing tapes to Leumadair, but not when he had tourists aboard. He switched off the engine and turned up the volume. The song *Fear a' Bhàta* went out over the water, but the woman in the boat showed no recognition, though she had sung it as she skipped about the kitchen in her clumsy shoes, as if there was no furniture in her way, until the mantle of the lamp collapsed on the flame.

Then Leumadair leapt.

'*Seall sin!*' he spoke excitedly to Eilidh, turning her round by the shoulders.

As the dolphin rose again out of the water in a shower of spray he saw the transformation in the face of his sister as the years of fear and confusion fell away. She was young, smiling, not yet the innocent victim of her own brain, gripping the gunwale with both hands and watching intently.

'We'll sit quietly,' he whispered to her.

They had had a game as children. He would ask her to close her eyes and then he would put something into her hand, a shell, a little crab, asking her to guess what it was. He took her right hand and put it over the side into the water, then played the tape of the Gaelic song again.

> '*An tig thu 'n-diugh, no an tig thu màireach?*
> '*S mur tig thu idir, gur truagh a tà mi.*'

> Will you come today or will you come tomorrow?
> And if you don't come at all I'll be distressed.

He wasn't watching the water; he was watching his sister. He knew that the dolphin had made contact because of the way her face lit up with delight.

'I call it Leumadair,' he whispered to her.

She nodded, smiling. After all the electric shocks they had put through her head in the asylum she still appreciated the fluid movement of the Gaelic word as the old man and MacCallum would have savoured it.

'Look,' he whispered to her.

Leumadair was lying on its side, watching her. He saw their eyes meeting, saw a signal passing between them. Her hand rested on its body and now she was singing the Gaelic song she had sung that day in the school when there seemed to be no wall between the classrooms.

> *'Dh'fhàg mi 'n seo na shìneadh e,*
> *Na shìneadh e, na shìneadh e;*
> *Gun d' dh'fhàg mi 'n seo na shìneadh e*
> *Nuair dh'fhalbh mi bhuain nam braoileagan.'*

> I left my darling lying here,
> Lying here, lying here,
> I left my darling lying here,
> To go and gather blaeberries.

He sat listening, the sun in his face, feeling sleepy himself with the lullaby and the rocking of the launch. They sat out on the sea for an hour, her hand on the dolphin that was transmitting peace to her as she sang the remembered songs of her childhood in the clear beautiful voice that MacCallum had admired so much, saying that she would be a great Gaelic singer who would take the Gold Medal at the Mod and other honours. She was singing as if it were her child in the water beside her.

He didn't want to start the engine, but they had to be getting back. As he eased open the throttle Leumadair went ahead of them, leaping high, planing on its belly while his sister clapped, enthralled. The dolphin led them into the bay and then its fin did a circle before it disappeared.

'It'll have gone to feed,' he told her. 'We'll need to get you something to eat before you go back.'

He realized too late that he shouldn't have said that, but she wasn't upset as he carried her ashore on his back from the dinghy as he had done when she was a wee girl. He had bought cold meat and a lettuce which he washed carefully under the tap. As they ate she questioned him in Gaelic about the big fish. He explained that it wasn't a fish but a mammal, and that it had to come up for air. He saw the understanding rising in her mind, and she asked if there was any of the trifle left. He let her clean out the bowl with her finger as màthair had let her do when she was baking.

'I'll come again to see Leumadair,' she said.

'You'll have to come, now you've made friends with it.'

'Will it be still here?' she asked anxiously.

'Oh, it'll still be out there waiting for you,' he assured her. 'It took a real fancy to you.'

They went for a walk hand in hand, but when they came to the slope above the ruined village she stopped.

'I need to do the bathroom,' she told him.

He kept her handbag as she went down the slope, parting the bracken with her hands as if she were entering the subterranean world of the little people in màthair's enthralling tales. He gave her five minutes, then ten. Whatever she was doing she should be finished by now, so he went down the slope.

'Eilidh! Eilidh!'

He looked into the empty windows of the tumbled houses, but couldn't see her. He found her sitting in the last house with the window above the sea, talking in Gaelic.

'We'll need to go because Donnie will be waiting,' he told her.

'I was just telling Flòraidh about the big fish and she said she would like to see it herself. Is it all right to take her with us the next time I come?'

'That'll be fine,' he said, smiling sadly.

He took her hand along the path in the fading light. She was animated now, as if she had just discovered that she could speak Gaelic.

'Will you get a picture for me of the big fish for the lounge?'

At first he didn't know what she was talking about, until he realized that it was the lounge in the asylum where she lived with the other women, the hopeless cases who would never be released because nobody wanted them home, or because they had no relatives. If things continued to go well with the trips out to see Leumadair maybe he could do up the house and bring her home. It wouldn't be easy, and he might not be able to leave her alone, but it was worth thinking about.

'I'll get you a picture of Leumadair for the lounge,' he promised.

Donnie was waiting in the Land Rover at the road end.

'Did you have a good day, Eilidh?' he asked as he switched on the engine.

She didn't answer.

'Donnie's speaking to you,' Seumas said, nudging her gently.

'It was a lovely big fish,' she said dreamily in Gaelic, falling asleep with her head against her brother's shoulder.

Fourteen

A television crew from London wanted Seumas to take them out for the day in his launch to film the dolphin for a wildlife series. They would stay at Donnie's hotel and would pay him £150 for the hire of the launch.

He took the four of them out after breakfast. He hadn't seen Leumadair on the way up and was worried that it wouldn't show as he turned the launch out into the choppy sea, though he knew he would still get paid. The cameraman had his camera on his shoulder and the sound-man was ready with the boom. The pages were flapping on the production assistant's clipboard and the director was standing by.

He stopped the engine off Sgeir nan Eun so that they could get shots. The camera was sweeping the open water as they proceeded, but there was no sign of a fin. When he reached the entrance to his bay he was still wondering what to do. If he took them in it would be an invasion of his privacy, but if Leumadair was in there he wanted them to get shots for their money.

The dolphin leapt as they were entering the bay. But it wasn't going inshore. Instead it headed out of the bay as if drawing them away from his home, bucking, sinking, showering spray. The camera crew shouted excitedly as the camera tracked the creature, the throttle of the launch opened to its limit. Leumadair allowed them to catch up to get close-up shots, as if showing off its prowess, diving as if it weren't going to come up again, then suddenly shooting under the bows so that the cameraman almost went overboard in getting the shot.

After three hours Seumas took them back to the harbour. They were soaked but exhilarated, and the production assistant said that the cheque for £150 would follow.

'You've got some dolphin there,' the director told him. 'I've filmed dolphins all over the world and never seen one so lively. You're going to get a hell of a lot of people up here after we show the programme.'

'When is it going out?' Seumas asked anxiously, worried now about the effect on Leumadair. Publicity like that could drive the dolphin away.

'I'll let you know,' the director informed him. 'Come up to the hotel for a drink.'

Seumas thanked him, but told them that he had to get home in case the weather worsened. He was filling the tank with more fuel when a young woman shouted to him from above. He signalled that there wasn't going to be another trip that day, but she still came down the steps. She was wearing denims, a sweater and trainers, and her blonde hair was pulled back in a ponytail.

'Can I come aboard?'

He shrugged and she climbed over the gunwale.

'My name's Feona Bradwell-Price. I live in the old school house.'

That was where MacCallum had lived with his sister. He recognized her as the woman in blue oilskins who had come off the yacht to his door, asking for lobsters.

'I'd like to help you on the boat,' she told him, squatting on the heels of her trainers as she fondled the dog's ears.

'I don't have a job.'

'I don't need paid,' she persisted. 'I want to be on the boat so that I can study the dolphin.'

'Then come out as a paying passenger,' he suggested sarcastically.

'I need to be out every day to study it for my thesis. I'm at Cambridge doing a PhD about dolphins in the wild.'

'There must be ones off the English coast you can study. I have to get home. The dog needs fed.'

'Please.' She caught his arm. 'I won't get in your way. I can help you with the boat. I've got a yachtmaster's certificate.'

But he had started the engine. She jumped off, ran up the steps, lifted the rope from the bollard and threw it down to him. He watched her disappearing along the pier as he backed the launch out. The old man had been right: there were too many incomers in the Highlands. That was why Gaelic was dying. A yachtmaster's certificate: was he supposed to be impressed?

When he went into the hotel Donnie asked: 'Did a lassie with her hair in a ponytail come to see you about a job on the launch?'

'Aye, an English girl.'

'Her name's Feona Bradwell-Price. She's got a yachtmaster's certificate. She could be a big help to you with the boat. She was telling me that she's writing a thesis on dolphins, and that if you would take her on she wouldn't want paid. She could tell your customers about the dolphin.'

'It's bad luck, having a woman on board,' Seumas said defensively.

'But you've had your sister out.'

'That's different. She belongs here.'

'And you've been taking female tourists out to see the dolphin,' Donnie added. 'Suit yourself,' he shrugged. 'You always were a stubborn bugger, but if I were you I'd take her on. You might find yourself a wife.'

Seumas didn't appreciate the joke. But there was sense in what his best friend had said about the woman telling the people on board about the dolphin, because it would make the trip more interesting, and would attract new customers.

'What's this woman's number?' he asked impatiently.

Donnie smiled. 'I'll phone her myself.'

She was down on the pier in fifteen minutes.

'I'm very grateful to you for taking me on.'

'Let's get one thing straight,' he lectured her. 'You're not to get in the way of the passengers while they're looking out for the dolphin.'

'I won't get in the way,' she replied pleasantly. 'I'll tell them about dolphins.'

She went out with him for the first time the following morning at ten. They had a full group and she lifted the rope from the bollard. She pulled a video camera from a holdall and knelt in the bow as the launch ploughed out of the bay. He was watching the curve of her hips as he moved the tiller.

'Dolphin!' she shouted, pointing.

She conveyed her excitement to the passengers, and they had binoculars and cameras raised as he followed Leumadair, but not too fast to frighten or endanger the creature. He saw her taking a big notebook and stopwatch from her bag. He shut off the engine, letting the launch drift to allow Leumadair to come closer. When it jumped his new crew member pressed the watch, stopping it when it reappeared and writing down the time. She seemed to know where it was going to come up better than himself, and he resented this. As she was working she was telling the passengers about the way of life of dolphins.

'The next trip's at twelve,' he reminded her abruptly, stepping past her and going up to the hotel to get something to eat without inviting her.

'How are you getting on with her? She's a good looker, isn't she?' Donnie added with heavy innuendo.

'I haven't noticed,' Seumas said morosely as he tore open the plastic pouch to put sauce over his scampi and chips.

'Aye, you never noticed these things,' his best friend said sadly. 'I could have set you up with a lot of feels in the school lavatories if you'd hung about. I think it was MacCallum with his Gaelic who put you wrong.'

'MacCallum was all right,' Seumas said defensively.

'All right to you,' Donnie corrected him. 'Remember that day he hammered me?'

The map of Canada was slung across the blackboard for another lesson. Seumas would always remember looking that day at the tray of fragile birds' eggs behind glass in the case at the back of the room, as if they were of special but undefined significance for what was to follow. MacCallum picked up the brass-tipped pointer and touched Hudson's Bay. He explained how men who had gone out from the Highlands bartered with the Indians for the furs they trapped. He told how Gaelic speaking men had tramped on snowshoes for hundreds of miles, and how some of them had married squaws.

Had Heather fallen asleep in the sunlight at the back of the room, at her desk in front of the glass case containing the fragile collection of eggs? MacCallum ordered her to come out and handed her the pointer, telling her to locate Hudson's Bay on the map, which she did correctly. As she went back up the passageway to her desk, Seumas saw Donnie, who was sitting beside him, putting his hand up her kilt.

MacCallum proceeded with his lesson.

'The fur trappers didn't treat their squaws very well,' he noted.

As the schoolmaster turned from the board Seumas saw the telltale sign, the lid of the right eye beginning to sink.

'They abused the squaws,' MacCallum continued. 'They had no respect for women.'

He laid the pointer in its groove on the blackboard and went to his desk, which sat on a low platform so that he could observe the classes.

'Morrison, come out here.'

Donnie shuffled to the front.

You don't treat the opposite sex very well, do you?' MacCallum stated.

He was taking off his Harris Tweed jacket and draping it carefully over the back of his high chair before rolling up his sleeves. The pupils had never seen these preparations before and were both fascinated and frightened. MacCallum was wearing the blue short-sleeved pullover which his sister Sèonaid, who spent her spare time with her needles, had knitted for him.

He opened the lid of his desk and took out the coiled strap. It had two prongs, like the forked tongue of a snake, but its bite was usually mild. This time, however, it was clear that it was going to be an exceptional belting. He lifted his victim's right hand and studied the palm, as if reading its grimy lines for a sign of some promise or redeeming feature. Seumas could see the bravado look on his best friend's face as MacCallum raised the boy's palm level with his chest.

The schoolmaster stood back. Not satisfied that he had the distance right, he took a small step forward and lifted his right arm. Seumas saw the scene in slow motion in the utter silence of the classroom, and would see it many times in the course of his life when some act of violence external to himself prompted the memory. The forked tongue of the belt hung behind the schoolmaster's right shoulder. Then it came up, until it seemed to stand vertically above the wielder's shoulder before falling, like the erect cobra poised to strike in the educational film.

Donnie made the mistake of dropping his palm as the belt came down, smacking the wielder's thigh. MacCallum's baleful eye was now fully closed, as if the belt had struck it. He raised his victim's palm again, and this time when the prongs came down they made contact with a cracking sound, as if the palm had split in two.

The procedure was repeated, three times on the right hand, the same on the left, a total never witnessed before by the pupils in the classroom, in which the only sound was the swish and smack of leather. Donnie had looked arrogant after the first stroke, but by the fourth the pain was on his face, and some of the girls who had been enticed across into the boys' lavatories by him so as to explore their anatomy were smiling in satisfaction. At the sixth stroke Seumas saw the trickle coming down the bare leg of a nervous boy called Norman Graham across the passage, the piss running into his boot. For the rest of the morning Donnie was blowing into his hands at the back of the class, and at the interval the girls went unmolested. One of his previous victims even called Donnie across to the wall and popped a sweetie into his mouth, telling him: 'You have to keep your hands to yourself today, which makes a change.'

That night MacCallum came round to the house in his launch in his tweed jacket and seaboots, with the usual bottle of whisky, the usual box of Black Magic. Seumas sat beside him by the lamp for his lesson in writing Gaelic, but the letters were all jumbled when he thought of the blows his best friend had received from the quiet patient man beside him, who had also brought the gift of appetizing fairy cakes from his spinster sister.

'By Christ, it was some belting from the old bugger,' Donnie recalled from behind the counter of the bar. 'How the hell did he see me having a feel at Heather? I've puzzled over that one for years.'

* * * * *

The postman tramped across the moor with the cheque for £150 from the film company, and Seumas took it to Donnie at the hotel.

'Can you cash it for me?'

'I can't. You need to take it to the bank, to open an account.'

'I don't like the new manager.'

'Aye, Alan Maclachan is missed. I'll tell you what to do: take the cheque to the post office and open a savings account. You'll get interest on it.'

The woman behind the grille in the post office had been in school with him, one of the girls who went willingly across to the boys' lavatories.

'In the money, are we, Seumas? I'm looking forward to the programme on the dolphin. I must come out with you in the boat to see it when I've got a free day.'

She completed the transaction and pushed under the grille his savings book, explaining that he could withdraw money as necessary. The old man had grown up in a cash economy and hadn't liked the idea of his money being taken away from him, so Alan Maclachan had made no attempt to recommend opening an account to the fisherman when he came into the bank with cheques from the sale of lobsters. The manager cashed them himself for this favoured customer with his beautiful Gaelic.

Seumas took the box of groceries down to the launch and motored home, contented with his own company and that of Dìleas, feeding her a whole tin of meaty chunks, the chipped enamel dish clattering at his feet as he made a meal for himself. He cleaned his own plate with the piece of bread and rolled himself a smoke, lying back in the old man's chair with the mug of tea within reach to listen to the Gaelic request programme on the radio. The young woman from Barra who was singing a cradle song made him think of his sister, reminding him that he must take her out again soon, so that she could meet Leumadair again.

He fell asleep by the peat fire, and was wakened by knocking on the door. Nobody ever came to visit. He sat still but the dog started growling.

Alice put her head round the door.

'Anyone at home?'

He was clumsy in his embarrassment, tripping over Dìleas as he got to his feet. His supper dishes were still on the table, and he was ashamed of the primitiveness of the house.

'I ordered a new book about dolphins for the library and it came in this afternoon,' she told him, putting it down on the table.

He stood awkwardly, not knowing what to do.

'Can I sit down? It's quite a walk over the moor.'

He sorted the cushion on màthair's chair as she slipped off her short camel coat, hanging it over the back of the chair. She was wearing a tight ribbed green sweater and light coloured slacks. He knew that it was for his benefit to show up her figure as she sat on the edge of the chair, holding her palms to the fire as she looked around.

'This is a cosy room.'

'I haven't done anything to the place since the old man died,' he said, by way of an excuse.

'Leave it as it is. It's got character, not like the houses in the town, with their insides ripped out by these bloody incomers. Some days I hardly hear a local voice in the library. They want books on French cooking and continental holidays. When I was a wee girl my father used to take me for walks round the crofts above the town to see the cows. They've all got kit houses on them now, which is why you've got to keep this place as it is.'

Seumas made himself a cigarette as he listened.

'I hear you've got an assistant on the boat.'

So this was why she had come over the moor.

'She's not working for me,' he said defensively. 'She asked if she could come aboard because she's studying dolphins.'

'Her parents come into the library. They're very grand. The mother orders book on antiques. Evidently she collects Georgian silver.'

'I don't know anything about her people,' he reacted dismissively. 'She's only here till the beginning of October, when she has to go back to university.'

Alice was sitting in silence now. He should light the lamp, but was awkward about doing it in front of her. Besides, he was intrigued by the way the firelight was showing up her face. She had a lot of make-up on, particularly round the eyes and mouth, and he felt himself attracted to her even more than in the library.

'How's Donnie?' she enquired.

'Busy. He's doing well in the hotel.'

'Donnie always did well at whatever he tackled,' she said with a wry smile. 'I miss the rogue.'

There was more silence, but she wasn't going to go.

'I'll make some tea,' he said, leaning over to lift the kettle on to the peats. 'I'll light the lamp.'

'Let me,' she offered, rising to stand beside him. 'Show me how.'

He could smell the perfume as he held the globe while she struck a match.

'Turn up the wick,' he told her.

He watched the flame going from blue to white, but his hand was shaking so much that as he replaced the globe the mantle collapsed.

'Is it serious?' she asked.

'I don't have a spare,' he said, angry at his clumsiness.

'I prefer to sit in the dark,' she told him, going back to màthair's chair again.

Màthair always kept a supply of candles under the scullery sink. He found one and carried it through, lit, to stand it in the saucer on the dresser while he opened the door, then remembered that he had sold the wedding china.

'You'll have to take a mug,' he told her.

It was the old man's and had a crack but she wouldn't see it in the poor light. She sat warming her fingers round the thick china.

'I'd love to live in a place like this,' she enthused, turning her green eyes on him. 'It's so peaceful. You're a lucky man, Seumas. Never leave this place.'

'I don't intend to,' he assured her as he smoked to overcome his nervousness.

'I hear your sister was here.'

'Was it Donnie who told you?' he asked, irritated.

'Donnie and I don't have any contact nowadays,' she informed him with a sigh. 'He has other interests.'

'What do you mean?'

'It doesn't matter. No, it was Tommy on his bus who saw you with Eilidh.' She shook her head sadly. 'I remember her in school; she was such a lovely person.' She sat in silence, drawing on her cigarette. 'She seemed so calm, so mature for her age as if she knew so much but couldn't get it out. I really respected her. There were some rough ones, I can tell you, but nobody ever lifted a hand to Eilidh. Did she enjoy her day here?'

'She liked the dolphin a lot,' Seumas told her, shifting in the chair. 'It was hard, putting her back into that place.'

'It doesn't have to be like that.'

'What do you mean?'

'You hear on the telly about handicapped people being released back into the community so that they can have normal lives. Maybe one day –' she speculated, offering him her cigarette packet.

He took one and held out a light to her from the fire. As her face came forward into the flame he saw the pouting red lips, and had a surge of desire that made his hand tremble, moving the blazing paper away from her cigarette. He was taking her hand and helping her to her feet, the way he had been taught at school to ask a girl to dance at the Christmas hop. He was lifting the candle from the dresser and leading her to the bottom of the stairs, telling here to go up first. Since he had sold màthair's chest of drawers there was nowhere to put the candle, so he set it down on the floor. His large shadow was on the wall over her as she lay back on the bed. She opened the zip of her slacks and he tugged them down, pulling down her pants.

But they hadn't moved from the fireside.

'I'd like to go out in the boat with you to see the dolphin,' Alice spoke.

'I'll take you out one evening,' he promised. 'I'll pick you up at the harbour.' It was a signal to her not to come back to the house because her presence disturbed him.

She held her wrist out to the firelight to look at her watch.

'Goodness, it's nine, I must be going.'

'I'll walk you to the road end.'
'Don't bother.'
'Thanks for bringing the book.'
'It's due back in a fortnight but I can always extend the time,' she told him as she pulled on her coat.

Fifteen

Before the last trip of the day Seumas went up the brae to the antique shop to buy back màthair's wedding china. It was still in the window, priced at £6. As he pushed open the door the bell went. The man was at the counter polishing a piece of silver with a blue impregnated glove.

'The tea set in the window,' Seumas said abruptly. He pulled out the wad of money he had collected as fares and threw the pound notes on the glass case.

'I'll wrap it up for you,' the man murmured, as if he didn't recognize the vendor. He counted the cash carefully before putting it into a drawer.

He waited while the man tore up the sheets of newspapers and wrapped each item. The man went into the back shop and as Seumas went out of the door with his purchase under his arm, he reached up and yanked out the connection for the provocative bell.

'Will you keep that safe for me until tonight, when I'm going home?' he asked Donnie, pushing the box across the bar counter.

'Have you been buying yourself a present?'

'You could say that.'

'Remember that business will be slackening off soon and you'll need to put money aside for the winter.'

'I'll manage,' Seumas assured him.

The student was on the launch, studying the large notebook on her lap.

'I'm getting a lot of good data,' she told him, smiling up at him in a way he found disconcerting. 'One of the things I'd like to know is its sex.'

'Why does that matter?' he asked morosely.

'The sex makes a difference to behaviour, just as in humans. But dolphins are physically more subtle than we are.' She pulled a sheet of paper from a big notebook and began to sketch. 'The sexual organs of both male and female are contained in slits under the belly.'

He turned away, embarrassed by this basic lesson in biology which he had read about in the library book.

'One day I hope I can swim with it,' she told him.

'No way,' he warned her vehemently.

'Why not?'

'It's a wild animal that should be left by itself.'

'But we're not leaving it by itself, taking people out to see it,' she argued, lifting her hair away from her face. 'Anyway, dolphins are sociable animals. People swim with them all over the world.'

'I don't give a damn what happens in other places. Nobody's getting into the water with Leumadair.'

She shrugged and resumed studying her data. Seumas went up to the shop to get tobacco for cigarettes. He knew it had been a mistake, allowing her on board. She was trying to take the dolphin over. You couldn't put it into a notebook; it was a wild animal.

He met Alice going up to the library.

'I enjoyed my visit,' she told him. 'Did you get a new bit for your lamp?'

'Thanks for reminding me.'

'I'd like to come again, if that's all right. Your place is so peaceful.'

'If you want.'

When he was on the pier the following morning he did something he had never done before: he tripped on one of the iron rings and came down heavily on his arm. The student had seen him and came running up the steps.

'Are you hurt?' she asked, helping him up.

'I'm all right,' he said, using a bollard as support. But his arm was hanging.

Feona touched it.

'I think you've broken something.'

'I told you, it's all right,' he reacted angrily, trying to pull away from her.

'You'll need to go up to the doctor,' she urged him.

'I can't. There's a full trip going at ten.'

'I can easily take the boat.'

'Stop bloody fussing. There's nothing wrong with my arm.'

'If there's a bone broken and it doesn't set right – '

He started shouting at her about interfering, but she stood there, watching him with her large steady blue eyes. In his anger he saw how attractive she was, but it didn't calm him down. Why wouldn't people leave him alone? Alice had come over the moor because she wanted to be ridden and this one –

'All right, I'll go to the doctor if you take the launch out. But watch the engine, it's temperamental.'

He had to wait half an hour in the doctor's surgery and was told that he would have to go to the hospital on the mainland to get an X-ray. The next bus didn't leave till the afternoon, when there was another trip. As he went down to the pier she was bringing the launch in, steering it expertly among the other craft as she stood at the tiller. He watched from the top of the steps as she took the fares, putting the money into a pouch at her waist. The passengers were talking excitedly about the dolphin as they came up the steps.

'It looked as if Leumadair was going to leap over the boat at one point!' she called up to him.

He resented her confidence and the way she used the name he had given to the dolphin, as if it were public property.

'What did the doctor say?' she asked, concerned as she came up the steps.

She always seemed to be touching him.

'I've to go for an X-ray to the mainland, but I'll leave it till tomorrow. I'll take out the other trips today.'

'If you don't go and get that arm attended to as soon as possible it could be weakened for life,' Feona warned him as she pushed the rope through the iron ring, tying it with an expert hitch because she had spent so much time on her father's boat. 'I'll take out trips. You go and get that X-rayed. I'll look after the dog.'

He was angry at the way she was ordering him about.

'The dog's coming with me. I'll be back this evening,' he told her. 'I'll see you in the hotel.'

He took the bus to the ferry terminal, and had to wait half an hour for the crossing. It was three o' clock by the time he arrived at the hospital in the mainland port. He told Dìleas to sit and wait for him at the entrance. There were two people in front of him, and it was half an hour before they called his name. They gave him his X-ray plates to take back along the corridor under his other arm. The doctor in Casualty took them away and came back to say that his arm was fractured at the elbow and would have to go into plaster.

It was four-thirty before he left the hospital, and the ferry home wasn't until six. He went into a cafe and ate a plate of fish and chips with a fork in his left hand, appreciating now how the stroke must have affected the old man. He took a box of chips out to the dog, which devoured them after her long wait outside the hospital. How was he going to manage in the house? How did you strike a match with one hand and open a tin for the dog? That student was trying to take over his life, and he was sorry that he had allowed her on board now.

He bought ready-made cigarettes, but they weren't the same strength as the ones he rolled. He sat smoking on the pier until the ferry came in, convincing himself that he could manage the boat with one hand.

Alice's husband Tommy took his fare in the bus.

'Been in the wars, Seumas?'

'I had an accident,' he told the driver, knowing he would take the news home to his wife.

There was no one else in the bus, so he ignored the no smoking sign on the window. Dìleas sat on the seat beside him, staring out of the window as if with genuine interest in the countryside she had never seen before. Seumas was watching Tommy at the controls. All Tommy had ever wanted to do since he was a boy was to drive a bus. He ran about the playground steering an imaginary bus, revving it with his mouth and stopping to take non-existent people on board, though he was in primary seven and due to go to the bigger school. Tommy couldn't draw a straight line with a ruler, but was a careful driver who had never had an accident. He pushed the gear stick gently as he slowed for the bend, his arms circling the wheel as if it were a revered woman's waist.

His wife had been mounted by Donnie for years while Tommy drove the bus to and from the ferry. What did he do when he got home at night, Seumas wondered as he watched him braking the bus, releasing the pneumatic door for an old woman who hirpled up the steps with a stick? Did he have sex with Alice, or did he fall asleep immediately, driving his bus through his dreams? It was said that the elder daughter belonged to Donnie, but maybe Tommy didn't care because he had his beloved bus.

Tommy was now taking the vehicle down through the narrow streets of the town, as if he had never been there before, as if every bend was a new experience to be savoured, the big wheel turned so much and no more, the engine singing under the pedals. He braked outside the hotel and released the door.

'Did you hear the news?' Tommy asked.

Seumas turned round on the step, waiting to be told that he had separated from Alice at last.

'I'm getting a new bus.'

'That's very good.'

'Brand new. It's going to have – '

Seumas stepped off the bus without listening to the specification and went into the hotel. The student was sitting on a stool in the public bar with a glass of lager.

'What did they say?' Feona asked, touching the plaster.

He was embarrassed by the attention she was giving him in front of the locals, who would be thinking they were having an affair.

'There's a bone broken,' he informed her reluctantly. 'It'll take a few weeks to heal. But I'll manage the boat.'

'We didn't see Leumadair until the last trip.'

He was pleased because it confirmed the special bond there was between him and the animal.

'Not that the passengers complained. I gave them a talk on the seabirds and they took a lot of photographs. Some of them are booked to go tomorrow again. Why don't I take you home in the boat and bring it back?' she suggested. 'I can come round for you in the morning.'

She said it loudly, as he was going towards the door, making heads turn. He knew he had to say something decisive.

'I'm perfectly capable of taking my own boat home,' he told her, leaving the door swinging behind him.

But he had difficulty starting the engine with his left hand, and it was awkward steering the launch out of the harbour. The dog huddled against him on the seat in the breezy journey. He held the tiller against his thigh as he worked at the packet, and when he couldn't get a cigarette out he tore the top off with his teeth. The first two matches went out. Though he couldn't see the creature, he had the feeling that Leumadair was travelling home with him in the light from the fitful moon.

When he went ashore there was the problem of feeding Dìleas. He tried to use the dagger-shaped opener with his left hand, stabbing at the tin's lid, but it was awkward and dangerous. The dog was sitting, looking up at him, her tail slapping the flagstones expectantly, so he went into the scullery and brought out the toolbox. What would open it? He rummaged with his good hand, but found nothing suitable and was becoming exasperated. He took the tin out to the step, laid it on its side and smacked it with the axe. The meat oozed out of the seam, and as he scraped at it the dog ate it.

Dressing was going to be difficult, so he lay down on the bed in his clothes, but couldn't sleep. It wasn't the pain of the broken bone; it was something sharp inside him. He kept thinking of the curve of the student's hips in her denims as she crouched in the bow, filming the leaping creature. But she was English, a different race from him, as the old man would have said. They came up to the Highlands with money from the sale of their fancy big houses, buying up fishermen's cottages and houses on decrofted land where in his boyhood sheep had grazed. They took over all the local organizations, the Women's Institute and the Historical Society, and they sang in the Gaelic choir, though they couldn't speak one word of the language. Even the conductor was a Sassenach. The old man had had utter contempt for them, though he had never shown it to their faces.

He had seen the girl's father at Donnie's hotel, loading a box of drink into the boot of his Volvo Estate because they were giving a party for other white settlers. Evidently he had been a Brigadier in the army. The mother was very posh, and when she came into the Spar shop, she asked for teas they had never heard of.

The following morning he took the launch out, steering with his left hand while the student gave a commentary on the different types of birds on the Sgeir and on the life of the dolphin as it leapt ahead and glided under the bow. At the end of the day he carried the box of groceries from the Spar shop under his good arm, and he and the dog went home.

It took him a long time to get the fire going to cook himself something, and to feed the dog with the axe on the tin. He smoked ready-made cigarettes, and as he listened to the Gaelic request programme on the radio he thought about the old man, who, as far as he knew, had never broken a bone in his life, despite the bare knuckle brawls he became involved in when he was aggressive on the drink.

Seumas went up to bed and was reading the new book on dolphins Alice had brought from the library when he heard the door opening below.

'Hullo! It's me!'

It was the student. He leaned over and clamped his hand round the dog's muzzle because she always welcomed visitors with a whimper. He heard her going into the kitchen and through to the scullery. Now she was running up the stairs.

'I came to see if you're all right.'

'Why shouldn't I be all right?' he challenged her.

She crouched down, rubbing Dìleas's stomach as the dog rolled over.

'I love your house,' she enthused, looking round. 'It's so – right for this place.'

He didn't get up from the bed and didn't close his book. He reached for a cigarette, striking the match on the rusty metal of the skylight.

'Is there anything I can do for you? What about your washing?'

'I do my own washing. How did you get here?'

'In Daddy's rubber runabout. You don't need to come out tomorrow. I can take the launch back with me and leave you the runabout. You need to rest your arm.'

It made him uncomfortable, the way she was standing in the centre of the room, her hands in the slanted pockets of her denims. She was a good looking woman and he was attracted to her, but he was also angered by the intrusion.

'I can manage.'

'If you're sure. I'd better go.'

Dìleas wanted to go after her down the stairs, but he called the dog back. He listened for the outboard being started before resuming reading.

Sixteen

Seumas always knew it was clipping day because he came downstairs to the abrasive sound as the old man sat on the doorstep, using his spittle on the whetstone to sharpen the shears. The dog knew it too because she was restless, tugging at her master's trousers, wanting to get up on to the moor for the round-up. There were only a dozen sheep, but they had scattered in their search for feeding.

The old man stood on the hillock, his hands cupped round his mouth, shouting in Gaelic to Dìleas's predecessor, telling her to go wide, to lie down in the heather. When a sheep broke loose the dog streaked after it, and the old man brought them both back with a shrill whistle. It usually took the morning to get the flock into the fank the old man had built with driftwood behind the house. Màthair called that dinner was ready, always a hearty meal with plenty of potatoes because she thought that both men needed their strength for the afternoon.

It was Seumas's job to let the sheep out of the fank one by one. The old man wrestled the animal on to its back and sat with its head twisted to one side as he used the shears to cut away the fleece, its fringes filthy with dung and tangled briars. He worked quickly, but never drew blood, and when he turned the animal on to its hooves again it was skinny and snow-white. He gave it a shot in the mouth with the worming gun before it scampered away, a different creature. Seumas spread the fleece out on the heather, rolling it into a bundle while the old man was shearing the next one.

In the late afternoon the shorn sheep were back on the moor in their cool summer coat. He and the old man waded out to the launch, their arms full of fleeces, piling them in the stern to take them round to the pier where the van that was going to the wool merchants would be waiting. The cheque that came back for the fleeces was a welcome addition to the family income.

At sale time it was too expensive to drive the lambs on foot across the moor to a float waiting in the layby on the road, so the old man took them four at a time in the launch round to the town, wading out with them round his neck, like a Viking raider of old. Once one of the lambs had jumped overboard and drowned off Rubha nan Ròn, but the old man had fished out the carcass and they had eaten it because *struidhe*, waste, extravagance, was one of the few words he excluded from his Gaelic vocabulary, including sexual terms, particularly *pit* for the female organ, since he was essentially a prude.

* * * * *

When the old man had taken his stroke and couldn't go out on the moor again, Seumas had sold the sheep because he couldn't attend to the animals as well as to the invalid. In the old man's time you could run a croft and fish and bring up a family, but there wasn't a living in these diverse activities nowadays. He was thinking about the shearing and the conversations he had had with the old man over the clacking shears as he steered the launch out into the bay with his left hand, his plaster cast resting on the gunwale. Feona the student was giving the passengers a commentary on what they could expect to see. Seumas knew that he was attracted to her and that annoyed him. He drew the last of the smoke from his ready-made cigarette before flicking it into the sea, and, as if it were a signal, Leumadair breached spectacularly in front of them. The passengers shouted, and he leaned forward to push the throttle.

'Can I help you with your shopping?' Feona asked at the end of the trip.

'I can manage.'

'If I can do anything just ask.'

He went home with the dog and the box of groceries in the launch, glad to be by himself again. He was putting the tin on to the step to open it with the axe to give the dog its dinner first when he saw the student swerving into his bay in the rubber roundabout. She had seen him and was waving, otherwise he would have hurried over the hill with the dog.

'I brought you this.'

She put the basket on the table, though she hadn't been invited in, removing the cloth to show him a loaf.

'I baked it myself.'

He was waiting for her to go so that he could put the steak pie from the freezer in the Spar shop into the oven, but she was sitting on her heels, fondling the dog's ears. He found himself roused as he watched her, and turned away.

'Your dinner's on the step,' he told the dog in Gaelic, but his visitor didn't move.

'Is this your mother?' she asked, pointing to the photograph, its corners curled by the heat, propped against the tea caddy on the mantelpiece.

'That's her,' he said, moving restlessly about the kitchen.

She lifted down the snapshot and took it to the window to study it. He had taken it himself with the box camera he had got for next to nothing at a jumble sale, shading the little window on the top with his curved hand, surprising màthair as she came round the corner of the house in her floral apron with a peat for the grate in her hand. It had been the photographer she had smiled at, not the camera.

'She looks a gentle lady,' Feona said.

He had been angry that the student had touched the photograph. But nobody had ever called màthair a lady before. He was struck by the choice of the word and looked at the student, her back to him at the widow. Màthair had been more of a lady than the white settlers who went into the Spar shop to ask for special teas in loud voices.

'Do you have a photograph of your father?' Feona asked.

But he wasn't going to go into the dresser drawer for her.

'You're really lucky to have grown up in a place like this,' she said wistfully at the window, looking out over the bay where her rubber boat was pulled out on the shingle.

'Where did you grow up?' he asked out of curiosity, though he wished she would go because he was hungry and it would take an hour for the steak pie to defrost in the oven.

'In all sorts of places.'

'What does that mean?'

'Daddy kept being shifted about because he was in the army, in the Royal Engineers. We lived in Germany for a time. I was sent home to boarding school and I hated it. It was so lonely, though there were three hundred other girls. The teachers were beastly.'

He was struck by the look of sadness in her face as she was speaking.

'What took your family up here?'

'Daddy was retiring from the army, and we'd been coming to the area for holidays for years. We spent most of the summer here, renting a house and going sailing. I used to wander about a lot, but didn't know this place existed. Anyway, do you have a knife? It's better to eat the bread while it's still fresh.'

He opened the sideboard drawer and brought her the carving knife. She had a round cheese in red paper in the basket, so he lifted two plates from the press and sat opposite her.

'This is good bread,' he said appreciatively.

'It's the only thing I learned to do well at school.'

She produced fruit from the basket, but he refused it. She peeled a banana and carefully laid the skin by his plaster cast on the table.

'I'd like to learn Gaelic,' she announced.

That took him by surprise.

'I tried to find someone in the town to teach me, but there wasn't anybody. I sent away for a book, but it's hard doing it by yourself. It's the pronunciation.'

'It's not worth learning it when there's no one to speak it to,' he told her abruptly, because it was a sensitive subject with him.

He was trying to strike a match by pressing his plaster cast on the box, but the head broke as it fizzed. She lit a match for him and held it to his cigarette, earnestly studying his face by the flame. It embarrassed him, the cigarette trembling in his mouth as if it were avoiding the flame.

'But you speak Gaelic,' she persisted. 'You could teach me.'

MacCallum rowed into memory with his black notebook and red correcting pencil in the top pocket of his tweed jacket. The schoolmaster had taught him to write Gaelic, but he had never had the chance to use the skill, doubting if he could write a sentence now.

'Gaelic's been finished for a long time,' he told her bitterly. 'That's what the incomers have done to the place.'

She sat opposite him, her folded arms on the table.

'I understand how you feel. It must be so sad, having a language and seeing it dying.'

'That's the way it is.'

'But surely the way to keep it alive is to teach people to speak it?'

'It wouldn't be the same,' he told her, uncomfortable at her presence and the topic.

'It can never be the same as it was, Seumas, but at least the language would survive in some form.'

But it was too personal, too painful to speak about, so he rose and moved to the window.

'I'd like to go for a walk,' Feona suggested.

It was a way of getting her out of the house. They went over the hill with the dog, up past the sheep fank with its broken posts, on to the path where màthair had trekked from the bus with heavy message bags. He felt he was betraying her by walking with this woman. He was also anxious that Alice would come on a visit and see him with the student. He didn't want people talking about him, since his family had always kept to themselves. He had never even invited Donnie to the house.

The light was going when Feona pulled her rubber boat down to the sea, sitting in it with the short red oars.

'Thank you for a lovely evening. I'd like to come again,' she called.

But he didn't extend an invitation as he pushed off her boat, and when she waved he turned his back and went up to the house.

* * * * *

'How's Feona getting on?' Donnie asked when Seumas was having his supper at the bar.

'She seems all right.'

'She thinks a lot of you,' Donnie revealed.

'What was she saying?' he asked, irritated.

'She doesn't have to say it. I can tell by her eyes when I mention your name. She seems to think the sun shines out of your arse.'

Seumas pushed away the unfinished plate of fish and went out.

It took him all evening to do his washing with one hand, rubbing it against màthair's ribbed board. He pegged the clothes out on the line in the breeze, then went upstairs to tidy his bedroom. When he came down he opened the door of the room which had been kept for special occasions, but since MacCallum was the only visitor and preferred to sit in the warmth of the kitchen, it was only used at Christmas. He and Eilidh hadn't been allowed in this room unless they removed their footwear because of the square of carpet on the flagstoned floor which màthair rolled up in the spring and beat on the clothes line outside, to the accompaniment of *port-a-beul*, Gaelic mouth music, as the dust drifted out over the bay. However, it had become Eilidh's bedroom for the all too short a time before she went into the asylum.

Seumas sat on the red plush sofa with the scrolled ends which had been brought round in the launch from the manse sale before he was born. The room was chilly and smelt of damp, and he had a vague recollection of his grandfather's coffin lying between the two chairs before it was taken away by sea for burial in the town. Màthair used to wind up the black marble clock on the mantelpiece, but it had been stopped for years.

He had a sudden compulsion to lay a fire in the empty grate, as if it would bring back màthair's presence. He went behind the house to the shed for sticks, breaking them up with his boot on the step, and kneeling to pile them with one hand on an old newspaper before going out to take peats from the stack. Instead of lighting the fire he closed the door and went upstairs. He was lying on the bed reading when the student shouted up the stairs.

'Hullo?'

He dared the dog to make a sound, but the visitor was coming up.

'Are you not feeling well?' she asked anxiously.

'I'm reading,' he told her abruptly, letting her know that she wasn't welcome.

She came across and sat beside him on the bed, looking at the cover of the book.

'You don't need books on dolphins when you see Leumadair every day.'

He still had the book open, waiting for her to go away so that he could continue reading.

'I learnt some Gaelic today,' she announced.

'Oh,' he reacted, unimpressed.

She took a pencil from her pocket and began to write on the plaster on his arm.

'What are you doing?' he demanded, pulling away.

He saw what she had written.

Tha gaol agam ort, I love you.

He spat on the plaster and tried to rub off the writing that seemed to him a profanity, like what had been written by Donnie and others about some of the girls on the doors of the boys' lavatories in the playground.

'Why are you so defensive?' she wanted to know.

'I'm a very private person. I happen to like my own company.'

'And I happen to like your company.'

'Listen: you asked me to take you out in my boat so that you can study the dolphin. That's all.'

'No, it's not all as far as I'm concerned. You're a very attractive person, different to most of the men about here. You don't get drunk; you keep your own company; you care about the environment. You care about Gaelic.'

'What's all that got to do with you?'

She leaned over him and kissed him, and his hand went to her thigh. She pulled down the zip of her denims, lifting her tee shirt over her head and stepping out of her panties. She stood naked in the sweep of the beam coming up from the lamp on the floor. He lay watching her from the bed. The dog had gone quiet, lying in a corner. Her hips were wide and her breasts showed as shadows on the sloping wall, like the silhouettes of two faces with noses.

She came and lay beside him on the narrow bed. His back was pressed to the wall, his arm in plaster up on the pillow. She was kissing him, and his *bod* was up, though his mind had fought against it.

'This is awkward for you,' she said.

She moved his shoulders and was astride him, fitting him inside her. He tried to pull out, but the plaster was impeding him, their fluids already mixing. Her hips were heaving in the lamplight, her ponytail brushing the skylight. He had never dreamed it was going to be as good as this, worth waiting for until he was in his late thirties. He was coming now and he tried to get out, but she pressed down on him, keeping him inside her.

He groped in his pocket, but the cigarette packet was crushed. She opened it and put a flattened smoke into his mouth, striking the match on the buckle of his belt. She held the flame even after he had lit up, as if she were studying his face.

'I do love you,' she said earnestly.

He didn't respond because he was taking smoke into his lungs. She dressed quietly and kissed him, ruffling the dog's head before she went downstairs.

He was angry with himself for having let it happen in that way. He hit the wall with his plaster cast, feeling the pain in his arm as a punishment. She had done it for her pleasure, not his. Donnie was always saying that the women who came to the holiday cottages rode like rabbits.

But he slept well and steered the launch in the fine morning, with Leumadair surfacing off Sgeir nan Eun, leading the way ahead into the harbour. How could she face him after what had happened? She was sitting on a bollard, talking to the passengers for the first trip, and when he reversed away from the pier she put her hand on his on the tiller.

Seventeen

On the last trip on Friday Feona lowered something over the side of the launch, trailing it in the water.

'What's that?' he asked suspiciously.

'A hydrophone to pick up the sounds of the dolphin.'

'What do you mean, sounds?'

'Dolphins communicate by sounds. They also use this part of their head' – she touched her forehead – 'to send out echo-location signals. Listen,' she instructed him, putting the headphones on him.

He couldn't believe that the clicking and whistling sounds were coming from the creature.

'That's the dolphin sending out a signal to find out where this boat is,' she explained, removing the phones and putting them on her own head. For the rest of the trip she sat listening.

When the last passenger had gone up the steps at the harbour he gave her £10.

'I told you, I don't want paid,' she insisted, pushing away his hand. 'You let me come on the boat so that I could do my research and I'm very grateful.'

'Take it or you'll never be in this boat again.'

It was the first time he had seen a lack of confidence in her face.

'Look, Seumas, I know you're independent and I respect that, but I'm not trying to – '

He thrust the money into the back pocket of her denims. She was biting her lip and sobbing as she went up the steps with her camera bag. He watched her hurrying along the pier and getting into the Volvo, starting it up quickly and driving away. He turned and spoke to the dog.

'That's you and me got the place to ourselves again, Dìleas. I'm going up to Andy the butcher's for the biggest bone he's got.'

* * * * *

It was autumn now and there weren't many visitors to the hotel, apart from retired couples who wanted to see a dolphin before they became too old to travel. He was busy at the weekend with people coming from the mainland, but because of the darkness the last trip went at two. His arm felt stronger and one night when he went home he got the hammer out of the toolbox under the scullery sink, held the plaster on the wall outside and broke it open. He used his returned dexterity to clean the house, filling it with great Gaelic singers of the past as he washed and cooked. One night he put on the tape of *Fear a' Bhàta* and opened the door.

> *''S tric mi faighneachd de luchd nam bàta*
> *Am fac iad thu, no a bheil thu sàbhailt,*
> *Ach 's ann a tha gach aon diubh 'g ràitinn*
> *Gur gòrach mise ma thug mi gràdh dhuit.'*

> Often I ask of the crews
> If they've seen you, or if you're safe,
> But every one of them says
> That I'm foolish if I've given you love.

The rolling fin was in the bay. He thought about Feona, sitting with her supervisor in the laboratory in Cambridge, watching her films of the dolphin. He had the real creature on his doorstep, a creature which understood Gaelic, as if the water were conveying the sounds out to it like a sonic language, a language that made it leap with joy, as if into the lighted door of the house itself. The old man and MacCallum would have loved this performance.

* * * * *

One evening when he came home a letter had been pushed under the door. He lit the lamp to read it. NEWNHAM COLLEGE, CAMBRIDGE was written on the flap. He eased it open slowly with a finger and sat in the old man's chair to read it.

Dear Seumas,

I have been trying to write to you for a week, but couldn't find the words. However, today I watched the film of Leumadair breaching and it seems to have given me the courage. I'm pregnant. I don't know what to do. I haven't told my parents, but I know they'll be so angry.

Newnham is Mummy's old college, and she was thrilled when I won a place here. She'll think I've thrown it all away. I don't want to have an abortion because I don't believe in denying life its opportunities. I'm coming home next weekend to see my parents and will come round and talk to you about it.

I hope you're continuing to see Leumadair. I miss it and you so very much.

Fondest Love,
Feona.

He crushed the letter in the fist of his healing arm and threw it into the fire, thrusting it among the peats with the poker, as if that obliterated the charge of paternity. It couldn't be his, not after only one time, with her on top. It was probably one of her fancy white settler friends in the town, or maybe one of the students at Cambridge. It wasn't him she was after; it was Leumadair. She wanted to come and stay with him so that she could study the dolphin.

He wouldn't answer the letter. But when he had rolled himself a cigarette slowly and crudely, having lost his touch after the plaster cast, he knew that she would still come to his house. What was he to do? He took the dog with him and went down to the shore. He pulled in the rope for the dinghy and went out to the launch. The seabirds were gone from their breeding sites on the Sgeir, and after their clamour the silence was eerie.

Donnie was behind the counter of the bar.

'I need to talk to you,' Seumas told him.

They went into the chilly sun lounge and sat on wicker chairs in the light from the street outside.

'I've had a letter from Feona. She's pregnant.'

'When did you hear this?' Donnie asked cautiously.

'Today.'

'Right. Did you shag her?'

The question was abrupt, but Seumas knew he had to answer it.

'Not really.'

'Now listen,' Donnie said, his face coming into view as the match burst into flame for one of the small cigars he habitually smoked, 'you either shagged her or you didn't. Let's put it another way: was your cock in her fanny?'

'Yes.'

'Were you wearing a French letter?'

'No. But she was on top.'

Donnie drew in smoke for the next part of the lesson.

'It doesn't matter where she was, if you shot your load inside her.'

'It was only once.'

Donnie had always helped him. He had lent him money and given him advice in the past. He was going to help him again as he blew the strong smoke out in the sun lounge, the wicker chair creaking under his bulk.

'Have you checked out the dates?'

'What do you mean?'

'When did you do it?'

It was a few days after his arm had been put into plaster.

'About six weeks ago.'

'So she must have missed only one period. She may not be pregnant; it could be a false alarm.'

'Do you think so?' Seumas said hopefully.

'It could be, but she's a scientist. I also think she's a pretty straight person. As far as I know nobody else was riding her when she was here, so if she's pregnant it's probably yours.'

'How will I know for sure?' he asked his best friend.

'You won't; it's a question of trust.'

'She's coming home this weekend to see her parents,' Seumas disclosed.

The glow of the cigar moved in a slow arc from Donnie's mouth.

'So what are you going to do?'

'I don't know,' Seumas admitted, having hoped that Donnie would tell him, after his experience with women.

'Her parents have plenty of money.'

'What's that supposed to mean?' Seumas challenged him.

'Money makes life easier,' Donnie said factually. 'Have you met them?'

'No.'

'Mind you, I don't think they'll like their daughter's news.'

'What would you do?' Seumas asked.

There was a pause while smoke was taken in, as if it aided inspiration.

'If I'd married all the women I've put in the family way I'd be in jail for a long time. What men have between their legs is a strange thing; it gives so much pleasure and causes so much trouble.' He leaned forward, the chair creaking, as if it were going to split as he slapped Seumas's knee. 'I think you could do a lot worse. She's a genuine person, unlike most of the incomers here.'

He had a full complement of dolphin watchers on board at the pier and was about to start the engine when the constable shinned down the ladder.

'What do you want, Hughie?'

'Stop that engine.'

'Why should I?'

'Because I'm ordering you to. I want to see your boat hire licence.'

'Is this you harassing me again, Hughie? You've never liked me since the time we were in school. You hated the fact that MacCallum and me spoke Gaelic. Did you think we were speaking about you? These folks have paid to see the dolphin.'

'It's not harassment; it's the law. Your boat hire licence,' the constable demanded, holding out a hand.

'I don't know what you're talking about.'

'Before you started taking paying passengers on trips you should have applied to the local authority for a boat hire licence. You're in breach of the law.'

'That's a big phrase for you, Hughie.'

'I've just told you, you must have a licence.'

'Look: I've been handling this boat since I was a boy, and I know these waters so well that I could practically go about them blindfold. If I need a licence I'll get one.'

'It takes time, and has to go to the Chief Constable for approval.'

'Ah, I see, Hughie, this is more victimization because I stood up to the police.'

'It's for the Chief Constable to determine if you're a fit person to operate a pleasure boat.' He was consulting the paper in his hand. 'The boat needs to be given a thorough check, and you need to have insurance for five million pounds in case anything happens to your passengers.'

'Five million?' Seumas repeated, laughing. 'You used to make up stories when you were in school, Hughie, but that's the best you've come up with yet.'

'This boat isn't sailing because it hasn't the proper certification or safety equipment, or insurance,' the constable told the passengers. 'Please leave now.'

Seumas went up to the hotel to report the confrontation to Donnie.

'Did you know that I needed a licence?' he challenged his best friend.

'I did.'

'Then why the hell didn't you tell me?'

'You could have gone to the trouble and expense of getting a licence and then found that the dolphin had disappeared. I wanted to give you the chance to put money from the fares aside when the going was good.'

'So that's the dolphin trips finished,' he said bitterly.

'It looks like it, because you might not get a boat hire licence, after your confrontation with the police, and even if you did, it would cost you, not to mention the insurance and other requirements. You could spend a fair sum, then find that the dolphin has disappeared.'

'So I'll have to go back to the fishing.'

'Unless you can get a job in the town. I can give you a few hours a week.'

'There are no suitable jobs here, and you know that I can't rely on the fishing.'

'I'm sorry, Seumas. I tried to help. If you're short I'll lend you whatever you need.'

'You could be dead by the time I'll be able to pay you back, Donnie.'

Feona knocked on the door on Saturday night. He had tidied the house and had a big fire burning. She stepped out of her wellingtons at the door as if she were entering a shrine, placing her big red torch on the table beside the lamp. He embraced her awkwardly, missing the mouth he meant to kiss. The dog gave her a warm welcome.

'I'm so glad to see you, Seumas.'

He had pushed màthair's chair closer to the fire for her, and she sat warming her hands before she spoke.

'I'm sorry about the way I broke the news to you.'

He nodded.

'Do you want a cup of tea?'

'That would be nice after my hike.'

'Well,' she began, when she had her fingers wrapped round the warm mug, 'I told my parents.'

'Are you sure you're expecting?' he interrupted her.

'Oh, I'm sure. I've had two tests. I told them tonight.'

'Did you tell them whose it is?' he questioned her, then realized that he had just admitted paternity.

She glanced up.

'Yes, I told them. What's the point in lying about it? They're furious.'

'But if it had been someone at Cambridge?'

She sighed. 'You're right; they don't want a fisherman for a son-in-law. They both had big plans for me.'

'Then it's settled. Get an abortion.'

Her eyes were angry now.

'I told you in the letter, I don't believe in abortions. I'm having this baby. It's yours, but if you don't want to have anything to do with it I'll bring it up myself.'

'How would you manage that if your parents are against it?'

'I've got money coming to me from Granny's will. She died last year, but her estate hasn't been settled yet.'

'What are you going to do?'

'No, Seumas, it's what *you're* going to do. I'm not looking for an answer tonight. The baby's not due till May. But it's going to be born and it's yours. How is Leumadair?'

'I'm not allowed to take any more passengers out to see it because I don't have a boat hire licence. I didn't know I needed to have one, and Donnie didn't tell me. Hughie the policeman came to tell me that I'm breaking the law by not having a licence.'

'Apply for one,' Feona urged.

He shook his head. 'It's too complicated and expensive.'

'I can pay for it out of Granny's legacy.'

'Thanks all the same, but the police will probably say that I'm not a suitable person to hold a licence because of my run-in with them. I'm back at the fishing.'

'We'll manage,' she reassured him, taking his hand across the firebars.

He walked back across the moor with her, the powerful beam of her torch wavering over the heather.

'There's something I want to say,' she spoke as they approached the Volvo parked in the layby. 'Living together doesn't mean having to get married.'

She kissed him on the mouth before driving away. As he and the dog went back with his much weaker torch he was working out her remark. Màthair had had him and raised him in the house, but it wasn't suitable for a woman like Feona who was used to electricity and other modern conveniences. If she were expecting him to move into the town there was no way he was going to do that because that would be cutting himself off from all sorts of things. Gaelic was as much part of the house as the peat-stack by its gable wall, and there was no Gaelic now in the town, with MacCallum and his sister, and Alan Maclachan the banker in their graves.

By the time he reached home he was angry with Feona.

Eighteen

Seumas was using màthair's blue-lined pad to write to Feona as he sat at the table by the lamp. It would be easier to write in Gaelic because he could express his feelings.

> *Dear Feona,*
> *I've been doing a lot of thinking since you were here for the weekend. I know I'm the father of the baby, but I don't think*

He looked at the dog as if for inspiration, but it was sleeping by the fire.

> *that it would be suitable for you to live here with a baby. There isn't any electricity and there's no bath. It would be too expensive to put these things in.*

He rolled a cigarette for inspiration.

> *Maybe if you continued to live with your parents in the town I could come to see you and the baby every day. Anyway, we can discuss this when you come home for Christmas.*

He blew out smoke ruminatively between pursed lips, then picked up the pen again.

I see Leumadair almost every day when I'm out fishing.

Love Seumas.

He wasn't satisfied with the letter and wanted to tear it up. However, he folded it into the envelope because he didn't know what he wanted to say. He sat by the lamp, his face cupped on his hands, thinking of her coming into the room above. Sometimes in his sleep she was on top of him again.

He was reading one night when the door was knocked. The dolphin book in his hands was overdue from the library and he thought it was Alice come to collect it.

'Anyone at home?' a man called round the door.

Though Seumas didn't respond the visitor came into the room. Donnie had pointed out Feona's father sitting in the sun lounge with his wife, having a bar lunch. He had the florid face of a drinker and was wearing a deerstalker, a wax jacket and green wellingtons with buckles.

'Cyril Bradwell-Price, Feona's father,' he introduced himself, holding out his hand.

'What do you want here?' Seumas asked, angry at the intrusion, refusing the proffered hand.

'I think you know why I'm here,' he said, sitting in màthair's chair without invitation, putting the deerstalker over the knee of his corduroys and laying his red torch by his feet. 'My daughter's pregnant and tells me you're the father.'

'So?'

'I beg your pardon?'

'So what has it to do with you?'

'It has everything to do with me. I'm her father. I'm supporting her at university and I live in this community.'

'You came two miles over the moor just to tell me this?' Seumas challenged him, hating the man more with every minute that passed. He had seen his like before on the moor with the laird and his paying guests, with ghillies carrying the shotguns that blasted the birds from the sky. One of them had wounded a merlin which came down near the house. The old man had tried to make a splint for the broken wing, but on its first flight it had drowned in the bay, and the old man had cursed the shooter.

'I came here to put a proposition to you. I believe that you no longer take visitors out to see the dolphin because you don't have a boat hire licence.'

'You're well informed.'

'You know how news travels in a small community.' The Brigadier took a folded magazine from his jacket and held it out. 'Have a look at this boat. It has a big cabin with a table and there's a toilet. It could take a dozen passengers comfortably.'

'Why are you showing me this?' Seumas demanded.

'I'm willing to put up the money to buy this boat and to apply for a licence,' the Brigadier disclosed. 'You can run dolphin trips with it for a share of the profits – provided you don't marry my daughter.'

Seumas's hand had become a fist at his side.

'Is that what she told you, that we're getting married?'

The Brigadier was taken aback.

'She didn't discuss it with me, but I assumed so since she *is* pregnant by you.' He leaned forward. 'Are you saying that you don't want to marry her?'

'Why should it concern you so much?'

'It concerns me because she's our daughter and has a brilliant future ahead of her as a marine biologist. We don't want anything to happen that would jeopardize that future.'

'You mean, you want her to marry one of her own class?'

'Feona mixes with two different types of people. When she's up here in the summer she mixes with the locals and loves them, as we do. But when she's in Cambridge she has her own friends.'

'Let me get this right. If I don't marry her I get a new boat with you as a partner.'

'I knew you were a sensible chap.'

'What about the baby?'

'She's against abortion and so are we, but it can go for adoption.'

'And if I do marry her?' Seumas asked, still keeping his temper under control.

'Then she's no longer our daughter.'

'So I'm not good enough for her?'

'I didn't say that,' the Brigadier retracted hastily. 'We just think it wouldn't be right for her. There's the big age gap, apart from other factors.'

Seumas took the magazine from him and pushed it between the firebars, then went to open the door.

A-mach à seo,' he told his visitor.

'I beg your pardon?'

'It's Gaelic for clear out.'

The Brigadier was getting to his feet.

'You won't treat me like this, Macdonald. I've had thousands of men under my command in my lifetime and by God –'

'You're disturbing the dog.'

Dìleas was beginning to growl at the green wellingtons with buckles.

'You'll soon find out who you're dealing with,' the Brigadier threatened as Seumas kicked the door shut behind him.

He sat down again, not even able to roll a cigarette because of his shaking hands. The old man would have kicked out at him, the English bastard who had ruined MacCallum's house that had been full of character and Gaelic. Christ, no wonder the Welsh were burning down holiday homes to save their culture, as the Gaelic news reported. It was that bitch his daughter's fault, coming here, looking for sex, knowing his arm was in plaster, that he couldn't even handle his own boat, never mind his *bod*. He didn't want a share in a new boat and he didn't want a wife.

But there was the baby to consider. He paced about the room in his anger and uncertainty. When a sheep rejected a lamb the old man would find it another mother by putting the skin of a dead lamb of hers over it. This was different, though. He couldn't allow his child to go for adoption. But the way that bastard had spoken, they wouldn't allow their daughter and her baby to stay with them.

Feona and the baby couldn't come here. The house wasn't his; it belonged to the estate. They wouldn't do it up for him without increasing the rent, which he wouldn't be able to afford. So if he were to live with her and the baby he would have to give up the place. He could put his name down for a council house in the town, but there were very few and one rarely became vacant. Anyway, the way she had been brought up she wouldn't want to live in a council house.

He didn't know what he was going to do, and suddenly he didn't care. He called to the dog and they went out into the night. It was calm, with a big moon. He stood at the tide's edge for a few minutes until he saw the fin gently rising and falling in the smooth bay. It calmed him to stand there watching it in the autumn night. He couldn't leave this place, even though the Brigadier bought him his own house in the town in return for not marrying his daughter. Out there was a solitary creature also that seemed to have made the bay its home.

The dog was in the water. He called her back, but she was swimming out towards the fin. He thought she was going to attack Leumadair out of jealousy at the attention her master was giving it, but the dolphin was coming in to meet her. The two animals seemed to be having a game, with the creature's beak pushing Dìleas away. He shed his own clothes and began to swim, immune to the cold because of the energy and delight in joining in their play, being knocked over with a flipper, the dog butting him with her head. He came out of the water and picked up his clothes, carrying them up to the house while Dìleas shook the ocean from her coat.

When he went round to the town the next day he told Donnie about the Brigadier's visit.

'He and his wife are good customers in here,' Donnie disclosed. 'But I'm not keen on him. He thinks he owns the town. So he offered to buy a new boat and give you a share in it?' he repeated, intrigued.

'A glass fibre one, with a cabin.'

'That would cost a lot of money. He's obviously desperate not to have you as a son-in-law, though he wouldn't mind you as a boatman,' Donnie said with a wry smile.

'I don't want to marry her.'

'But do you want to live with her?'

'I don't know,' Seumas admitted. 'The house isn't suitable, and it isn't mine.'

'There's a way round that.'

'What do you mean?'

'That croft's been in your family for a long time. Under crofting law you're entitled to buy it. Alastair Beaton was in the bar recently, celebrating after buying his croft from the estate.'

'He obviously had the money to do it,' Seumas pointed out.

'You told me that Feona had money coming to her. She can buy your house off the estate.'

'I wouldn't allow that.'

'Why not? It's her baby as well as yours, and it's going to need a roof over its head. The only problem you've got to worry about is her father, but I don't see what he could do to you except run you down in the Volvo. You wait, before you know it he'll be the devoted grandfather. You'll end up in MacCallum's old house yet.'

A letter arrived from Feona.

There's no way that I'm going to live with my parents after I've had the baby – not that they want me. I'm being bombarded with letters and phone calls by them. They even arranged for a woman from some society in London to phone me up to 'chat with you about adoption.'

You say that it wouldn't work, living in your house with a baby. I agree. But surely it can be modernized without losing its character. I know it would be expensive, but it would be a wonderful place to bring up a child. We have family friends who have a remote cottage on Deeside. They've put in a generator for lighting, and have a super bottled gas stove. With Leumadair in the bay I would have a lab on my doorstep.

I wrote to the lawyer (daring him to tell Daddy), asking how much I will have coming from Granny's will. He says that it shouldn't be less than £40,000! I never dreamed it was anything like that, and there's no way my parents can stop me getting it, so there's plenty money to buy your house from the estate and do it up.

I wish you had a phone so that I could talk to you because I miss you so much. I don't think you appreciate how much I'm in love with you. Will I prove it by learning Gaelic so that our child will grow up speaking it?

> *Fondest love,*
> *Feona.*

* * * * *

'As I told you before, you should buy your croft,' Donnie advised Seumas when he next went into the hotel. He pulled a phone directory from under the counter and thumbed through the pages, then lifted the phone across to Seumas. 'Call the factor and tell him you want to buy your croft. This is the number.'

He was apprehensive, but did as his best friend urged.

'Just like that?' the English voice responded. 'You'd better come and discuss it.'

'When?'

'Let me consult my secretary.' A pause, then: 'Wednesday afternoon, three o' clock. You know where we are? In the stable block.'

Seumas walked up the hill out of town and a quarter of a mile up the eerie avenue of trees, arriving ten minutes early for his appointment. He had never been at the big house before. At the prize-giving in school the laird always gave a lecture on private property, saying that trespassing was a 'serious offence,' a warning to Donnie and his friends about raiding the big house's apple orchard. He went round the side of the large grey house with battlements and towers, to where a woman was kneeling in a flowerbed.

'Can you tell me where the estate office is?'

She looked annoyed, pointing with the trowel, watching him go as if she were suspicious of him. He went under the arch into the courtyard. The stable units had been turned into offices with arched windows. He had to wait half an hour before he saw the factor, who was dressed in breeches with leather patches on his elbows.

'I want to buy our croft – the house and the land.'

'You can't, Macdonald; it's not a croft. I checked the estate records,' the factor stated, laying his hand on a ledger, as though it were a Bible. 'It was a gamekeeper's cottage, but the occupant was killed in the Boer War and he wasn't replaced because there was a shortage of skilled men. Your great-grandfather was given the tenancy at a modest rent because of the condition of the property. There was no lease; it was a verbal agreement between the estate and your great-grandfather. So it wasn't classified as a croft. Your family have made their living from the sea trout netting in the bay, and that is reflected in the rent, since the estate owns the netting.'

'It was and still is a croft,' Seumas insisted. 'I'm the fourth generation to work it. I had to look after my father, but now that he's gone, I'll get on with it.'

'I've just told you, it didn't come under crofting law and therefore you don't have a right of purchase under crofting law. Even if you wanted to buy it as an ordinary house and piece of land, Colonel Carlton-Ashington won't sell it to you. He wants to keep the estate intact for his son when he's finished his degree in agriculture and forestry at Oxford.'

'I'm fucking telling you, it's a croft, and I'm going to force you to sell it to me, because that's my right.'

The factor ignored the expletive.

'Go ahead; you'll be wasting money on lawyers, because we'll oppose you. We have very experienced lawyers in Edinburgh – including an advocate who'll plead our case. The judgement will go against you, and we will certainly be seeking our costs from you for bringing the case.'

'We'll see about that!' Seumas threatened as he rose from the obnoxious man's presence, who seemed to get satisfaction in humiliating him. He was shaking with rage as he went down the road. Alice was at the desk in the library, deserted except for an old man reading the local paper at the table, the sheets trembling between his fists.

'Do you have a book on crofting law?' Seumas asked her.

'Is this your latest interest? I'm afraid not. Is the laird trying to put you out?' she asked, concerned. 'He's a real bastard, that one. He had a small fine on an overdue book about shooting and he wouldn't pay.'

'I want to know my rights,' Seumas told her.

'You could phone the Crofters Commission for advice. I'll get you the number.'

He went to see Donnie.

'He's lying, the slippery bastard,' his best friend pointed out. 'He knows it's a croft, and that you have the right to buy it. I'll phone Alastair Beaton and ask what the procedure is. Come in and see me tomorrow morning.'

He couldn't sleep for thinking about what the factor had told him. It had to be a lie, because the old man must have known that it was a croft when he always called it *croit* in his conversations with MacCallum, saying that *am balach*, the boy, would take it over.

'I spoke with Alastair Beaton last night,' Donnie told him. 'He says he was told by someone from the Crofters Commission before he went to see the factor that if the estate wouldn't come to an agreement with him about buying the croft, he could appeal to the Land Court. He didn't need to because his place was registered as a croft, so the estate had to sell it to him. However, Alastair says in your case, if you decide to appeal to the Land Court, you'll have to make two separate applications: one for the conveyance of the croft house site and garden ground to you; the other application is for the acquisition of the croft land. Alastair says that if the estate hires lawyers to act for them at the Land Court, you may have to do the same; and that the Land Court has the power to decide who has to pay the costs, so you could end up with hefty bills.'

'It's too complicated,' Seumas said bitterly.

'Alastair was all ready to go and plead his case at the Land Court in Edinburgh if the estate wouldn't sell to him. He didn't need to, but you could.'

'Thanks for getting in touch with Alastair, but I'm not going to bother.'

'But you should bother. People – probably some of your own family – fought to get the crofting laws passed. You've got rights; don't let the bastards scare you off with lies. Remember what the landowners did to the people, clearing them off the land and putting sheep in their place. I'll never forget MacCallum talking about the Clearances the day the poor bugger died in front of us in the classroom. I'll tell you this, he would have been disappointed in you – and so would your father – if they thought you were giving in to the descendants of a man whose forebears cleared the estate and sent them in overcrowded ships across the Atlantic. He has a double-barrelled English-sounding name, but he's descended from the owner who cleared the estate on the island here in 1850, because his father inherited the estate from a cousin. It's still the same ruthless bloodline.

'This isn't about the croft, Seumas; it's about you. The laird and the Brigadier are close friends. I believe their wives are related. He's asked the laird not to sell the place to you to stop you marrying his daughter in the hope that you'll move away, and the factor's quite willing to lie about your place not being a croft. Feona's got money coming from her granny; use it to go to the Land Court and fight your case. Alastair Beaton says that he got his croft for fifteen-hundred – fifteen times the annual rent. What a bargain, and he's getting a big grant to build a new house on the croft. You can get the same, Seumas, and provide a modern home for the three of you. But you'll have to get your application in to the Land Court soon so that you can settle down to married bliss, like me,' Donnie added, winking.

'I'll think about it. Thank Alastair from me.'

Nineteen

He lay in bed under the skylight sprinkled with stars, thinking not about becoming a father and buying the croft, but about MacCallum and the dinner money. The headmaster had told màthair that it would be twopence a day for Seumas to have his dinner in school, and the same for Eilidh when she arrived. The pupils from both classrooms lined up to pay their dinner money at MacCallum's desk while he wrote the amounts in a lined jotter, putting a tick beside names with his fountain pen after he had counted the money from each pupil. One day of reckoning Donnie was sixpence short, and the way the schoolmaster's eye half closed showed Seumas that MacCallum suspected that his best friend had tried to cheat him. He didn't belt Donnie, but warned him: 'Don't ever try that trick again.'

The dinners came in a van, driven by a man the pupils called Desperate Dan because he had a jaw on him like the comic hero's, and was said to be daft. MacCallum sent out the boys in primary seven to bring in the aluminum containers Desperate Dan slid from the back of the van, telling them: 'You're going to enjoy this today. It's tripe.'

'What's tripe?' one of the boys asked.

'You don't know what tripe is?' the driver asked, ruffling the questioner's hair.

But Seumas knew. When the old man killed a sheep no part of it was wasted. What couldn't be chewed as meat was boiled in a pot to make soup. Even the sheep's head was cooked, though Seumas found it ghoulish, sitting on the table, with its hair singed, the old man eating its clouded eyes as though they were a delicacy. The sheep's intestines were scrubbed, then cooked by màthair in the blackened iron pot and served up as creamy white strands. That was tripe, but he wasn't going to say in front of the other boys that he knew what tripe was, because they would make a fool of him for eating the guts of a sheep their parents would only feed to their dogs. The word tripe was never used at home because the Gaelic was *maodal*, and the old man never liked English words in his mouth. Anyway, Desperate Dan was joking; it wasn't tripe today.

At half past twelve the two dinner women, heads wrapped in white scarves, came into the school, the wall between the two classrooms pushed open, trestle tables set up. Seumas liked the macaroni and cheese the best, and was always at the head of the queue for a second helping. The women served him with a smile, pouring the custard from a ladle over his big portion of sponge. The schoolmaster took his dinner in his house with his sister, but came back through to make sure that the tables were folded away again, the wall between the classrooms restored.

'What did you have at school for dinner, sonny?' màthair would ask, and he would sit down and go through the menu with her, telling her about steak pie that came with a crust, and tapioca pudding, like the clusters of frog spawn in the jam jars on the window ledge in Miss Maclaren's room in spring. He would still be talking about the tapioca as màthair lifted away his cleaned plate of habitual mackerel and potatoes, with no pudding to follow. Only after màthair's death did he realize that he might have hurt her by going on about the school dinners, as if they were superior to the meals at home.

After MacCallum died they had let his sister stay on in the schoolhouse because the next schoolmaster had invested in a house in the town. Seumas had started going to see her, taking Dìleas with him because she adored dogs. She and her brother's dog had died a few months after the schoolmaster's passing, belying its Gaelic name of Sona, happy.

'He was a good man, so careful about everything,' Miss MacCallum said as she fondled Dìleas's ears by her chair. 'I never saw a neater writer.' She hobbled over to a drawer and pulled out a blue exercise book. 'I saved this from his desk in the school before they threw all the stuff out, including his collection of birds' eggs.'

Seumas took it on his knee. It was the dinner book for the last year he had been in MacCallum's room. His fingers went down the column of names: the Macgregor sisters, Sandy, Alice, Donnie, with the amounts they had paid weekly marked in columns. Then he came to his own name: Seumas Macdonald. He had only paid twopence a day, not ninepence as MacCallum had written.

Seumas began to weep, his tears dropping on the page, blotting the blue ink, smudging the money that the others had paid for their dinners.

'What's the matter?' Miss MacCallum asked, concerned.

But Seumas couldn't tell her what he had just discovered. In all the years he had been in the primary school MacCallum had been subsidising his dinners out of his own pocket, and Eilidh's also.

Lying in bed under the visible stars, Seumas could still weep at MacCallum's generosity. The schoolmaster had paid for him and Eilidh, not because he knew that they came from a poor primitive house, but because he and his sister were the only children in the school who spoke Gaelic. It was a kind of bursary MacCallum had given his family all those years. *I'll feed you food and you'll feed me Gaelic because I'm starved of it in this place.*

He couldn't sleep, so he put on his clothes and went downstairs. Dìleas was waiting for him because she seemed to be able to read his mind even at a distance, and was always alert for a nocturnal excursion. They walked together along the shore under the immense moon. One evening MacCallum and the old man had a discussion about people in the future going to live on the moon, which was filling the window that night, laying a white mat on the flagstones. The old man was staring beyond the schoolmaster's shapely bald head, as if looking for figures moving in the heavenly body. He asked MacCallum if he thought that there could be life on other planets.

'Perhaps even in Seumas's lifetime they'll send a spaceship to Mars to find out,' the schoolmaster speculated in Gaelic.

Since he didn't know if there was a Gaelic word for spaceship among modern coinages, MacCallum had to break his rule of not using English words in his fluent sentences. That made the old man frown, not because he thought his native tongue was deficient and old-fashioned, but because the term had had no use in the culture in which he and his forebears had been raised, where the majority of people had never even seen a train. Certainly there was a word for Heaven, *nèamh*, but that had nothing to do with interplanetary travel, since not even the most powerful telescope which man could devise would ever see *nèamh*, nor any spaceship ever reach it.

As Seumas and the dog were walking along the shore he noticed the cherished fin rising and falling fifty yards offshore, as if accompanying them. As he waded in the dolphin rubbed against his leg. His hand was caressing the belly turned up to him, like a dog's, and he felt a slit. It was like a sexual experience.He went up to the house and lit the lamp, banking up the fire so that the dog could dry off. He took out the blue-lined pad and began a letter to Feona.

> *Dìleas and me have just been taking a walk in the moonlight.*
> *Leumadair came inshore to meet us. I was thinking about you as*
> *I played with it. We are both missing you.*
>
> *Love, Seumas*

* * * * *

He was fishing again in the bay, with Leumadair driving the shoal inshore. He took the twenty sea trout round to the hotel and had a bar supper with part of the proceeds while Donnie fed Dìleas from an audible dish in the passage. Seumas was sitting eating by the fire when Feona came through from the lounge bar.

'When did you come?'

'Yesterday morning. I was going to walk over the hill to see you, but I'm carrying this extra weight.'

'Do you want something to eat?' he asked solicitously.

'No, thank you. My parents think I'm at home. They're at my godparents for dinner. They don't want me wandering about, showing everyone my condition.'

'I'll walk up the road with you,' Seumas offered, and went to the bar to pay for his supper.

On the way up the dark brae she felt for his hand and he allowed it to be taken. Then she stopped as if the climb had suddenly become too much in her condition.

'Have you thought any more about us?' she turned to him. 'It's not all that long until the baby's due. My parents want to pay for it to be born in a nursing home down south, well out of the way, before it goes for adoption, but I want it to be born up here.'

He didn't tell her that he had been to the factor to see about buying the house and land, to be told that, since it wasn't a croft, the laird wouldn't sell the property to him. He hadn't made up his mind about appealing to the Land Court.

'The fishing's picked up again, thanks to Leumadair. It drives in the fish to the bay. I'm having some good catches.'

'Dolphins are intelligent sensitive creatures. It must know you need help.'

They had reached the gate of the schoolhouse.

'Do you want to come in? They won't be back for ages.'

'No, I'd better get home. Where did you say they were?'

'Up at the Carlton-Ashingtons. Vanessa is Mummy's cousin.'

'What kind of people are they?'

'Very pleasant. She's my godmother.'

She held out her cheek to be kissed.

'Can I come round tomorrow?' she asked.

'I'll leave a message with Donnie.'

When she went in he didn't go out the gate. Instead he walked down the garden and went through the gap in the wall into the girls' playground. He went down into the shed where the Macgregor sisters had lifted their cute little kilts for him. He stood, rolling a cigarette in the darkness. So her mother was related to the laird's wife, as Donnie seemed to know; so that was why he wasn't getting to buy the croft. He struck a match on the stone wall and looked up to the window where MacCallum had sat at his desk beside the long strands of raffia which hung in front of him like a mare's coloured tail. If you needed another strand to decorate the brush you were making you went out and chose a colour, tugging it from the cluster.

He went through the gap into the boys' shed. On wet days some of them had swung backwards and forwards along the rafters in a contest to see who could hold on the longest. Donnie had usually won and had dropped off to go into the girls' playground to choose someone to coax, with sweets, across into the boys' lavatories.Seumas swung the rafters but this time he had to bend his knees, and when he came to the wall he turned deftly and went back again, the wood polished by several generations of aerial pupils making his palms smart. He dropped off and went up the playground, through the gap in the wall again, opening the gate into the former schoolhouse to which the Bradwell-Prices had added a large extension with a conservatory.

Down in the garden a big garage stood where Miss MacCallum had dug up potatoes with a graip during the morning break for her brother's dinner. He knocked the door and the fanlight lit up.

'I'll take that coffee,' he told Feona.

She was wearing a white bathrobe which made her look even bigger, and her feet were bare. He heard running water.

'I was about to have a bath,' she revealed, leading the way upstairs into her bedroom. She took the robe off and threw it across the bed, then put her arms round him, her hands going up under his jacket.

'I've thought about this for a long time, darling.'

He moved his body back so as not to crush her stomach.

'It's all right, pregnant women are more robust than men think. Sex doesn't do any harm to the baby. You can do it from behind.'

It was a strange feeling, his hands round Feona's belly as he pushed into her, not needing to worry about protection now. But it didn't feel like love; it felt like a form of anger against her money and her parents' connection with the laird.

She lowered herself into the bath and he sat on the cork-lined stool in the fragrant steam, looking at the gold hoops holding the snowy towels, the glass shelf of jars with coloured tablets of soap in them.

'Would you do my back?'

Seumas took the sponge, lathering it on the expensive scented soap. Màthair had washed him in front of the fire in a tin tub on Sunday evenings before he went to school for the week.

He watched her gently soaping her belly protruding from the foam.

'How is Leumadair?' she asked.

'Fine. How's your work going?' he enquired, finding that soaping her was rousing him again.

'I was hoping to start writing it up in the spring, but I'll have to leave it to the summer because of the baby.' She turned her head to him. 'I don't know what's going to happen. Mummy and Daddy have made it clear that they don't want the baby in this house, so we'll buy yours off the estate.'

'I've been to see the factor about it, Feona. They won't sell the place to me because they say it isn't a croft, and they want to keep it as part of the estate.'

Feona sat up in the foam.

'What's on your mind, Seumas?'

'I think your father got to the laird.'

He was expecting a protest, but she sank back into the foam again.

'You're probably right. It's the kind of thing he would do.'

Seumas couldn't believe he was hearing her say this.

'It's understandable. They love their only child. They've always thought they knew what was best for me. A good school; Cambridge; maybe a fellowship; marriage to someone of my own class, or better; kids whose school fees they'd pay; and so it would go on, the upper middle class reproducing itself. Then you came along, or rather, I went along to you and now this.' She put a hand on her belly. 'This isn't supposed to come with a retirement house in the Highlands.'

'So what's going to happen about my house?' Seumas asked.

'You mean, can I go and plead with my godmother to get her husband to sell it to you? I can, but she'll say that you're putting pressure on me, and that'll only make it worse. So we're going to have to teach them all a lesson.'

'What do you mean?' he asked apprehensively.

She was rising from the water, pointing to the rail. Seumas brought the big white warmed towel across to her.

'We're going to have our baby in your house, as it is.'

'But it doesn't have electricity or a proper toilet.'

'Your mother had you there, didn't she?'

'Yes, but that was different.'

'In what way?'

'Well – she was used to it.'

'I can get used to it too.' She turned so that he could dry her back with the towel. 'I can get an advance on Granny's legacy. We can put in a generator for light and a gas stove to give us hot water. We can find space to put a toilet and shower in. What more do we need?'

'The house isn't mine,' Seumas reminded her. 'I can't make any improvements without the permission of the estate. Donnie spoke to a man in the town who knows crofting law. He said since the estate says it isn't a croft, I can apply to the Land Court to decide if it is, in which case the estate would have to sell to me. But I could end up with a big bill, because the factor said they would use lawyers to fight me, and the Land Court may decide that I had to pay at least part of their expenses.'

'What did Donnie advise?' Feona wanted to know.

'He thinks I should go to the Land Court.'

'So do I. We can use Granny's money.'

'I don't want that.'

'Why not?'

'We'll talk about it later. You'd better put on your dressing gown in case you get a chill,' he advised her.

'You mean the sight of my nakedness disturbs you?' she asked, turning in the looking glass. 'I think pregnancy is rather beautiful.'

'I have to go,' he excused himself abruptly. 'The light's going.'

'Are you going fishing tomorrow?' she enquired.

'That depends on Leumadair.'

'When you're free come round to the town. Donnie will phone me to let me know you're there, and we can go back to your house together to discuss what we're going to do. We'll show them yet. Daddy needs a defeat in his life to teach him a lesson.'

It was dark on the way home, so he went slowly, despite the light at the bow, keeping clear of the black bulk of Sgeir nan Eun. In summer the breeding birds had roosted like raucous city folks in high tenements, but had gone to feed out at sea with their young. They were starving because it was hard to feed in rough seas, and their emaciated bodies were thrown back on to the shore by ferocious storms. As he steered past the deserted Sgeir he was becoming irritated by the suspicion that Feona was trying to take over his house, not for the sake of their baby, but to prove something to her parents. He didn't know if he could allow that. He was confused and suspicious, and that made him angry, feeling that both Feona and Donnie were putting pressure on him.

He carried the oars up to the house. It was late but he would have to tidy the place for her coming tomorrow. He raked out the ashes and set a fire of criss-crossed sticks and peats, swept the floor and tidied up the scullery. He took the torch out to the *taigh-beag*, shining it inside to make sure it was clean, and that there was paper. The beam wavered on the crude hole in the plank from which the old man had toppled forward into the fragrant flowers.

He had always liked sitting on the plank in the *taigh-beag* on a still night, with the door open, his trousers round his boots, looking up at the stars. MacCallum had taught him the Gaelic names: *geal-shruth nan Speur*, the Milky Way, translated as the white tide of the sky. He went to bed reciting the Gaelic names, like the prayer *màthair* made him say every night, sitting on his bed. He felt that he wanted to burst into song at the beauty of the heavenly bodies.

Twenty

He picked up Feona at the pier and on the way round to the house she sat in the bow of the launch, but there was no sign of Leumadair.

'Maybe it's gone,' she said sadly after Seumas had shut off the engine.

'It's about somewhere,' he reassured her. 'We'll probably see it on the way back.'

He helped her carefully into the dinghy, wanting to carry her because she wasn't wearing wellingtons, but she laughed at him as she waded ashore. There was a big fire going and she held her bare feet to the bars as he made tea.

'It gives a wonderful heat,' she enthused.

'Mother used it all her married life,' Seumas told her, more at ease now in her company. 'She cooked on it and baked in the oven.' He leaned over her and opened the door. 'Put your hand in and feel the heat.'

'But it doesn't heat the water and we'll need hot water with a baby in the house. Maybe I should go up and have a word with my godmother about recognizing this place as a croft and then we can buy it.'

'No, don't get involved,' Seumas reacted apprehensively.

She sat up, snapping her fingers.

'Got it. I know how we solve the problem without touching the house just now. We'll buy a mobile home.'

Seumas associated mobile homes with the tinkers who used to camp in the layby outside the town. There had been complaints from some of the white settlers about their caravans spoiling the view, and someone had started a petition to have them removed to a specially built stance out of the way in the disused quarry. The tinkers – *ceàrdan* in Gaelic – were among the last people in the district who had Gaelic, and MacCallum had said that they knew more about horses than anyone else in the land.

The *ceàrdan* had come across the moor when Seumas was still in his mother's womb, and though she already had a drawerful of clothes pegs from their previous sales trips, she gave them a shilling and filled their tea cans. In return they blessed the foetus, asking for a long life for it. They sat on the bank of Allt a' Ghobha-Uisge, drinking their black brew and eating the bread and cheese that màthair had cut for them. The old man – young then – sat with them, conversing in Gaelic, enquiring about the health of their horses and hearing about the spectral soldiers they had seen while camping on the site of a bloody battle. The old man shared his tobacco with them, telling them that they would always be welcome at his door because, like him, they were Macdonalds, and that, if he was related to them, he was proud of it.

An old woman with a furrowed face put her ear to the expectant mother's abdomen and listened intently. 'It's a boy,' she pronounced in Gaelic. 'He'll be a strong handsome fellow with blue eyes and black hair, and he'll know the sea like the back of his hand. The ladies will fancy him,' she added with a toothless smile.

* * * * *

'How would you get a mobile home down here?' Seumas asked Feona sceptically.

'Tow it slowly across the moor.'

'It would bog down. It'll have to come by sea, by barge,' Seumas told her.

'That's fine. We could put it beside this house. They're fitted with a kitchen and bathroom. All you need is a water supply.'

'And electricity which we haven't got,' Seumas added.

'We'll get one that's fitted out for gas cylinders.' She reached over and caught his hand. 'Don't you think that's a brilliant idea?'

'How much would a mobile home cost?' he asked apprehensively.

'That depends on the size and quality. You can probably get a good second hand one for a few thousand. I can get an advance on the money I've got coming from Granny.'

Three days later when he went into the town Feona was waiting for him in the Volvo at the end of the pier. Seumas was self-conscious about getting in beside her in front of the fishermen, but she leaned across and opened the door.

'I got this sent up,' she said, handing him a magazine showing mobile homes for sale. 'I've put crosses beside the ones I think will be suitable.'

When she had driven away Seumas took the magazine to Donnie.

'Aye, she's a clever one,' his friend and adviser said, turning over the pages on the bar counter. 'That would be just the thing for you. Some of them are better than houses. How are you going to pay for it?'

'Feona wants to pay for it, but I'd rather take a loan from a finance company.'

'You'd need a regular income to pay it off. You're doing well at the fishing just now, but how long will that last? Let Feona pay for the mobile home. You've got a smart woman there, Seumas. I'd hold on to her. Not that you've got any choice,' he added with a smile. 'But her old man's not going to be too happy when he hears that she's living in a mobile home with you. How are you going to get it round to your place?'

'Feona thinks it can be towed across the moor, but it would get bogged down. I was thinking that it could come by barge from the mainland.'

'That'll be very expensive,' Donnie cautioned. 'Wait a minute. Hugh MacFadyen at the other end of the island has a barge which he uses to bring heavy plant from the mainland for his construction business. He was in school with us, so I'll speak to him about doing it for you for a reasonable rate. Besides, he owes me a favour.'

When Seumas left the hotel Feona was waiting for him.

'When will I see you again?' she asked anxiously.

'Probably not till after Christmas,' he said evasively. 'I'm going to overhaul the engine of the launch.' It was a lie, but he needed time to himself to think about what he was getting into.

She put something into his hands.

'That's your Christmas present, darling.'

He stood watching Feona walking away to the Volvo. He felt like running after her and giving her the gift back without opening it, but he pushed it into his pocket and went home in the darkness. Once in the house he laid the small package in Christmas paper by the lamp. It was tied with a red ribbon, and there was a robin on the label with a written message. He wanted to get up and open it, but something kept him in the old man's chair. He made himself two cigarettes, ignoring the Christmas gift as though it would vanish. The lamp was beginning to smoke because the paraffin level was falling, and after he filled it with the funnel and can he took the Christmas gift into the dark room opposite.

On Christmas Eve màthair would take Seumas and his sister through so that they could hang their stockings from the mantelpiece. Seumas couldn't sleep in the room above for puzzling how a sledge pulled by reindeer could halt in the sky while the white bearded man in the red coat squeezed down their chimney. Eilidh would come into his room in the dawn and they would go downstairs together. Màthair would be waiting with the lamp to kiss them, wishing them *Nollaig Chridheil*, Christmas Greetings, before opening the door of the good room, where the fire would be burning. The two stockings that they had hung up under the brass candlesticks on the mantelpiece the night before sagged with an orange at the toes, and a small toy – if the fishing was good.

Seumas placed Feona's gift to him on the mantelpiece, closing the door behind him.

Next day he went into the Spar shop to get his messages in for Christmas. This year there would only be himself for dinner. He stopped at the deep freeze cabinet, looking at the fowls wrapped in cellophane. When he knocked the breastbone it felt as if it was made of stone.

Two nights before Christmas the old man would kill a hen. You could see he didn't like it, the way he kept moving in his chair, lifting the punctured lid of his pipe to put a flame to a bowl that only contained ashes. The dog knew what was about to happen, because when the old man got up suddenly she didn't move. Seumas followed the old man because someone had to hold the torch. Its wavering beam went round the corner of the house, sweeping up the peat-stack, shining on the door to the henhouse as the old man drew back the bolt. The dozen hens that were roosting on the spar started cackling, as if they knew the purpose of this nocturnal intrusion.

'Shine it! Shine it!' the old man was shouting as he waded in hens' *cac*.

Seumas moved the beam, catching the baleful eye of the cockerel. It pecked the back of the old man's hand as he grasped one of its harem by the neck, yanking the hen's claws from the spar. He brought it outside and in the frosty night with its wings lifting to the stars the old man drew its neck over his knee. It would be twitching when he carried it by the legs into màthair, and once one of his victims had struggled free from màthair's hold, and in the last minute of its life spread its wings, fluttering up to the sideboard from where it fell back.

Màthair sat by the fire, her knees open, a basin by her shoes. The dead hen was in her lap, and as she pulled its feathers she sang as if she were plucking a clarsach. Seumas watched the white feathers floating upwards like snow, his sister running round the room, trying to catch them before they reached the floor. A feather would swirl in the vortex of the lamp's globe until it spun down to burst into flame, shrivelling without breaking the mantle, while the old man snored in his chair through nervous exhaustion after executing the hen.

Seumas still kept the old man's hens for their eggs, large brown speckled ones, some with the gift of a double yolk. The hens announced their laying by strutting into the house, cackling loudly, so bold that they flew up on to the table to peck at crumbs. However, unlike the old man, he couldn't kill a hen for the pot, nor did he have màthair's skill and patience to pluck it. So it had to be either a ready-roasted chicken or an oven-ready one complete with giblets from the deep freeze cabinet in the Spar shop. He took the one he would have to roast himself and carried it to the check-out in the basket along with the plum pudding and a tin of custard. He left the bird to thaw in the scullery sink and peeled a pot of potatoes. He was conscious of màthair's presence in the house as he went about his chores before going up to bed, having banked up the fire with peats.

On Christmas morning he was down early, listening to a Catholic service from a church on South Uist in Gaelic on the radio as he put the chicken into the oven. He left the front door open in the clear morning with a lot of light over the bay. He went for a walk with the dog along the shore. Màthair had felt she was in touch with forces in the island she had come from, and though Seumas couldn't see the fin, he felt that he was in touch with the creature out there. He would never explain this to anyone, not even to Feona, because it was like having a secret love.

The chicken was sizzling away in its own juices, the skin turning brown. He put the pot on the radiant peats, prodding the potatoes from time to time with a fork as màthair had done. For Christmas she had always given the old man a pair of socks she had knitted herself, but he hadn't given her anything. Seumas could see now that that had been very wrong, that she must have yearned for some kind of sign of his affection, since the creaking of the bedsprings under her didn't count.

He set out knife, fork and spoon on the tablecloth, remembering that he had forgotten to put the plum pudding in the oven. He went through, reading on the label that it would take two hours before it was ready, so he would eat it later.

Before he himself ate he opened the tin of quality dog food, which he had bought as a special treat for Dìleas, wishing her *Nollaig Chridheil* before scraping the contents into her dish, its loud clattering showing her appreciation of the succulence.

When the dog had stretched out to dream by the fire he lifted back the skin from the breast of the chicken and carved himself thick slices of the white meat, laying them neatly on the plate as màthair had done, spooning out six potatoes, leaving the others in the pot. There was no other vegetable and he sat down to eat slowly, savouring the meal, thinking about Feona, wondering what kind of Christmas lunch she would be having with her parents. No doubt there would be plenty of wine.

He would leave the pot and plates until later. He sat at the fire, listening to the radio, smoking one of the small cigars from the packet of Hamlets that Donnie had given him as a present. He was taking in the pleasant smoke when the song came on the radio, a request from someone in Mull. He turned up the volume until the voice filled the house. It was *Muile nam Fuar-bheann Mòr*, Mull of the Cool High Bens, and he felt the tears rising as he saw MacCallum standing at the tiller of his launch as it came round Rubha nan Ròn, with the mountains to the east under snow, the half bottle of whisky and box of chocolates in the haversack he had carried through the Second World War, come to share Gaelic and goodwill.

On the day of their schoolmaster's funeral primary seven had lined the gravel path from the church. Seumas's knees were knocking, not with cold, but with terror as he saw the coffin being carried from the church. The Gaelic word for a coffin was *ciste*, but it was also used for the chest in the good room which had belonged to màthair's seafaring brother, and in which Seumas kept his few toys. It had always been a delight to lift out a toy, but as MacCallum's *ciste* approached, Seumas saw that the lid was screwed down with brass bolts. His eyes were brimming with tears for his teacher who had come with the gift of Gaelic words and chocolates. Beside him Heather had lifted his right hand to his head for the salute that Miss Maclaren had practised with them, and when the coffin was being slid into the hearse Heather had hugged him, whispering: 'I know how much you'll miss him, Seumas.'

Now Heather too had disappeared in a *ciste*, and her sister Myrtle hadn't returned in her nifty little sports car to claim him as her lover.

He went to the door and saw the fin in the bay. He leaned against the lintel, smoking the cigar, letting the song go past him, out across the water where Leumadair was now leaping, as if going up and down a musical scale. When the song had finished on the radio he went back inside, through to the good room where the fire was smoking as if there was an old nest in the chimney. Once a jackdaw had come tumbling down, and as it flew around the room, squawking in its frantic search for a way out, Eilidh had stood in the doorway giggling. But when it flew past her face, into the kitchen, she had started screaming. He had managed to get the bird out while màthair soothed his hysterical sister.

He remembered Feona's present and felt ashamed as he lifted it from the mantelpiece beside the stopped clock. He stood looking at the little package, as if using extrasensory powers to see through the Christmas wrapping of a robin in the snow on a bough to what it contained. The toy that màthair gave him for Christmas always came crudely wrapped in paper through which he could feel plastic wheels.

He studied the writing on the label with the robin.

TO SEUMAS WITH ALL MY LOVE: FEONA.

He broke the bright Christmas seal and exposed a black box, lifting the watch with buttons on the side from its satin bed and taking the instruction leaflet to the window. It not only told the time; it was water-resistant to a depth of 200 metres, gave the date, and showed sunrise and sunset.

Eilidh had been in the asylum for six months and màthair was visiting her. Seumas was watching the hill for her coming back because he hoped that she would bring his sister. When she appeared she was walking slowly, her head bent. He carried her message bag into the house and put it on the table. She sat down and asked him to put on the kettle. She looked old and exhausted after her day with her insane daughter.

'Will she be coming back?' Seumas asked anxiously, because he loved his fragile sister.

'I hope so,' she answered as she reached into her bag. 'I bought you this.'

It was a watch made of tin. It had no inside but the hands moved. Seumas strapped it to his wrist and all that day he kept looking at it constantly, as if it were capable of telling him the time. When the old man came in Seumas held it to his parent's ear, as if it actually ticked. He was frightened to wear it in bed in case he rolled over and crushed it, so he put it on the chair.

Next day he was helping the old man to cut the peats, watching his boot pushing the blade of the *tàirsgeir,* the special spade with a long wooden handle and an angled blade on one end. The old man sliced through the peat with a downward motion and, pulling back the handle, dislodged a rectangular block of peat which he threw aside. Seumas lifted the blocks and stacked them in the way that he had been shown by the old man, so that they would dry out before being carried back to the house in a creel on the old man's back, the way his ancestors had gathered their fuel, because he couldn't afford even a second-hand tractor. When it was time to go home and he saw in the fading light that the watch wasn't on his wrist he started to sob. The old man had had a tiring day, but he helped him to search, moving all the peats in case it had fallen there. It wasn't among the peats, so Seumas searched the heather until it was too dark to see.

He couldn't tell màthair that he had lost the watch, so he pulled his sleeve down over his wrist as he ate his supper. When he went up to bed he felt on the floor as if it would come back by some mysterious force, like the force màthair described on her island, when planks moved across the joiner's shop because a coffin was going to have to be made soon for someone not yet dead. For days Seumas kept going back to the moor by himself to look for the watch, but it wasn't there and màthair never mentioned its loss.

As he stood with the fancy watch from Feona on his wrist he was thinking of the tin watch, of his sister in the asylum, of the present he hadn't sent her, of the old man now under the earth in the town, with no stone to mark him, but at least having the consolation of the company of that obsessed Gael Alan Maclachan half a dozen graves away. The numbers changed on the dial of the watch, but Seumas's sense of time was in the past, the gravity of a stocking with an orange in the toe, the sisters with their kilts lifted and no sign of the thing he most wanted to see, and then Feona initiating him into the mystery of the act fundamental to life in the room above as he lay with his arm in plaster, her declaration of love written on it.

He sat by the fire in the good room until the glowing pyramid of peats collapsed in a shower of sparks. The room needed a lamp but he sat on, thinking of the gift of Gaelic on Christmas Day, and how one Christmas MacCallum had come wading ashore with his flannels tucked in his seaboots, carrying a cake from his sister for their household and for him, a wooden pencil box. You put your thumbnail into the groove and pushed open the lid and there were pencils lying in the slots. Then you twisted it and there was another tray below, with a pair of compasses and a protractor.

MacCallum had come bearing gifts and had spent Christmas afternoon with them in the good room by a blazing fire, with whisky and conversation, two of the most welcome gifts of the Gàidhealtachd. MacCallum said that Mary MacDonald the Mull bard who had composed *Leanabh an Àigh*, the carol that had been translated as *Child in a Manger*, had been related to him.

'You sing it,' MacCallum had urged Eilidh, who was enchanted with the scarf the schoolmaster's sister had knitted as her present. She had stood by the lamp, her hands clasped, wearing the scarf though the room was hot, as Seumas accompanied her on the mouth organ.

> *'Leanabh an àigh, an leanabh bh' aig Màiri,*
> *Rugadh an stàball, Rìgh nan Dùl;*
> *Thàinig don fhàsach, dh'fhuiling nar n-àite,*
> *Son' iad an àireamh bhitheas dha dlùth.'*

Child who was wondrous, infant of Mary,
Born in a stable, king of all.
He came to our desert, furthered our penance,
Happy those persons who follow His call.

As he blew into and sucked the instrument between his hands Seamus was watching MacCallum while Eilidh sang softly by the lamp, her big head inclined to the side, fingers interlocked, all her awkwardness gone as if she had been reborn. The schoolmaster's face was shining as he joined in quietly, so as not to interfere with the beauty of the child's voice. It came to the schoolmaster that if strangers had come into that room that night, they would never discern that the singer was retarded, and the words she expressed so movingly, diction and pronunciation perfect, she would never be able to read on a page, or write down.

> *'Seo leanabh an àigh, mar dh'aithris na fàidhean;*
> *'S na h-ainglean àrd, b' e miann an sùl;*
> *'S e 's airidh air gràdh 's air urram thoirt dha,*
> *Is sona an àireamh bhitheas dha dlùth.'*

> Child who was wondrous, as prophets related,
> And the high angels, the desire of their eyes;
> Our love He does merit, our honour deserving,
> Happy those persons close by His side.

The schoolmaster pondered the phrase *miann an sùl*, as if he were hearing it for the first time, though it had been sung every Christmas since his infancy in the family home on Mull. Why had the high angels desire in their eyes, and for whom? Were they present at the birth in the stable? The word desire carried sexual connotations, but this wasn't the meaning in the image in the hymn. The word desire expressed their love, their wish that the Son of God would fulfil His Father's hope in Him.

* * * * *

'Seumas!'

At first he thought his name was being called by the dead. Then he saw the outline of Feona's stomach in the doorway.

'How did you get here? You didn't walk,' he said, concerned.

She slid her arms out of the haversack on her back.

'I came over the moor.'

'Happy Christmas and thanks for the watch,' he said, kissing her.

'I've walked out on them,' she told him, squatting down at the fire, offering it her palms.

'How do you mean?'

'We were having Christmas lunch at my godmother's. Daddy was very drunk and started talking about you. Mummy tried to stop him but he wouldn't shut up. He said that you should be run out of the place after what you'd done to me. He didn't do it, I said. What do you mean? Mummy asked. Was it someone else? Someone at Cambridge? Darling, why didn't you say instead of putting us through all this? It wasn't Seumas who fucked me, I said: I fucked him. Daddy slapped me in front of them all and called me a slut, so I walked out and went home for my things.'

She began to weep. Seumas hadn't had any experience of another person weeping since the day they told màthair that Eilidh would be in the asylum for the rest of her life, with no one there to talk with her in Gaelic, no one to appreciate the sweetness of her singing. Feona was sobbing as she sat by the fire. He remembered the whisky in MacCallum's last half bottle before his death that màthair had kept for emergencies, and went through to the press for it, but Feona pushed the proffered glass aside.

'I know what you need,' Seumas said.

He went through for the battery driven cassette and the tape of *Fear a' Bhàta*. He took her hand, leading her outside and turning up the volume at the lines:

> '*Thug mi gaol duit 's chan fhaod mi àicheadh,*
> *Cha ghaol bliadhna is cha ghaol ràithe.*'

> I gave you love and I can't deny it,
> Not love that lasts a year, nor that lasts a season.

It seemed that Leumadair wasn't touching the water as it leapt towards them. They stood on the shore together with the cassette recorder at his feet. Feona's face was transfigured as she held her arms out above her big belly, as if inviting the dolphin to leap into them. She was laughing and calling and when the song ran out the fin settled into the water and then disappeared.

Seumas led her by the hand up to the house and into the good room. He pushed the sofa towards the fire and undressed her. Her belly was shining in the firelight as she turned over and he entered her in that room where Eilidh had sung about the pure desire of the high angels, the burden of her head raised. Afterwards he and Feona shared the Christmas pudding and he gave her his present, a box of chocolates.

'You can sleep on the sofa,' he invited her.

'I can't impose on you. I've arranged to stay in the town with Eleanor, a girl I go sailing with. If you take me back in the launch I'll be very grateful.'

Twenty One

Feona went back to Cambridge after New Year. Though Seumas had enjoyed her company over the festive season he was glad to see her go. It might make her father hate him less, to know that his daughter still had a will of her own.

The first he knew of the frost's severity was when he turned on the tap and there was nothing. When he went outside his breath was visible, the bay lipped with ice. He looked for the fin in the bay before he went up the burn, a bundle of papers and sticks under his arm. He started a fire under the exposed section of the zinc pipe to try to thaw it, but it still wasn't coming through the tap, so he took the kettle off the range.

On freezing mornings màthair had taken this sooty kettle across to the burn, breaking the ice with a stone. She tilted the mouth of the utensil to the slow flow and when it was filled she put the lid back on and carried it back to the fire. By the time he and Eilidh came down the kettle was boiling, their porridge being stirred in the pot.

Seumas filled the kettle at the burn and sat it on the peats, leaving the tap open in the scullery to tell him when the supply came back. He took the dog a walk along the shore, his boots sliding on the ice-domed stones. It was as if the frost had brought another dimension to the world, making his hearing more acute. The call of the curlew going overhead seemed clearer, sharper, and when he spoke its name, *guilbneach*, he saw the Gaelic written in his breath like the frosted Merry Christmas greeting that màthair pinned to the mantelpiece in the good room.

When Dìleas barked in the frost it was an explosive sound, as if she were young again, as if the frost had penetrated into her being, making her keen, alert. He stood on the shore calling, his hands cupped round his mouth: 'Leumadair! Leumadair!' He heard the name go out and come back to him as an echo. Its splash was the loudest he had heard as it came leaping inshore, its belly even whiter in the clear air, so distinct that he could see its eye and the fine spray from its blowhole.

It was just five yards from the shallows now, swimming around, and he began to speak to it, as if he had just acquired Gaelic and was using it fluently for the first time, marvelling at the sound and shape of the words. He felt that the creature moving quietly with its wise eye on him was answering him, not through speech, but directly by some signal into his brain that made him shiver with pleasure. He was suddenly aware that a part of his brain was older than the rest and that some memory lay there which he couldn't quite recover, but which had to do with himself and the dolphin which had come inshore to his call. The book he had borrowed from the library said that the dolphin had once been a land creature with legs, maybe related to the cow, and certainly it had the soulful eye of a cow, reminding him of their one which màthair had milked until her arthritic hands could no longer work the teats.

It was an extraordinary experience in the frosty morning, and he felt exhilarated as Leumadair breached again. He had difficulty starting the engine of the launch because of the cold, but eventually it fired. He went round to the town to deliver his latest catch of fish to the hotel and to return the dolphin book to the library.

'Congratulations,' Alice said.

'For what?'

'I hear you're going to be a father.'

'So?'

She kept her head down as she tidied the stack of books, but Seumas could see that she was agitated.

'I didn't think you would have picked someone like her.'

He couldn't let that go.

'What do you mean?' he asked aggressively.

'You're one of the last Gaelic speakers in the place, so I'd have thought you would have been against white settlers, especially a family that's in the MacCallums' old house.'

'I don't like them,' he conceded.

'Yet you've put one of them in the family way.'

'It's my business, Alice,' he warned her, his voice rising.

She bit her lip in vexation, raising her head, her angry green eyes confronting him.

'I'd be very careful if I were you. Her father's a bastard.'

'I can look after myself.'

'I don't think you understand who you're dealing with. He's on the Community Council with me and always gets his way by bullying the others. He'll make it very difficult for you because he doesn't want his daughter marrying a fisherman. He was probably the one who told the police that you didn't have a hire licence for your boat. He's trying to drive you away to the mainland for work, away from his daughter. You're too good for her, Seumas.'

'I don't want to talk about it,' he told her, pushing the dolphin book across the counter and walking out.

He didn't go into Donnie's after this encounter, but shopped and went home. The pipe had thawed and water was splashing into the sink. He built up the fire and took the Gaelic dictionary from the shelf, his personal prize from MacCallum. Sitting by the lamp as a boy, turning the pages, it became a quiz as he asked his parents the Gaelic for animals and birds.

'There weren't any *brocan*, badgers, on the island I came from, so we wouldn't have needed the word,' màthair said.

It was as if Seumas could still hear them speaking as he leafed through the dictionary, wandering in an old world of songs where they waulked the tweed and trimmed the sail, where *na mairbh*, the dead, were seen about again.

'I'm sorry about this afternoon.'

Alice was standing at the door, the collar of her sheepskin jacket turned up. 'I shouldn't have said what I said.'

She was waiting for an invitation to the fire, which she was eyeing appreciatively after her walk over the moor. Seumas pointed to màthair's chair and she sat down, turning her palms to the flames.

'What are you reading?'

'A Gaelic dictionary.'

'No one asks for one in the library now. That's what's happened to our culture. My parents both spoke Gaelic.'

He looked at her with surprise and respect.

'They spoke it to themselves, but they wouldn't speak it to their three children because they thought we wouldn't get on in the world if we spoke Gaelic. English is the language of advancement, my father was always saying. Well, I didn't advance very far with English. I think I hate my parents for depriving me of Gaelic. It's as if a vital part of me is missing, the way a woman must feel when she has a breast removed.' She looked at him. 'You were lucky, having parents who knew what was important. So did Mr. MacCallum. Do you remember how he taught us Gaelic songs, writing them up on the board? I used to hate it, but I wish I was back in that classroom learning from him.'

She began to sing *Muile nam Fuar-bheann Mòr*, Mull of the Cool High Bens.

'O Eilean mo rùin tha maiseach don t-sùil,
'S ann ann a chaidh m' àrach òg;
Bu bhòidheach do shnuadh air mhoch-mhadainn chiùin
'N àm èirigh don driùchd sna neòil.'

O Isle of my love, beautiful to the eye,
It was there that I was brought up;
Lovely was your appearance on a calm early morning
When the dew rose to the heavens.

MacCallum's pointer moved across each word, making them repeat it. He had sung the song about his native isle with them, his eyes bright, the brass ferrule tapping in tempo on the board.

Seumas went for his mouth organ.

'O, b' àlainn leam riamh bhith coimhead 's a' ghrian
A' ciaradh san iar mar òr,
'S Caol Muile mo ghaoil fo dhubhar nan craobh,
'S na luingis a' sgaoileadh sheòl.'

O, it was beautiful for me to see the sun
Setting in the west like gold,
And the Sound of Mull that I loved in the shadow
                              of the trees,
And the ships unfurling their sails.

MacCallum the Mull man had had his wish, going home up the Sound of Mull in a *ciste*.

'I'm sorry about what I said to you this afternoon in the library,' Alice apologized. 'I said it because I care for you; I don't want to see you getting hurt.'

'I can take care of myself,' he told her, but with no truculence this time.

He felt for her, with no Gaelic and a sham of a marriage, with Donnie having sex with her until he had become tired of her.

'I brought you this,' she said, taking a book from her handbag. 'It doesn't belong to the library; it's a Christmas present.'

It was an illustrated book about dolphins, showing them suspended in blue water with their permanent grins.

'Thanks, I'll make a cup of tea,' he offered, stretching over to the kettle.

He knew he had a problem. He had two women interested in him, one of them pregnant by him. But he felt more attracted to the one sitting by the fire, holding the hot mug gratefully in her chilled fingers after carrying the torch across the dark frosted moor. She didn't have any of the airs and graces of Feona.

Alice was watching him now, smiling at him. She stretched out a hand and their fingers touched as if an electric charge were flowing between them. She stood up and pulled down the zip on her hipbone, stepping out of her skirt and hanging it over the back of the chair before pulling her sweater over her head. In the light from the firebars he saw the wide hips, the dark spread of pubic hair.

He was out of his clothes quickly, as if he hadn't undone the laces of his boots or any buttons. He went upstairs naked and brought down the quilt from his bed draped round his shoulders, Indian style, spreading it on the flagstones in front of the fire.

When he touched her between the legs the fluid of desire there had the elasticity of a burst raw egg in his fingers. She seemed to be too big, too slippery for him until she pressed her thighs together.

'It's all right, I'm on the pill,' she whispered, as if there were other people in the room.

One day at school he had felt sick and MacCallum had brought him home in his launch. The doctor came across the hill with his medical bag in the June evening and left a thermometer in Seumas's mouth while he spoke to his parents outside the door. It was pneumonia and that night his temperature kept rising. The old man went down to sleep on the sofa in the good room, and Eilidh moved across the landing to Seumas's bed so that he could be carried in beside màthair. She kept the lamp burning all night, with the wick turned low, the old man lying downstairs with his clothes on and his boots within reach in case he had to go round in the launch for the doctor, guided by the light in the bow.

Seumas was soaking with sweat, as if he had fallen into a boiling hot sea. The shadows the lamp threw on the wall became terrifying animals that he had never seen before, not even in the educational films about the jungle and its inhabitants, the massive snake coiled round a bough, the ferocious tiger. He seemed to leave his own body, to be standing in a corner, calm and cool, watching màthair rocking him in her arms and singing a Gaelic lullaby. He knew he didn't have to go back into his own body, to face the fever and the frightening animals on the wall again, but màthair looked so sad, he couldn't leave her.

He was out of his own body again now, standing in a corner, watching Alice lying in front of the fire, her bouncing buttocks cushioned by the quilt on the flagstones as his *bod* went in and out. He could hear her whimpering like an animal caught in briars. Then he was back inside his own body, lying beside her while she stroked him.

'That was good, very good,' she whispered, as if awarding him a mark against Donnie.

It was strange to think that his best friend also had used her in the same way for years. Everything was so strange about the experience he had just had that he wanted to lie in front of the burning peats and not even think about it. She was lighting two cigarettes in her mouth at the one time, sitting, knees drawn up, her back against màthair's chair.

'What will you do now?' she asked dreamily.

What did she mean?

'What will you do about the English girl?'

'I don't know,' Seumas answered in a subdued voice.

'I could tell you something about her mother, but I won't, something that would shock you,' Alice spoke.

'You must think I'm easily shocked,' Seumas reacted as he looked at the dark bars like brands that the fire was throwing on her body.

'You're too decent a man to get mixed up with these kinds of people.'

Her cigarette was finished and she took his from his fingers, throwing it into the fire, telling him to relax as she lowered her face to his body. His identity was disappearing into the red circle of her lips, so that he didn't know where he was and had to get out of his own body before she consumed him.

* * * * *

He had been in bed for six weeks with the pneumonia. The doctor told màthair that he would have died if it weren't for a drug, M & B. For years he would repeat these letters to himself, like a silent prayer. The day he was to get up màthair brought a basin of hot water up the stairs and sponged his body, and after she had dried each foot with the towel she kissed his toes. He went down the stairs slowly into a new world in which the kitchen looked different; the fire in the grate brighter, clearer. When he went to the door the air tasted new and the bay looked changed, as if replaced with bluer water. The oystercatcher that flew over the roof sounded different, sharper, as if it had just learned its call and was thrilled by its timbre.

But when he went inside for his dinner he found that he couldn't remember simple Gaelic words, as if he had sweated them out of his being in the fever. He felt frightened, but màthair reached over and covered her hand with his.

'Your being with us still is a gift from God.'

His parents talked a lot to him in Gaelic. The old man took him out in the boat and used Gaelic words for the sea, for lobsters, for the wind. Màthair named the various foods on his plate in Gaelic as she put it in front of him, and when he was in bed she went over the Gaelic prayer with him, word by word. MacCallum came to visit, bringing tablet his sister had made, and many everyday words of Gaelic which he fed slowly to his attentive pupil. Within a month Seumas had more Gaelic than before the fever.

He rose naked from the quilt and carried a flame from the grate to the lamp like an entranced man in a fire ceremony, until the lighted paper scorched his fingers. As Alice dressed her limbs were like a starfish on the wall.

After he put on his own clothes and took the torch he didn't need to call on Dìleas. The three of them went out into the freezing starry night, the bay looking strange to him as if he were seeing it for the first time, the torch wavering as if he had forgotten the way over the moor. Ice that was forming splintered under his boots in the strange bare landscape, and when he looked up and saw the stars all the correct names from his heritage flowed back into his brain. *Grigleachan*, a constellation. 'But the same word is also the word for the Pleaides, the Seven Sisters,' MacCallum said by the lamp. 'All things in the firmament are the same source of wonder to the Gael, and Gaelic can be stretched over the heavens.'

He took Alice's hand under the stars across the treacherous moor, and when they came to the layby they hugged. He scraped the frost from the windscreen and waited as she turned the key in the ignition, the car shuddering into life in the cold, her glove waving to him out of the window as she drove away. But as soon as he went back into the house and saw the quilt on the floor in front of the fire he was overcome with remorse. He had taken it from màthair's bed for his own. Every spring she had washed the quilt, pegging it out on the line to dry in the breeze, a lucky golden flag to himself and the old man coming in with the prize catch of lobsters. Sometimes he would go up to his bedroom and bury his face in the soft feathers of the quilt, as though they were màthair's skin to which she had held him, to cool the fire of his face in his fever.

He could wash it and the stains would come out, but it would never be the same again. Màthair would have been heartbroken that he had sullied their house as well as her bed linen through having sex with a married woman.

He bundled up the quilt and carried it down to the shore. He held the wavering match to the corner of the quilt heaped on the shingle, and as the golden pyre burned, flaming feathers drifted out over the bay. When he went back inside he put on a kettle, getting down on his knees to scrub the flagstones in front of the fire in an act of purification. When he went upstairs he was exhausted, but before he fell asleep he understood why Alice had pressed his hand before she had got into her car. It was like the Masonic handshake the old man was always complaining about. She was telling him that he could continue with her while he was living with Feona, just as Donnie had done for all those years while still living with his wife.

He fell asleep between two women.

Twenty Two

He was varnishing the upturned dinghy on the shore, singing a song he had learned at màthair's knee, when the barge with the mobile home came into the bay. He stood watching in wonder and apprehension as it approached, its bottom beginning to grind on the shingle.

'How are we going to get it up to the house?' he asked Donnie, who was accompanying it with Hugh MacFadyen, owner of the barge.

'It's got wheels,' Donnie pointed out.

'Aye, but there are big stones higher up.'

'Then we'll just have to lift them out of the way, my friend.'

It took the three of them two hours to clear a path and to haul and push the mobile home, planks under its wheels, to within a few feet from the peat-stack at the side of the house, large stones round the wheels to stop the wind from moving it.

'Well, here are the keys to your new home': Donnie handed them over ceremoniously. 'I should have brought a bottle of whisky to break over the door, to launch your new life. This is the connection for the cold water supply,' he instructed, having difficulty bending to point to it because of his bulk. 'Where do you get the water for the house from?'

'Up the burn there.'

'So you need to buy a roll of plastic piping and bury it in the ground, then connect it to the mobile home. It shouldn't freeze, not like a metal pipe. This is the waste pipe. Do you have a septic tank? I've got a glass fibre one lying behind the hotel. I bought it when I built the extension but it was too small. You can have it. All you have to do is to dig a big hole and we'll connect the tank to the toilet in your new home. Now, power. It's fitted out for gas, so bring a couple of big cylinders round in the launch. You're going to have a damn good place here.'

'What do I owe you for bringing it?' Seumas asked the barge owner.

'Nothing,' Donnie answered for him. 'I've settled that. Let me give you some advice,' he went on to say, slapping the side of the home. 'Don't let the laird make you move it by telling you it's against planning regulations.'

After waving to his two helpers as the barge swung out into the bay Seumas went into the mobile home, though the brush was drying across the mouth of the varnish can by the upturned dinghy he had been treating before the arrival of the cargo. He wasn't used to door keys, and had difficulty getting the knack of opening the metal door. The mobile building had an unpleasant smell he identified as plastic. He felt unsettled and pulled the door behind him without inspecting the interior. It seemed a betrayal of the family home to place this ugly box beside it.

From the plumber in town he purchased a length of plastic piping which he brought back coiled in the launch. There was a lot of satisfaction in stripping to the waist in the mild day, using a pick and shovel to break into the side of the hill to make a trench in which to lay the pipe for the water supply from Allt a' Ghobha-Uisge. In the evening he took all his clothes off and walked naked into the sea, splashing himself clean, his breath coming in gasps, the coldness shrivelling his *bod* to a small boy's. He was walking back up the shingle, watching his feet for shells, when Alice came over the hill, carrying a basket. He thought of running into the house for clothes, then realized how absurd that would be, since she had already seen him naked.

'What's this then?' she asked, putting her hand against the mobile home.

'It's for living in, when the baby comes.'

'She must have money, that's for sure,' she remarked, looking through the window into the lounge. 'It's better than my house.'

But Seumas knew from her tone that she wasn't annoyed.

'Do you always wander around naked?' she enquired, slapping his buttocks lightly.

'I'm putting in a water supply,' he explained as they went to the house.

'I've brought you some food.'

She put the basket down on the table and lifted out a bundle, unwrapping the cloth to show him a pie with a golden crust. 'And I made this for you,' she added, parting the greaseproof paper to reveal a fruitcake.

'You shouldn't have bothered,' Seumas protested.

'Well, you've got to keep up your strength for all the tasks you have to do. Do you want me to heat up this pie?'

'Aye, you could put it in the oven. I'll away up and put clothes on.'

'You'll just have to take them off again,' she said, lifting her dress over her head. She took his hand and he thought she was leading him upstairs, but she opened the outside door. She led him naked into the mobile home, down the narrow passage into the bedroom, as if she already knew the layout. She pulled him down on to the bare mattress and he was immediately inside her, finishing within seconds, rolling on to his back, exhaling with satisfaction.

'You're just like Donnie was, in and out. That's what I disliked so much. He had no tenderness, no consideration for me. He used the word ride, but I didn't like it because it degrades women. We're not bicycles. Be gentle, I used to say to him, but he doesn't know what the word means. Why would I have expected anything else, when he wasn't gentle with me or his other victims when he enticed us into the boys' playground with sweeties, so that he could drag us down to the lavatories and grope us? I'm not saying that some of the girls didn't enjoy it, because we were at that age. We'll do it again, Seumas, but this time slowly, with feeling.'

He found it difficult, holding back, but her hand was restraining him, the experience becoming better and better as she guided him to the pleasurable zones of her body, cautioning to 'touch gently,' not to invade her with his fingers.

He lay beside her, his arms by his side, listening to his heart quietening. Yet despite the tenderness of the experience he was still suspicious. She had led him into the mobile home because she wanted to use the bed before Feona, to demonstrate her claim over him. He felt that he was in the grip of powerful opposing forces between two women, and that it would be dangerous to surrender, like letting the tiller go on a day with a shifting wind.

They went back naked into the house. He went upstairs to put his clothes on, and when he came down the pie was on the table and she was bursting the golden crust, spooning him out a big helping. She watched him eat as màthair used to do, and when he was finished she cut him a thick slice of her cake, the richness of the fruit in his mouth.

'Take me back in your boat,' Alice asked him.

'Someone will see you,' he said anxiously.

'You mean Donnie? I told you, that finished months ago. He's got someone else now.'

'Who?'

'I can't tell you. What does it matter if someone sees me? You could be taking me out to see the dolphin. I'd like that since I've never seen it. My car's in the layby at the end of the road. If you take me back in your boat I'll walk up from the town and get it.'

Seumas rowed her out to the launch. As they curved out of the bay Leumadair came alongside, pacing them. The sight of her leaning over the side, the breeze lifting her dress as she fondled the dolphin's beak, was so erotic that he almost put the launch on to Sgeir nan Eun.

When he helped her off at the steps there was no one about, and he reversed the launch out quickly. He didn't leave the house for the next few days, wanting to be by himself, to see if a solution to his situation would come to him as he worked, hacking at recalcitrant rock with the pick. There was satisfaction in fitting the pipe into the trench he had dug, covering it again and coupling it up to the mobile home. He stood in the kitchen and turned on the tap, waiting, as if his mind were flowing down the narrow plastic with the water which was now splashing into the stainless steel sink. He swivelled the tap, put his mouth to it and drank from Allt a' Ghobha-uisge.

Two days later Donnie's Land Rover came over the hill, towing the bell-shaped septic tank on a trailer with a stack of pipes. When they had lifted it off Donnie leaned on the bonnet of the vehicle, drawing a sketch to show how it should be installed.

'I've got the water supply in,' he told Donnie.

'Good man. All you need to do with this thing is to dig a big hole and use the small pipe I've brought to make an outlet for the overflow. It's too far to take it down to the water, but you can take it to the burn there.'

'But that'll pollute it,' Seumas pointed out.

He had played a game with minnows as he lay on the bank of Allt a' Ghobha-Uisge, trying to scoop the tiny fish up in his palm, but they were always too quick for him, darting between his fingers to under the bank. It was also the burn where the sea trout ascended in autumn to spawn, their grey shapes caught in the beam of the old man's torch. And it was the territory of the water ouzel, which had given its name to the purling flow seeking the sea.

'Then dig a hole and cover it with something,' Donnie suggested. 'The overflow will seep away into the ground.'

They sat down for a smoke. Seumas waited but Donnie didn't say that he knew Alice was coming to see him.

'Have you heard from Feona?' his visitor asked.

'I had a letter this morning. She's fine. She'll be back before Easter.'

'She phoned me last night to see how you're getting on,' Donnie revealed.

Seumas was surprised at this.

'I better get back to the hotel,' its proprietor said, having to hold on to the septic tank for support to get himself to his feet. 'There's a party of a dozen Germans coming in next week for the shooting.'

He started digging the hole for the septic tank that afternoon. It was strange, going so deep and finding so many shells, as if there were ancient beaches layered below him. He found a horn-shaped shell and blew the earth out of it before he put it to his ear, listening as if he could hear the roar of a prehistoric ocean.

He was up to his shoulders in the hole, hacking at the ground between his feet, when he heard a motor. Two people were coming over the brow of the hill on a vehicle that looked like a tank with its top sliced off. The factor shut off the engine and he and the laird came down the slope, but Seumas stayed in the hole as they wandered about.

'Have you lost something?' he called to them.

'Who gave you permission to put a mobile home here?' the factor demanded.

'I don't need permission. I've got the tenancy of this croft!' Seumas shouted back.

'You need planning permission as well as the estate's permission,' the factor said. 'This is an area of outstanding natural beauty.' He struck the septic tank with his knuckles. 'You can't install this without permission.'

'Look: I pay my rent and don't bother anyone, so clear off,' Seumas warned them.

The laird who had tried to buy the old man's ivy-entwined *cromag* was standing on the lip of the hole.

'This is my land, Macdonald. You've applied to purchase it under crofting law and the estate is opposing it because it isn't registered as a croft.'

'You know fucking well it's been worked as a croft for generations.'

'Keep a civil tongue in your head, Macdonald,' the factor warned him.

'It's your type who have given the Highlands a bad name,' the laird said, 'ignoring planning law.'

'This mobile home has to go,' the factor spoke. 'I'll be back in two days. If it's not away we'll get it towed away. And get that hole filled in again.'

Seumas came out of the hole with the shovel in his hands.

'It'll still be here when you come back in two days, and so will reporters from the papers, and the television people, especially when your ancestor was one of the worst clearers in the Highlands and Islands last century,' he threatened the laird. '*Thallaibh!*' he ordered them, motioning with the shovel.

They went back over the hill in their buggy, and Seumas resumed digging. He was still in the hole when the moon came up over the bay, his anger having evaporated with his sweat, knowing he had done well. The old man would have been proud of him for keeping his temper. He enjoyed the rhythm of shovelling in the dark, the scrape of the metal on the shingle of an earlier age of the planet, throwing it over his shoulder and hearing it slithering away. He didn't want to think about Feona or Alice: all his energy was concentrated on the excavation, the moon overhead now, and when he paused for breath the metal in his hands was sheened, as if the spade were made of silver. He climbed out of the hole, measured his height against the septic tank, finding that he had gone deep enough. He would install it tomorrow.

He ate the remains of Alice's steak pie and had a thick slice of her cake. The letter from Feona was lying on the oilcloth beside the lamp, with Newnham College at the top. He wouldn't reply to it tonight because Donnie would have told her that the mobile home had arrived and that he had already installed a water supply, and was working on the septic tank. Was it possible that Donnie had been with Feona, he considered as he rested his elbows on the table as he smoked, because there couldn't be many women in the town he hadn't seduced? Maybe it was Donnie's baby and not his. But Donnie wouldn't do that to him.

He switched on the Gaelic request programme, and stood naked at the door. The moon had gone. The septic tank was a dark silhouette like a huge shell that had been thrown up in a storm, and beside it the mobile home was an alien presence. Sometimes the storms had brought a *cnò-bhachaill,* a smooth brown nut that had come on the warm currents from the other side of the world. He felt at peace after his day's efforts, and what he had said to the laird and the factor had restored his self-respect.

Then Seumas saw the lights.

At first they were indistinct, like weak searchlights sweeping the horizon, but he knew what they were. Màthair had called them the *Fir Chlis,* the lively leaping men. He went down to the shore to watch the Northern Lights, as if he were the sole spectator in an immense auditorium. As the *Fir Chlis* came over the horizon they grew into gigantic figures, weaving and swirling. Then he saw the dolphin leaping out at the edge of the bay, as if it too were part of this nocturnal ballet. The lights wove and moved like dancers going down on a knee in supplication to the creature leaping across the horizon, backwards and forwards, bending as if they were about to catch Leumadair and lift it into the sky.

Seumas knew he was having the most powerful experience of his life. There had been nothing to compare with this, not even being introduced to the sexual act by Feona, or Alice's lowered mouth.

The lights were a show accompanied by the request programme still playing on the radio from the open house. He had seen Gaelic words moving like this before in his head as the old man told the epic tale of the Irish warrior Naoise's and the beautiful Deirdre's blissful bower on Loch Etive-side. Now the *Fir Chlis* were taking a bow and the show was over, Leumadair's splashing as it leapt out to sea sounding like fading applause.

He went up to the house like a man sleepwalking, shutting the door on the fire to keep it in for the night. The light seemed to be coming from inside his own head as he carried the lamp up the stairs, setting it down on the floor. Tonight he was going to sleep in his parents' bed for the first time since he had had pneumonia. He changed the sheets that he had left on after the old man's death because it was too harrowing at the time to strip the bed, as if he were trying to remove the memory of his male parent from his life. Màthair's Gaelic Bible was still on the table with the thread of the marker in the pages. Though she felt that she couldn't read Gaelic properly, she had an understanding of the Bible in her native tongue through following preachers reading it in church.

Seumas read her Bible as he sat in the old man's chair, in the comforting circle of the lamp. He wasn't reading it for the story of David and Goliath, but for the expressive resonance, grateful that MacCallum had taught him to read and write the language of his birth. As he closed the book and sat ruminating, he had the impression that MacCallum had returned from the world of the dead, travelling over the sea from his grave on his beloved Mull, and that the schoolmaster was sitting beside him at the table, the sharpened red pencil in the pocket over his heart, Dwelly's Gaelic dictionary in front of him. Athair was in his chair by the fire, màthair in her usual chair.

He heard distinctly MacCallum's voice by his elbow.

'*Steàrnan* is the Gaelic name for the tern. Where does this name come from? From the Latin *Sterna hirundo*, a swallow tern, probably comparing it to the tern's forked tail, like the swallow's. *Steàrnan* and *Sterna* show the relationship between languages, Seumas.'

As MacCallum spoke the word *steàrnan* it was as if the birds of that name had come winging out of the shadows and were flying round the heads of the four occupants of the room, their white wings creating shadows on the wall, like the blades of oars rising and falling. The experience was so real that Seumas felt faint and had to close his eyes, gripping the table as though it were the gunwale of a pitching boat.

But when he opened his eyes again the *tannasgan*, ghosts of his schoolmaster, of his parents, of the circling flock of *steàrnanan*, had vanished. The fire was going out and the room was cold. Time to go up to bed, alone.

Twenty Three

'It's a bad sign to hear the *cuach*, the cuckoo, with no food in your stomach,' the old man had asserted to his son, and màthair, who was also full of the old superstitions, hadn't dissented as she served the old man his ample breakfast, brown eggs from the hens, fish from the net, bread new from the oven.

The *neòinean-cladaich*, the seapink, daisy of the shore, was out and Seumas took care not to tramp on them, because even when he was a child the old man had instructed him to watch where he put his feet, and never to stand deliberately on a plant which, he maintained, had as much right to the earth, and to its safety, as a human.

On early summer afternoons MacCallum would make them line up in two columns in the playground. Seumas might have the small hot hand of one of the Macgregor sisters as they went up the steps to the road where Miss Maclaren waited, a silver whistle in her mouth to signal when it was safe to cross, though there wasn't much traffic in those days. They went up the lane and began climbing the track that led to the sisters' croft. MacCallum stopped them and made them gather round him as he stooped, raising the head of the flower so delicately and carefully between two fingers.

'The marsh marigold.'

The class repeated the name after the schoolmaster, but that evening MacCallum rowed round to the house and said to Seumas: 'You saw the marsh marigold today. But what was the point of giving the others the Gaelic name, *beàrnan-Bealltainn*, because they wouldn't have appreciated it?'

'Now I know the word *beàrnan*,' the old man announced from his habitual chair, his pipe going. 'It means something notched.'

'It does indeed,' MacCallum confirmed, 'and it also refers to a person with broken or uneven teeth, which shows you how expressive our native tongue is.' He turned to his attentive pupil again. '*Bealltainn* is the first day of May, when a great Druidical festival was held in favour of the god Belus, when fires were kindled on the tops of mountains, for sacrifice. The cattle were driven between these fires to preserve them from contagion until the next May-day.'

'And all the fires on the hearth were put out, so that they could be rekindled from the purifying flames': màthair made her contribution to the discussion.

'I remember being told that the young people gathered on the moors on that day,' the old man reminisced. 'They cut a trench in the ground to hold the whole company, kindled a fire and made a cake of oatmeal, which they toasted at the embers of the fire against a stone.'

'So you see what can come from a small flower like the *beàrnan-Bealltainn*, like the bees spreading pollen,' MacCallum told Seumas. 'And sometimes the same flowers have different names in Gaelic, since in some places the marsh marigold is referred to as *bròg an eich-uisge*, shoe of the water-horse because of the shape of the leaf.'

That night in Seumas's dream the moor beyond the house was illuminated by fires, revealing an equine-like creature with yellow hooves emerging from the lochan, like the fairytale film that had come to the school one magical Christmas.

* * * * *

In spring the schoolmaster produced the key to the cupboard from his desk and handed it to one of the sisters to go and lift out the tray of eggs.

'The wren, among the smallest of British birds,' MacCallum announced.

The tiny egg, the life in it long since blown out through the holes at each end, was passed round the class. It had no weight as it lay on Seumas's palm, and when he tilted it to pass to Myrtle Macgregor it almost rolled off, but she righted it and smiled at him before stroking it with a finger. Even Donnie took it carefully on to his big clumsy hand, passing it on to boys in the back seats, who fought with their fists and boots in the playground, but who treated the tiny egg with curiosity and reverence.

'Please, sir, what like is a wren's nest?' Heather Macgregor asked.

MacCallum produced the keys again and went back up to the cupboard.

'This is a wren's nest,' the schoolmaster said from the front of the class.

It too was passed round. When it reached Donnie he tilted it on to the hand of Heather and put a finger into the hole. She went so red that Seumas had a vision of the little ball of grass in her trembling hand bursting into fire.

On a warm spring afternoon MacCallum passed round a curlew's skull with the long curved bill still attached, like broken compasses. The schoolmaster also distributed mother-of-pearl razor shells from his cupboard. Seumas watched Heather fanning her face with it, like a geisha girl in the film which had come recently to the school and during which he had been allowed to feel her again. But the way she stroked her face with the shell, then held it to her lips like a flute, had a queerer effect on him than the small mound he had been allowed to touch through her knickers when the man at the back was changing the reel on the projector. But this time in return she had touched his trousers.

* * * * *

Leumadair seemed to be charged with the spring, leaping far out of the water and driving fish inshore to make it easy for Seumas, who collected the glittering gifts in a bucket as he waded in the shallows.

'What are you going to do about the Land Court?' Donnie asked.

'I'm not going to bother,' Seumas told his friend. 'It's going to be too expensive. Anyway, there isn't the same need now; the mobile home is there for the baby.'

'All the same you should think of the future,' Donnie urged him. 'You mustn't give these bastards the idea that you're quitting.'

Some evenings Seumas took the key from the drawer and went out to unlock the mobile home. He sat on the unmade bed, staring out of the picture window over the bay, wondering what it was going to be like being a father. Things would change, that was for sure. He wouldn't have so much freedom, going off in the launch when he felt like it. But he was excited at the prospect and knew that he wanted a son. He could see himself walking along the curve of the bay with him, holding his hand as he stumbled on his wee legs, teaching him his first words of Gaelic, though that wasn't the way the old man had taught him. The son seemed to have been born with Gaelic, to know what they were saying to him even before he could speak, as if he had a newly formed ear to the wall of màthair's womb.

One afternoon when he was out in the launch at the lobster creels in the bay he saw Leumadair playing with a salmon, but when he took the launch closer he saw that it was a young porpoise which the dolphin was throwing up in the air on its beak, lifting it again as it hit the water with a splash. Leumadair's eye was bright, looking as if it were enjoying itself as it threw the dead porpoise into the air, diving to devour it. The violence of the spectacle depressed Seumas, because he had not seen that part of his friend's nature before. He was sitting brooding at the table with a mug of tea when Alice appeared.

'Is something wrong?' she asked anxiously, setting the basket down on the table.

'No, nothing.'

She unwrapped the quiche she had made for him and went through to the scullery tap to wash the leaves of the lettuce she had brought. She sliced the cucumber and laid the food out for him on a plate, but he didn't have an appetite.

'There *is* something wrong, Seumas. Have you had news about Feona and the baby?' she persisted.

He told her how Leumadair had played with the dying baby porpoise before consuming it.

'Why are you shocked? It's people who see dolphins as gentle creatures to swim with. But they're wild animals, hunting and fighting. You know something?' She was lighting two cigarettes in her mouth, a trick that intrigued him. 'I think you're in love with that dolphin out there.'

'Don't be daft.'

'I'm being serious. It came along when things were difficult for you and gave you a boost, didn't it?'

'I suppose so.'

'It's become like a woman you have to see every day or else you pine. What about me? I walk two miles across that moor, yet you hardly notice I'm in the room.'

They went out into the mobile home and this time he tried to be patient and gentle as she had taught him, but he was thinking of the dying porpoise tossed up on the beak of the surging dolphin, and for the first time he failed.

'Any word from your fancy English friend?' Alice asked as they lay together naked by the window overlooking the fading bay.

'She'll be coming soon,' he informed her because it was better to tell the truth.

'Which means I can't come here.'

'That's right.'

Her fingers were walking across his chest.

'But we can still meet?'

'I don't know, I haven't thought about it,' he said evasively.

'Things don't need to change,' she reacted with the same calm. 'God knows, Donnie and I were both married, yet we kept our affair going for years without anyone getting hurt.'

'*You* got hurt.'

'That was because of the way he dumped me so brutally, as if I was nothing to him.'

It must have been strange for her, two men having sex with her, Seumas was thinking as he looked at her profile beside him.

'I'd better be getting back. Tommy will be expecting a meal when he comes in with the bus.'

Seumas walked her across the moor.

'It's over,' he told her when they reached her car.

'What's over?' she asked, sitting on the bonnet.

'What's between you and me.'

She seemed to give all her attention to lighting the cigarette.

'No, it's not over; it's only begun. She's the wrong type of woman for you; you'll learn that soon enough.'

'It's got to be over,' Seumas reacted harshly. 'I'm going to be a father.'

'That didn't stop Donnie.'

'I don't want you coming to the house again,' he found the courage to say.

'Of course I won't come to the house, but I'll tell you what I'm going to do: I'm going to drive up here every Thursday night at eight and sit in the layby above the deserted village just along the road there for an hour. If a car comes I'll put my head down. If you don't appear I'll go home. But you'll come one night, I know you will. You forget, Seumas, that I know a lot about men and what their needs are.'

Alice drove away with a wave. He was angry as he hurried home. The bitch. He wouldn't be at the layby at Socrachadh on a Thursday night, rain or shine. It had only been a fling with her because Feona was away and anyway, it was she who had come to him because Donnie had given her up. She was randy; that was all she wanted from a man. However, he ate the food that she had brought for him.

* * * * *

I've bought an old Land Rover for getting across the moor, Feona wrote to him:

I'll bring some things for the mobile home. I'm booked on the last ferry, so I'll probably be arriving quite late.

It was a fine evening. At eight o' clock Seumas was sitting on the shore with the dog, wondering if Alice was waiting in the layby for him. He felt the urge, and knew he could get there and back within the hour at a run, but that wasn't the way to treat Feona on her first night back.

He had brought cylinders of gas from the town in the launch and connected them up to the mobile home, then went inside to test the gas lights in their fancy engraved globes. He was listening to the radio when he saw the headlights sweeping the bay. The Land Rover was loaded to the roof rack. He opened the door and helped Feona out. She was so big with the baby, he could hardly get his arms round her.

'Isn't Leumadair here to greet me?' she asked, going down to the edge of the bay.

'I haven't seen it about tonight. You must be tired, after the drive.'

'It's a long way, but I stopped several times. I'd love a bath. Is the water hot?'

'No, but I'll go and switch it on.'

She followed him inside.

'Don't you think it's very nice?' she asked, looking around.

'I like it.'

'Any word about the Land Court?' she called through from the bedroom.

'I'm not going to appeal to it.'

'Because of the possible costs?'

'That's the reason.'

'I told you, we can use part of Granny's legacy to hire a good lawyer to fight the estate in the Court.'

'I couldn't take any more of your money, after you paying for the mobile home.'

'Why not? We're a couple, aren't we? I'm so grateful that I've got money of my own, and don't have to depend on my parents any more. I haven't heard from them all term. I could have been sick for all they cared.'

Seumas could hear the regret in her voice as she kissed him. He unloaded the vehicle, bringing the things into the mobile home. Feona broke open the pack of sheets, and he helped her to spread them on the bed.

'Look, there's a stain on the mattress,' she complained.

'Does it matter?'

'I don't suppose so.'

'I'll go into the house for blankets,' he told her.

'Blankets are a thing of the past,' she said lightly. 'Give me that black sack.'

She tumbled out the blue quilt.

'It's called a duvet. You don't need blankets with it.'

The water was now bubbling in the boiler. Feona was through in the bathroom with the things she had brought.

'Run me a bath, will you?'

It was a strange feeling, running the first bath of his life, putting the plug in the hole, watching the steaming water gushing out. She came through naked with a floral box, crumbling a fragrant cube from it into the bath. It wasn't big enough for her to stretch out in, so she sat in the steam, soaping her big belly.

'Go through to the bedroom and bring me the brush with the long handle on the bed.'

He knelt, scrubbing her back with the bristles as she sat, eyes closed in the steam, as if meditating. Then she sent him through for one of the new white towels which she wrapped herself in before going through to the bedroom, lying down and reaching out for him.

'We can do it as long as you don't get on top,' she told him. 'Why don't you have a bath first? You can use my water.'

He stood naked at the big window, looking out over the dark bay, wondering if Leumadair was watching him. The gable of the house he had grown up in and spent almost every night of his life in was a dark triangle against the stars. It wasn't màthair sitting at the mirror behind him. She had had no use for mirrors, no use for creams for her face. The woman who was carrying his child was listening to classical music on the radio as she smeared her face at the mirror.

He padded down the narrow passage and sat in the scented steam, his knees drawn up to his chin. Màthair wasn't there to wash his back with a cloth, as she had done in front of the fire next door, when he was a boy, sitting in the tin basin like a wee boat.

Feona was in bed when he went back through. He had lain in bed with màthair when he had had the pneumonia, but now he was lying beside a strange woman in new sheets. She kissed him and turned over, presenting her back to him, guiding him in. Afterwards he lay, listening for the soothing sweep of the tide, but the glass in the big window was too thick and the room was too hot. She was sleeping now, her shoulder rising and falling rhythmically.

He needed a *cac*.

There had always been freedom in the past, doing 'your

business,' as màthair called it. You just got up from your chair or your bed and went round the corner of the house to the *taigh-beag* without announcement. He went on tiptoe down the passage to the bathroom with the towel over the rail and the brush in the floral holder by the bowl, the roll of paper on the wall. But he was too self-conscious to use the facility, and opened the front door to go out naked into the mild night. He didn't need a torch. His hand touched the peat-stack as he went round the corner. The door had never had a lock because of the isolation of the place and *earbsa*, trust, was a prominent word in his parents' vocabulary. His *tòn* found the hole in the darkness and he sat looking up at the stars, seeing the sparkle of *Reul-iùil*, the Pole Star, then groped in the darkness for half a page from the local paper before he stood up. There was no handle to flush; it all went into the pail to fertilize the croft, since not even a bodily function could be wasted.

He went back round the corner of the house, but didn't go into the mobile home. He looked in the big window and saw her lying there, her mouth open, a fist under her face. She looked vulnerable, with the curve of her belly under the quilt. He had feelings for her, but he also had feelings for Alice. He stood watching her before going in for his tobacco. He sat on the step of the mobile home, rolling himself a cigarette, looking out over the bay. The bedroom window was throwing a corridor of light out over the water, and he saw the rising and falling fin in it.

'Seumas, where are you?' he heard Feona calling anxiously.

'It's all right. I'm having a smoke.'

She came out and sat beside him on the step, in her thin nightdress.

'You'll get the cold,' he warned her.

'There's Leumadair out there,' she said, pointing.

'Aye, I've just noticed. It must have come in to welcome you home.'

She put her face against his arm.

'Do you love me, Seumas?'

'Yes,' he heard himself say, but wouldn't have been able to say it with such sincerity in Gaelic.

'I know we're going to be very happy here,' she said, pushing against him for warmth.

Seumas was watching the dipping body of the dolphin in the corridor of light. Beside him his old home was deserted, like the ruined village along the track where his sister had talked to the departed, except that he had nobody to talk to in his native language.

'We'd better get to bed,' he said, helping Feona up.

Twenty Four

Donnie invited Seumas and Feona to his private sitting room to watch the television documentary on Leumadair, but he told his best friend that she was 'a wee bit tired, and sends her love.'

'Aye, you'll make a film star yet, Seumas. It's as well you don't have a phone, otherwise you'd be pestered by women wanting to see more than your dolphin. It's a pity you're not still running your boat. The hotel's full with people wanting to be taken out in the launch, and there have been a lot of phone calls wanting rooms, and by the way, Willie McFarlane's giving up the fishing,' Donnie informed him as he brought his friend his plate of food.

'I'm not surprised. There's no living in it now,' Seumas said, squeezing the lemon sliver over the scampi.

Seumas had been in school with Willie, but had never liked him. Willie had been a friend of Sandy's, except that he had played with toy boats instead of bulldozers.

'I suppose he'll be selling his boat,' Seumas said. 'Not that it's worth very much. Who's going to buy it?'

'He advertised it in the local paper and a stranger came and took it.'

'What's he going to do when he's giving up the fishing?' Seumas wondered.

Donnie was opening a packet of cigars.

'He's going to skipper a boat to take people out to see the dolphin. It won't be his boat; the Brigadier's bought it; it's a fifteen seater and it's coming at the end of this week.'

'So this is the Brigadier's way of getting at me,' Seumas said furiously. He pushed his unfinished food away and confronted his friend. 'Are you going to tell your guests to go with him?'

Donnie was taking his time lighting his cigar, making sure it was drawing smoke before he shook out the match.

'It's good for the place, all these people who'll come to see the dolphin after tonight's TV programme.'

'I've built up a special relationship with that dolphin. It knows my boat and it trusts me. What's a strange boat with noisy engines and a lot more people on board than on my launch going to do to the dolphin?'

'I don't think the Brigadier's boat will scare away the dolphin,' Donnie responded calmly. 'From what I hear from the guests it likes human company.'

Seumas stood up from the bar stool. He was beginning not to trust Donnie, sensing that there was more behind this than he was saying. The Brigadier and his wife often ate at the hotel, so maybe Donnie had put him up to it so that he would get more and more visitors looking for hospitality after they had been out to see the dolphin.

Feona was sitting at her typewriter in the lounge of the mobile home when he arrived home.

'How's the work going?' he asked as he stood in the doorway, still uncertain about telling her about her father and the new boat.

'I should finish it before this arrives,' she estimated, patting her stomach. 'Then after I get my doctorate I'm going to try to publish it as a book. I think it's an important contribution to the study of dolphins; so does my supervisor. I'll get some more film of Leumadair to use in the book. You look angry. Is there something the matter?' she asked, leaving her writing to come to him.

He sat beside her on the sofa and told her about her father's purchase of a boat for trips out to Leumadair.

'I suspect that Daddy's doing this out of malice, not for the money; anything to drive you out of my life. A big noisy boat's bound to have an effect. Leumadair's used to yours. It knows it won't come to any harm. I've actually got a chapter on dolphins and the effects boats can have on them in my thesis. If they get too trusting they can get killed.'

'I still think Donnie's got something to do with this,' Seumas said.

Feona was at the picture window, her back to him, looking over the bay, her swelling bump raising the hem of her maternity dress.

'I should think he has.'

Seumas was waiting, but she didn't elaborate.

'What do you mean?'

'It's funny how easily words come when one's writing or speaking about a dolphin,' she mused, still with her back to him, as if she had seen something interesting in the bay. 'They seem so clean, so free, not like human beings. It's difficult, talking about one's own parents. Daddy was always on the move as an army officer. Settling here when he retired was the first real home we ever had. Mummy loves it. It's allowed her to express herself in ways she's never been able to do before. She doesn't have to leave her garden behind and pack up her things to move to another country at short notice any more. She loves it here, maybe too much.'

'I'm still not following you, Feona.'

She turned from the window. It was a moment he knew he was going to remember, not only for what she said, but because of the way her face was against the sky, like a painting.

'Donnie's been having an affair with Mummy since we moved up here.'

Seumas shook his head as if he had been struck a blow as he fumbled for his cigarette papers.

'It sounds so – degrading, but that's the only way I know how to put it. Last summer I was supposed to be out sailing with a friend, but it was too blowy. My shoes were wet, so I came into the house on bare feet. As I passed the drawing room I saw Donnie on top of Mummy on the sofa. I could see his big bare backside and Mummy's face at his shoulder. Her eyes were closed, so she didn't see me. I didn't say anything to her, but every time she went out to paint I would go into the hotel to ask for Donnie. He was never there.'

'Does your father know?' Seumas asked, having succeeded in making himself a cigarette.

'I shouldn't think so. That would hit him where he hurts most – in his pride. He wouldn't be sitting eating his dinner in Donnie's hotel if he knew. He would be at home, plotting some way to get him out of the hotel. Daddy's a very vindictive man, which I suppose is why Mummy took a lover, even a rough one like Donnie.'

His lifelong friend. They had shared everything since they had arrived at school together for the first day in primary one. They had filled the same jam jar with tadpoles; they had reported their first wet dreams to each other; and each year, faithfully, Donnie had shown him how much his *bod* had grown. He had lent Seumas money, handled the bookings for the dolphin boat, and, most likely paid for the delivery by sea of the mobile home. He had given him other things too, passing Alice on to him.

It was all too confusing, too sinister. He told Feona that he was going for a walk. Instead he went into the house and sat in the old man's chair with the dog at his feet, feeling that he had betrayed his parents by getting into this mess, after the calm isolation and contentment of his upbringing. He wished that the mobile home and the woman in it were gone, and that màthair and the old man were sitting in the room with him again. He wished he were sitting waiting by the lamp for MacCallum to come ashore with his gifts, the Gaelic dictionary, the mouth organ, his welcome and instructive presence. He wished now that he had taken the schoolmaster's help and gone on to study Gaelic at the university. He might even have come back to the school to MacCallum's desk, with the long streamers of raffia on the cupboard door, the coiled strap, unseen but never forgotten, under the lid of the desk, lying beside the dinner money book.

Even now, should he walk away from it all, leaving the launch at its mooring, going over the hill away from the mobile home with Dìleas at his heels? He saw himself striding purposefully across the moor, putting out his hand in the gloaming as the big red bus came round the corner, with Tommy caressing the wheel and fondling the gear lever as if it were a woman's leg.

He drops the fare into the Perspex slot and takes a seat at the back of the bus with the dog at his feet. He is going for a job on the mainland, with a council house, and then he will go and reclaim his sister from the asylum. It will be like the old days, and only Gaelic will be spoken between them as Eilidh goes about her slow chores, with her bad days, when the voices come back to torment her, speaking a Gaelic that crossed the Atlantic to Alba Neuve nearly a hundred and fifty years ago, a strange Gaelic with the names of plants that no longer grew because the sheep that replaced the people had eaten them, with the names of birds – *an coileach-dubh*, the blackcock – that no longer flew because the lairds had shot them to extinction.

He sat beside the cold heap of ash in the grate, his parents and MacCallum, more like an uncle than his schoolmaster, gone. You couldn't speak Gaelic to yourself. MacCallum had told the story of a man from Mull who had left to work in a shipyard in Glasgow. He had had an accident, falling into a hold under construction, and came home with a permanent crutch in his armpit. When MacCallum welcomed him back in Gaelic the disabled native looked at him as if he didn't understand.

'You see, even if there had been men to speak Gaelic with in the shipyard, it wouldn't have been possible to be heard because of the noise, the clang of hammers,' the schoolmaster explained. 'The man with the crutch who had excellent Gaelic had lost it through not using it, and couldn't understand the simplest greeting any longer.'

Seumas was frightened he was losing his Gaelic, having no one to speak it with now. The only way to retain it was to listen to the Gaelic programmes on the radio, to speak as if he and not the interviewee were being asked the question. He had never felt so alone, so vulnerable, now that Donnie seemed to be betraying him, yet he couldn't break with him. He had needed the fares from the tourists he took out in his launch to support the woman carrying his child next door in the mobile home where she was working at her thesis on dolphins.

The room was getting dark. For the first time in his life Seumas found the house eerie, as if màthair would come limping on her arthritic hip through from the scullery, carrying the pot of potatoes, a look of disgust on her face at the mess he was making of his life. He put on the radio and sat with his eyes closed, listening to the songs.

The door opened at his back.

'Why are you sitting here alone?' Feona asked. 'I thought something had happened to you.'

'I didn't want to disturb you with the radio.'

'You know I like Gaelic songs. What is it, Seumas? Don't you want me in your life?'

'It's just that I got a shock about Donnie and your mother.'

'Forget about them. And forget about Daddy buying a new boat for McFarlane. We can beat him at his own game.'

'What do you mean?' he asked, bewildered.

'We can get a boat ourselves. I'll apply for a licence to carry passengers.'

'I don't think we should get into competition with your father. It wouldn't be fair to Leumadair, having two boats out there, chasing after it.'

'I'm so sorry to see you so despondent, darling.'

'I'll keep on fishing – with Leumadair's help.'

The following week as he was repairing the large web of the net on the shore, Feona came down waving a letter.

'I wrote to my supervisor in Cambridge, telling him that I've used up all my research grant, but that I still need to collect data on the dolphin I'm studying here. He's written to say that he's arranged an additional grant of three hundred pounds. That means that you can be paid to take me out in the launch to study Leumadair, and at the same time we can keep an eye on it to make sure that it isn't disturbed by the other boat.'

A week later he lifted her into the dinghy because of her size and transferred her carefully to the launch. As they left the bay he saw a big launch ahead, ploughing the water. At first he thought it belonged to a rich tourist because it had two decks and two propellers, but then he saw McFarlane standing proudly at the big chromium wheel. He waved as he passed, but Seumas didn't respond. The wash from the new boat rocked the launch and Feona had to grip the gunwale with both hands. Leumadair broke surface, but without the spectacular leaps which Seumas had witnessed.

When he returned Feona to the house and motored round to the town for messages, a group of locals were standing on the pier, admiring the new boat, and the Brigadier was on the deck in a nautical cap. He looked at Seumas, who turned his back as he passed the mooring rope through the ring.

'This should give you a comfortable dolphin watching trip!' the Brigadier shouted up to the people above him, though Seumas knew it was for his benefit. 'It can do eighteen knots and we've even got a galley kitchen aboard for coffee.'

When Seumas reached the end of the pier he saw a newly painted board fixed to the railings.

WANT TO SEE THE DOLPHIN IN COMFORT?
THEN TAKE A TRIP OUT ON FÀILTE
SAILINGS: 10am, 2pm, 4pm, 6pm.
Book at the hotel.

He knew that naming the boat with the Gaelic for welcome was to taunt him. He felt like ripping the board from the railing and tossing it into the harbour, but that would give the Brigadier victory. He went into the hotel and ordered his lunch.

'It's some boat, isn't it?' Donnie said with admiration.

'It's too big; it'll disturb the dolphin.'

'I wouldn't worry about that.'

A woman in a checked body-warmer and matching hat appeared in the doorway. Seumas recognized her as Feona's mother.

'Could I have a bottle of champagne, Donnie?' she asked in a fancy voice.

'You sure can.'

Seumas saw her going down the pier, carrying the bottle. There was a crowd at the steps.

'Maybe I should have introduced you to your mother-in-law,' Donnie said with a smile. 'She's going to christen the boat. Good looking, isn't she?'

'I see you're taking the bookings for the new boat,' Seumas confronted his best friend. 'I hope the Brigadier's paying you commission.'

'I don't see the harm in handling the bookings,' Donnie said with a shrug. 'People who saw the TV programme are coming to the hotel because they want to see the dolphin, and as for the others – I'm giving folks employment in the town by taking on extra staff to clean the rooms and serve in the restaurant. You benefit too, Seumas, because with the hotel full, and the chance meals, I can take all the fish you can catch.'

'I'd better get back,' Seumas said, pushing the money for his meal across the counter.

He walked briskly down the pier. The Brigadier's wife was standing on the steps, holding the bottle of champagne which was attached to the railing of the bow. She swung it as Seumas passed.

'I name this boat Fàilte,' he heard her calling in a voice even fancier than her daughter's.

As the glass smashed Seumas turned. He wanted to go back and say something about a white settler using Gaelic. Instead he ran down the step, jumped into his own boat and pulled the cord violently to start the engine.

Twenty Five

Seumas and Feona were out in the launch when they heard, before they saw, the Brigadier's boat planing round Sgeir nan Eun, its shattering horsepower scattering the nesting birds, as if it was about to take off into the sky. Seumas was determined to keep track of the boat, to make sure it didn't harass Leumadair.

But would the dolphin show? It delivered fish to him, but would it be loyal and stay under the surface? Expectant cameras were lining the deck of the Brigadier's boat, and Leumadair leapt, as if it wanted to be recorded, in the future its leap projected in colour on to the wall of a southern house, the audience of neighbours exhaling audibly in astonishment.

Feona was filming Leumadair for her study, so Seumas stayed with it, but at a safe distance from the big new boat, circling so that the passengers could get steady shots. As McFarlane's boat tried to come in even closer, Seumas steered the launch between it and the leaping dolphin. When it had submerged the big boat turned for the harbour. An hour later, when Seumas came into the pier with his launch, McFarlane shouted from the wheel.

'Don't you ever do that again!'

'Do what?' Seumas asked innocently.

'Cut in in front of me like that. You could have caused a collision. I've a good mind to report you to the police.'

'You shouldn't be out there with that monstrosity, disturbing the dolphin. You should stick to the model boats you were always playing with in school, putting Miss Maclaren off her head.'

'I'm telling you, Macdonald, I'm losing patience with you,' McFarlane responded. 'You're nothing but a troublemaker and should clear off to the mainland and leave folk to get on with their business. This boat has a hire licence, and every sort of safety equipment, as well as insurance, which yours didn't have. You knew bloody well that you needed these things, but you took a chance with the lives of your passengers. You should have been prosecuted.'

When he reached home Seumas told Feona that he was going to take the dog for a walk. He was a boy again on the silent expanse of moor, going to meet màthair off the bus from the town, carrying for her the two brown bags weighed down with bones for making soup, the bottle of lemonade for himself which he would leave in the sea, then shake so that its chilled sweetness would foam down his throat as he drank. He had a basket with him as he went to the glistening black wall of the peat bank where the old man, tormented by flies, was pressing his boot down on the *tairsgeir*, whose blade went through the peat, as Macphail the grocer's wire had cut through cheese, the Gaelic word *càise* far more palatable. The old man took the lid off the dented can of milk and raised it to his mouth in both hands, saying a Gaelic blessing before he drank, long and deep, like a warrior flushed with success in battle, a reversed cap on his head instead of a helmet.

The moor had been a place of Gaelic. '*Sin iolaire,*' màthair pointed up to the soaring eagle, and suddenly the bags in the boy's hands were weightless as if he had been lifted up on the massive spread of the wings. There was that afternoon of oppressive sleepy heat when the flowers the old man was slicing through reluctantly with his spade seemed to give up their scents as they died, when the blade of the *tairsgeir* jarred on something. The old man had cut round the obstruction which Seumas hoped was treasure, loot buried by raiding Vikings with horns on their helmets and pitiless swords in their fists. The old man was holding up an old boot. How had it managed to get down into the peat, and was there a body to go with it? Was it someone who had lost the way in bad weather, a peddler perhaps? Màthair had spoken about the peddler who came to the island of her youth with his backpack of haberdashery, needles and other useful household items, and who also carried news from the outside world in Gaelic which contained the names of unknown cities and great persons. He had brought with bobbins of fragile thread the news of the deaths of ruthless emperors and haughty queens.

Everywhere else had changed, but the moor still held its Gaelic as it held the water in the bogs, and supported flowers, names Seumas had been given in his native language in boyhood by his parents and by MacCallum, in conversation with them. MacCallum's schoolhouse had been modernized, a television with a remote control where the schoolmaster had sat, talking in Mull dialect with his sister. But the *learga dhubh*, the black-throated diver, still came to the lochan on the moor every spring because Seumas had heard its eerie cry as he lay in bed in the mobile home with the window open.

One day the old man had taken his son to see the hill he called *Blàr Cathaich*, the battle plain. Seumas thought it was men who had fought there in ancient times, but the old man explained that it was the knoll where the blackcocks brawled each year for the hens. They went back pre-dawn, lying in the bracken to await the contest. The birds were fighting so fiercely that their feathers were mingling in the sky. When the victorious one flew off the old man went and picked up the other one with one hand, it was so exhausted. It had been blinded in the contest, so the old man put it out of its misery. After plucking the bird for the pot, màthair kept the sheened feathers in remembrance of the blinded warrior, *coileach-dubh*.

It was as if the moor had renewed his inner strength. When he went back Feona was lying naked on the bed and for the first time, against the light from the bay coming in the big window, he thought she was beautiful, even with her mountainous stomach.

'I want you,' she told him.

'But you've already got me inside you,' he said gently.

'Then I want the two of you, father and child, at the same time.'

As Seumas thrust at her curved back he could see the dark fin rolling in the bay.

'Leumadair's out there.'

'I can see it,' she said wistfully.

'It's as if it's watching us doing it.'

'Dolphins are sexy creatures, Seumas, especially the males. They're worse than men.'

'What do you mean?' he asked, stopping in his considerate stroke, learned from Alice.

'Men chase women singly, but male dolphins do it in pairs, or even bigger groups or pods. They'll go after a single female from another pod and herd her into theirs. I'm sure that what they do to females amounts to rape sometimes.'

Seumas found it strange, thinking of the power beneath the rolling fin as he entered her again, withdrawing to lie quietly at her back, the fin moving like a dark blade above her belly in the window.

'Do you think it's male or female?' he asked.

'What, the baby?'

'No, Leumadair.'

'You can't tell unless you get into the water with it. I could go and get a scan to tell the sex of the baby, but I don't want that; I want the surprise. Don't you?'

'Yes I do. When is it due?'

'In three weeks. But it could come earlier. Would you know what to do?'

'Aye, jump into the launch and go for the doctor.'

Her hand came over her shoulder, seeking his, and he slept deeply, clasping her hand at the bottom of a dream in which the shapes were dark and insubstantial.

* * * * *

When Seumas came into the harbour the Brigadier's boat was already in, tied up by the steps where he usually moored, and there was no other space. Seumas lowered the car tyre over the side to save damaging the new boat as he brought the launch alongside it. Though the engine was shut off he felt the launch moving sideways.

McFarlane's boot on his gunwale was pushing him out again.

'You're not lying alongside me with that thing.'

'You've taken my place!' Seumas shouted angrily.

'This isn't your private mooring. First in, first served.'

'I'm entitled to come alongside you,' Seumas protested.

'Then you're going to have to swim for the steps because you're not putting a foot on this boat. Anyway, there's bad weather coming, so you'd better find somewhere else to tie up.'

Seumas stepped forward.

'Just try it,' McFarlane warned. 'You've been in enough trouble with the police already.'

Seumas took his anger out on the engine, opening the throttle full out as he backed the launch out, turning it with a violent push of the tiller towards home, the wind freshening in his face. He had heard the forecast and knew that it was going to be a wild night.

Feona was in the mobile home, at her thesis.

'You look angry, Seumas.'

'McFarlane wouldn't let me tie up alongside your father's boat.'

'Was Daddy there?' she asked, surprised.

'I didn't see him,' he said abruptly. He wanted to tell her that it was all the fault of her father, all her fault for coming over the moor to the house that night to seduce him as he lay in bed, impeded by the plaster cast on his arm. He wished that the mobile home had never arrived on the barge.

'I'm going to take Dìleas for a walk,' he told her.

The wind was rising, sending spume ashore, soaking him, so he turned and went back to the mobile home which was now lighted and where she was now preparing the fish he had netted the previous day, the oil heating in the non-stick pan on the blue jets, the wires of the whisk click clicking round and round in his head as she made the batter. Màthair had slapped the herring into the black pan with butter she had churned herself, using the power of her arm and singing a Gaelic song as the thickening milk slopped in the small wooden barrel.

The wind was now rocking the mobile home, and as it tilted the bowl of batter slithered from the worktop, spinning, spattering over the floor.

'I'll need to rope it down,' Seumas told her.

He had to fight his way head-down to the shed behind the house, searching with the torch for the coils of varicoloured rope that the old man had been brought by the storms. It was the same principle as hay making: once you had the stack up you slung ropes over, weighing it down with stones. He threw the first rope over the roof of the mobile home and tied each end to boulders he lugged up from the shore. With three ropes across the structure was steadier.

The fish was burning in the pan, and Feona was lying doubled up on the bed.

'I think the contractions are starting,' she moaned.

Seumas had had moments of terror before: a big wave breaking over the launch, trying to force him away from the helm; seeing MacCallum lifting the lid of his desk and taking the coiled strap out to punish Donnie for his surreptitious feel. But this was worse than any of those terrors. He stood in the room rocked by the wind, not knowing what to do. He had carried the old man's body out to the launch and round to the town, but that had been on a calm day. It was too wild to take Feona in the launch on the same journey for new life this time, not death.

'Will you be all right if I go for the doctor?' he asked.

Her fingers tightened on his shoulder.

'Yes, but hurry.'

It would take too long to run over the moor to the main road, to flag down a vehicle to give him a lift into town, so he opened the passenger door of Feona's Land Rover for Dìleas to jump in. He was taking the dog for comfort and support. He had never driven before because they couldn't afford a vehicle, but he had sat beside Feona as she drove. He turned the ignition key, crashing the gears as the vehicle jolted up the slope. He pressed switch after switch, searching for the headlights, but the wipers came on. After trying more switches on the bewildering dashboard he found full beam as he reached the moor, wrestling with the wheel, trying to keep the tyres in the tracks Feona had made as she went to and from the town in the vehicle.

Clouds were being swept across the moon as he bounced along, the dog lying on the floor for safety, but still slithering about. He hit something and the vehicle veered off the tracks, careering fifty yards down the slope, its front wheels splashing. He opened the door to see that he was half way into a bog, but he couldn't find the reverse gear. He abandoned the Land Rover, having opened the passenger door to let Dìleas out, and began running, the strength of the wind at his back, but slowed down because of the stitch in his side, the dog going ahead, veering when a bog loomed. It was dark, but his feet knew the way because of the many times he had crossed the moor to and from school. When they reached the road end they began running along it towards the town. Coming round the bend, he saw the dim headlights of a vehicle parked in the layby near to Socrachadh.

Alice leaned over to open the car door.

'I knew you'd come eventually.'

'It's the baby,' he gasped. 'It's coming. She needs help.'

'Where were you making for?'

The town, to get the doctor.'

'Get in and I'll take you to the phone box along the road.'

It was a quarter of a mile away. He fumbled with the change she gave him, dropping a coin and scrabbling on the concrete floor to retrieve it before he pushed the coins into the slot, frustrated by the time the female at the other end of the line was taking to connect him to the doctor's number in the town.

'He's out on a call just now,' he told Alice as he left the phone box. 'His wife says he'll come as soon as he can. Will you come back with me? You've had children yourself.'

She squashed out her cigarette in the dashboard tray.

'I'll come on one condition.'

'What's that?' he asked, distracted.

'That you'll come here next Thursday.'

Seumas saw what she was doing, but had no time to think about it.

'All right, but hurry!'

He put the dog on the back seat and sat beside Alice as she drove her car down to the layby.

'This car's too low slung to take across the moor. The exhaust would be ripped off in the first hundred yards, so we'll have to hoof it,' she advised, taking a torch from the glove compartment.

The dog was out in front, navigating, turning her head in the torch beam to make sure they were following. The south wind was in their faces now, trying to push them back. He gripped Alice's hand and was almost dragging her along with him, and if he could have carried her on his back he would have, as he had done on the moor with his sister so many times when she was tired and fretful after school.

The torch flared on the grey metal of the Land Rover, already up to the windscreen in the bog. They veered round it on to firm ground.

'I was school sports champion, but that was on the flat,' Alice told him breathlessly. 'If this is what the fags do for you I'm going to give them up. But not sex. You and I will be doing it when we're both seventy.'

Feona was moaning in pain on her knees by the bed.

'Alice will help you until the doctor comes.'

He stood outside the door, smoking nervously, wanting to walk down to the shore to get away from the cries of his wife, but knowing that it was his duty to be there as father of the child being born. He thought he saw a fin close to shore, but couldn't be sure because a cloud moved across the moon. Then he heard a different cry at his back.

'You've got a daughter,' Alice came out to tell him.

He went through to the bedroom, to see his child, looking like a *tacharra*, a changeling, sometimes substituted by the fairies, màthair had said, for the newly born.

When Dr Murray arrived in his big wheeled four-track he checked mother and child, telling Alice: 'Why don't you train as a midwife?'

'I've never delivered a baby before, doctor. It was done instinctively, with a prayer. Though I'm not a religious person it seems to have worked. I think I'll stick to librarianship. Handling books is easier than helping out babies.'

'Thank you,' Seumas said, hugging Alice.

'My shoes are ruined. You owe me a pair.'

Before she climbed into the doctor's vehicle for a lift back across the moor she reminded Seumas: 'It's my turn next Thursday night.'

He gave Dìleas a hug before putting her to her bed in the house she had been brought up in, her head between the old man's knees, watching his face with intelligent concentration as he narrated a tale about a legendary sheepdog that had swam from the island to the mainland with a herd of black cattle. The dog had kept the herd of several hundred together on the drove of over a hundred miles to the Falkirk Tryst, where thousands of cattle were being sold. But its master had died from heart failure after the long hard drive through rain and wind, and from lying in his sodden plaid on the ground, with only oatmeal from the bag at his waist mixed with a little water from a burn to sustain him.

As the old man reached the climax of the story Dìleas's ears were up in expectation.

'This was an island dog, and he had no intention of going with a new master who didn't have Gaelic,' the old man explained in his slow expressive native tongue. 'So he headed for home by himself. He stopped at farms to kill a rat and lap water from the trough. He slept among the hay and the next day at dawn he set out on his journey again. But he wasn't going back the way he had come with the herd; he was taking a shorter way. He ran through villages and towns, and when children called to him and a woman threw a bone to him he didn't stop, as if he would lose the way if he did, though only God knows how the dog knew where he was going.' The old man stopped, to light his pipe, and for dramatic effect, though his wife and son and Dìleas were intent listeners. 'The ways of animals are often hidden from us, but many creatures are wiser than people. The dog I'm speaking of didn't stop for a second night's sleep. It was in the country now, running along tracks and through pastures, guided by *gealach bhuidhe nam broc.*' Seumas didn't need enlightenment: the old man and MacCallum had had a discussion on the evocative phrase, the yellow moon of the badger, explaining to Seumas that it was the harvest moon that was flooding the kitchen with light as they were speaking, as if the invisible hand of a former occupant of the house, long since dead, had turned up the lamp on the table to a more powerful luminosity without destroying the frail membrane of the mantle.

The sheepdog continued to run for home, across stubble fields cut by scythes swinging under the badger's moon, with that elusive creature dragging home fresh bedding, paying no attention to the speeding dog.

'When it reached the coast it swam across to the island, at the exact place it had crossed with the herd,' the old man narrated, his sweet pipe wisping in his fist. 'And when he ran into his home the drover's wife, who was sitting at the fire, stood up and crossed herself, because this was a Catholic household, and she knew that her man must have departed this life. That night she took the dog into her bed with her and he lay there night after night for years until he died, when the village bard made a song about him which Mr. MacCallum knows and which he'll sing to us the next time he comes. You're as clever as the drover's dog,' he complimented Dìleas, fondling the affectionate head between his knees. 'You would find your way back to us in the darkest, stormiest night, *m' eudail*,' my dear.

Twenty Six

Seumas adored his daughter. When he took her in his arms and put his face against her skin he was back gathering up the scented bundle of hay as it fell away from the old man's scythe. He changed her himself, lying her on her back on the bed while he spoke to her, wanting her first word to be *dadaidh*. It was a miracle, being a father at 37.

It was a wonderful spring of calm seas and blue skies. Seumas had to take two wire baskets in the Spar shop now, one for the pack of nappies, the formerly morose girl behind the till, a mother herself, smiling as she pressed the discordant keys of the till. But he didn't hide the pack from the locals as he carried it down the pier to the launch.

Feona had resumed work on her thesis, sitting typing with the baby in the portable crib by her feet.

'I'm coming back out with you on the launch to study Leumadair again, but I'll leave it till it gets warmer. My supervisor says to take my time. What are we going to call our daughter?'

He had been thinking about that.

'Flòraidh.'

'Say it again for me,' Feona requested.

'Flaw-ree. It's the Gaelic for Flora.'

'Flaw-ree. It's a nice name. We'll need to christen her.'

'But we don't go to church,' Seumas pointed out.

'We'll christen her ourselves.'

On the warmest day so far the infant was carried down to the sea where the mother scooped up the brine in her palm and held it out to the father.

'You do it,' Feona told him.

'I name this child Flòraidh,' her father pronounced, sprinkling the water on her forehead.

In the evening while Feona typed Seumas lay through in the room on the bed, with the baby sleeping in the crib by the window. He was recalling the debt he owed to Alice for the safe delivery of his daughter, and he had made a commitment to her that he must keep, so he swung his legs from the bed and went through to Feona.

'I'm going for a walk across the moor.'

He left the dog in the old house and walked in the soft fading light, in the hard tracks left by the Land Rover, passing the place where he had lost control of it the night Flòraidh was born. It hadn't been completely swallowed by the bog, but salvaging it would be too dangerous.

Alice was sitting in the layby up the road beside the car, cigarette ends around her.

'Where will we go that's private?' she asked.

'The old ruined village down the slope.'

He led the way, trampling the bracken's curling fronds where there had once been a track to the outside world. They went into the first ruin and she put her arms round his neck. Her need seemed even greater than his as she hitched her dress up to her waist, standing in the corner of the wall. Seumas thought that the unstable stonework was going to topple with the movements of her buttocks. But when he remembered that this was the house to which his sister had come to talk with her spectral friend Flòraidh, he lost his passion, as if the act he was performing was profane in that place of innocence and fond memories.

'You're not on form tonight,' Alice complained, giving him the first lighted cigarette from her mouth. 'How's the baby?'

'Fine. We've called her Flòraidh.'

'Will Feona be taking your name?'

He shook his head.

'It won't be easy for you to stop her. She's a very determined young woman.'

'What makes you say that?' he asked as he looked through the remains of a window on the sea, from which the inhabitants of long ago must have looked for the last time, trying to retain the view in memory before embarking on the brig in the harbour round the coast.

'She comes in to order books about bringing up children in that highfalutin' voice of hers.'

'I haven't made up my mind what I'm going to do,' he told Alice.

But he knew that he was never going to be able to leave his daughter.

'Well, I'll be at the road end next Thursday and I hope you'll be there too,' she said as she knotted on her headscarf. 'Will you walk me back?'

After the birth Feona seemed to have lost interest in sex, and when he made advances she turned her back on him with the excuse that she needed time. He was continuing to meet Alice for more than her body; he had to admit to himself. He felt freer, more himself in her company.

'Till next Thursday,' Alice said, blowing a kiss at him before she pushed the car into gear.

Seumas was troubled by the double life he was leading. It was like a path through the bog, where you didn't know if you were going to step on firm ground or go over your boots. The only thing he was sure about was his love for his daughter, and when Feona woke early to feed her he lay studying the way the light of dawn caught the globe of the breast, gleaming like one of the old man's glass floats as the baby took it in both hands before her tiny mouth found the vital nipple.

One evening when Seumas was lying on the bed studying the Gaelic dictionary he heard someone at the door and looked out of the window, seeing a woman in a headscarf with hounds, wearing a quilted jacket.

'My name's Veronica Bradwell-Price,' she said, holding out a hand.

'What do you want?' he asked roughly, without offering his own hand, recognizing her from the hotel and the Spar shop.

'I've come to see my daughter and grandchild.'

'You've a bloody cheek coming here after what you and your husband tried to do to me. Clear off before you upset Feona.'

'It wasn't me who did it,' she said quietly. 'It was my husband.'

'But you're related to the laird's wife,' he accused her, still barring the way in. 'You all put your heads together to stop me buying the house so that Feona would have to go home with you.'

'I never discussed it with my cousin. If there was any discussion it was with my husband.'

'Who is it?' Feona called through.

'Someone who's lost the way,' Seumas said, shutting the door.

But Feona had seen the visitor from the window in the lounge and she pushed past Seumas, hauling the door open and throwing her arms round the neck of the visitor.

'Mummy, I'm so glad you've come!'

Seumas pushed past them both and slammed the door behind him, leaving the home shuddering. He walked with big strides along the shore, calling angrily to the dog, as if she too had joined the enemy camp. He knew what he would do: he would take his daughter away with him to the mainland and bring her up by himself, using his mother tongue. He didn't want her growing up talking English with the accent of her mother and grandmother.

He sat smoking on a boulder at the mouth of Allt a' Ghobha-Uisge, watching the mobile home, waiting for the woman to go.

She would be holding his daughter now, drooling over it, seeing all the family resemblances on her side. It made Seumas so angry that he could smash his fist into something. He should go and confront her with his knowledge that Donnie had been riding her for years, and that he would tell everyone if she ever came back.

It was an hour before he saw the woman disappearing over the moor. He hurried back to the mobile home.

'She only came to see her granddaughter, Seumas,' Feona told him, seeing the anger still in his face.

'I don't want her back here. It's still my place until the estate takes it away from me. Understood?'

'No, not understood,' Feona said adamantly. 'She's my mother. She's been miserably unhappy with Daddy all those years. I saw it myself when I was young. The only happiness she's had in her life was when she moved to the island and met Donnie. I know what you're going to say, it's sex, but she's very fond of Donnie. And as for the dolphin boat, she says that Daddy didn't buy it out of spite towards you, but to give himself something to do. He's always been a very active man and he misses the army. Besides, he's a keen sailor.'

'I hope she's not coming back here.'

'Actually she's coming back at the weekend. She wants to bring something for the baby. It would be cruel to stop her, Seumas. We owe her a lot.'

'I don't owe her anything.'

'Yes you do. She asked my godmother to beg her husband to leave us in peace in the mobile home, with the baby due.'

When he was lying at her back that night Seumas hated the mother of his child. He could see himself wrapping up the baby in a blanket in the dawn and taking her away with him on the launch. They would catch the morning bus. But Flòraidh needed her mother's milk.

Next morning, when he went out in the launch to check his lobster creels before the Brigadier's boat began its trips, there was no sign of Leumadair. He felt that somehow it was connected with the woman coming to the mobile home, as if she had brought bad luck.

'Leumadair must have gone,' he told Feona in despair. She was feeding the baby by the window, her dress down to her waist.

'That's the way with dolphins. They come up to a boat and let people swim with them – even ride on their backs – but they're wild creatures with minds of their own.'

Seumas sat on the edge of the bed, his hands clasped. He hadn't felt like this since the loss of màthair, but at least he had been with her at the end, holding her hand, hearing her last words: '*Coimhead às dèidh t' athar, a mhic.*' Look after your father, son.

He felt intense resentment now at this woman lying beside him who had pushed her way into his life. Leumadair wouldn't have deserted him if he had stayed by himself in the old house.

It was Thursday night and Alice would be sitting in her car in the layby along the road, waiting for him to take her down through the bracken, her spine against the old wall of the ruins of Socrachadh where the *crùisgean* lamp of the cleared had burned fish oil, where his sister had stood talking to the departed. He would go to Alice because there was comfort there.

But as he was rising from the bed as the baby's mouth was giving up the nipple he saw the fin in the bay. He ran down to the water's edge, waving his arms and calling, but the fin seemed stuck as if the creature was grounded. He came back to the mobile home and carried the tape recorder down to the shore, turning up the volume, sending the song across the bay as he accompanied on his mouth organ.

> '*Thug mi gaol duit 's chan fhaod mi àicheadh,*
> *Cha ghaol bliadhna is cha ghaol ràithe.*'

I gave you love and I can't deny it.
Not love that lasts a year, nor that lasts a season.

But the fin wasn't moving.

The baby in her arms, Feona was watching him as he set the recorder down on the shingle and waded out up to his waist. He placed a hand on the creature's back, stooping to study its eye because the old man had maintained that you could tell if an animal was healthy by the clarity of the eye. But this wasn't the friendly mischievous eye that watched him as Leumadair sped past the boat; its eye looked old and bleary, as if it belonged to a different dolphin. He came ashore again with heavy strides through the sea, not conscious of the cold.

'Leumadair's sick!' he called to Feona.

She laid the child in its cot, covering it and pulling on a cardigan against the evening chill as she came outside.

'Is there a mark on it? Could it have been hit by my father's boat?'

He waded out again, going down on his knees beside the inert dolphin, the shock of the cold driving the breath from him. He plunged his head under, salt making his eyes smart as he examined the long graceful body. There were old scars his fingers investigated, but no sign of a new wound from a propeller.

'What else makes a dolphin sick?' he shouted to Feona as he came to the surface, his hair streaming.

'I don't know!'

'But you *must* know. You've been writing a bloody thesis on them.'

'I don't cover what diseases they get.'

'Go and look up your books,' he ordered her.

He stayed with Leumadair, his body acclimatizing to the cold, his hand on its fin.

'I can't find anything about diseases!' Feona shouted from the shore. 'Maybe it's just old.'

The old man had kept going, hobbling round the corner of the house to the *taigh-beag*, dying on the ground he had been turning over for most of his life. But this creature which Seumas was now encircling with his arms looked ill, its eye dull. The tide was going out and he pleaded with it in Gaelic to go with it. He kept most of his body underwater, on his knees under the sea as he pushed his shoulder against the dolphin, forcing it out, but it didn't move. The tide had dropped to his thighs now, the creature's back out of the water.

'Keep Leumadair wet!' Feona called, and he went ashore for the plastic bucket, pouring the water over its dark back.

The moon was up now, shimmering on the bay, the tide round Seumas's knees. Leumadair's beak was out of the water, its eye closed. He was running ashore, into the house, straight to the cupboard, clawing the contents out on the stone floor until he found the bottle of Old Mull, with whisky still in it, that MacCallum had brought and which màthair had kept for emergencies, but which the old man hadn't had the benefit of on the day of his sudden death at the *taigh-beag*. He went back into the sea, pouring the whisky down the creature's throat as he jammed open its beak with his arm. Then he was on his knees, pushing with all his strength against Leumadair with the balls of his hands, pleading: '*A Dhia, na leig leis dol a dhìth,*' O God don't let him die, tears streaming down his face.

Then it was gone.

Twenty Seven

The launch had been criss-crossing the bay and running along the coast for an hour, but there was still no sign of Leumadair. It must be dead, the carcass washed up somewhere, Seumas was convinced as he turned the tiller and headed back. Then the sea heaved ahead and Leumadair came out, appearing to stand on its tail in the sky to show that it was well again, pacing the boat on the starboard side, leaping and somersaulting. When he caught the dolphin's eye he saw in it gratitude, affection, the old mischief. Had MacCallum's Old Mull whisky revived it?

He heard a roaring sound as the Brigadier's boat approached, twin screws churning the sea. Seumas headed it off to give the dolphin clear passage on the landward side. He motored into the harbour and went to the hotel. A man with a big plastic book was waiting for him, and they walked up the road to the cemetery.

'This is the lair,' Seumas showed him.

The old man was on top of màthair, as he was so often in life in the room across the landing, and the turf still hadn't knitted on the humped earth.

'I want a nice stone for my parents,' Seumas instructed the man.

They sat on a bench, the salesman turning the cellophane-sheathed pages of the book, showing him photographs of stones.

'That's a very popular one': he pointed to a black stone with gold lettering.

'I don't think it's their style.'

The salesman turned more pages.

'What do you do in granite?' Seumas enquired.

Pages were flipped to the section featuring granite stones, with a choice of black and gold lettering.

'What about that one?' Seumas asked, pointing to a small Celtic cross.

'It's dear because there's a lot of work in it,' he was warned.

'How much would it be?' the interested customer asked.

'One hundred and thirty. The lettering would be extra.'

'I'll take that one,' Seumas said decisively, sure that màthair would have liked it.

'It's a good-looking stone,' the salesman agreed. 'We could have it up in about a month.' He took out an order book. 'Tell me what inscription you want on it.'

'It'll all be Gaelic.'

'Oh,' the salesman said, bewildered.

'I'll write it out and send it to you.'

'I'll need a deposit.'

After Seumas counted off the money from the proceeds of fishing through Leumadair's help, they shook hands.

Feona was feeding the baby when he went into the mobile home.

'I've asked Mummy round for tea a week Thursday.'

'I don't want her here,' he said angrily.

'I told you, she's got nothing against you,' Feona said heatedly. 'We have to make peace, Seumas. It'll be good for Flòraidh, having a grandmother.'

Was she hinting that they should get married?

'We'll talk about it later,' Seumas said.

Holding his daughter and smelling her natural fragrance always calmed him down. When she cried he walked her up and down the passage, crooning a lullaby to her, lying on the bed beside her cot until she had fallen asleep.

There were flat seas and blue skies day after day, with queues on the pier for the Brigadier's boat, and with Leumadair leaping as if it had an endless supply of energy. Feona's thesis was nearing completion, though she still needed to make several trips out in the launch for more film to study, financed by her additional research grant.

'I'll let you read it when it's finished,' she promised.

'I'm not sure I'll understand it,' Seumas responded affectionately. 'I'd like to bring my sister here this Sunday to see Leumadair.'

'I didn't know you had a sister,' Feona said, surprised and interested.

Seumas explained that Eilidh had spent most of her life in the asylum.

'Why are you frowning? Don't you want her to come? It would mean a lot to her. I've had her here before to meet Leumadair, and she loved it.'

'What illness does she have?'

'I don't know,' Seumas said, shrugging. 'I don't know if they ever put a name to it for màthair.'

'I wonder if it's inherited,' Feona speculated, half to herself.

He knew what she meant, and it frightened him as he looked at their daughter.

'Yes, bring her,' Feona urged. 'We'll go in the Land Rover for her.'

This was a new acquisition, the previous vehicle wrecked in the bog from the frantic night of their daughter's birth.

Feona had made a stew and Eilidh cleared her plate with a piece of bread, then sucked her fingers. When they went outside she wanted to hold the baby, but the mother kept a hand on it. Seumas played the tape of *Fear a' Bhàta* and Leumadair came inshore. Eilidh left her plastic handbag on the *cladach*, hitching up her old-fashioned skirt to wade out to the dolphin, bending beside it and speaking to it in Gaelic as she stroked it.

'I need to go to the bathroom,' she announced.

'There's a toilet in the mobile home,' he told her. 'Unless you want to use the *taigh-beag*.'

He made himself a cigarette and finished it while waiting for her, and when she still hadn't appeared he checked the toilet in the mobile home and then knocked the rickety door of the *taigh-beag*, but she hadn't fallen asleep in it as she used to do as a child, when her mental illness began to manifest. As he searched around, calling for her, he noticed that the bracken concealing the track leading above the shore the quarter of a mile to Socrachadh had been trampled down. He ran along to the ruined settlement and found his sister sitting in the ruined house she used to go to instead of school.

'I'm talking to Flòraidh.'

'We have to get back, Eilidh.'

'I'm not leaving Flòraidh.'

'We'll take her with us, Eilidh.'

They swung the invisible being, who would always be a child, between them through the bracken, back to the house. Feona drove them to the ferry, with Eilidh sitting in the back.

'We've left Flòraidh behind!'

'No, Flòraidh is beside you in her carrycot,' Feona said over her shoulder.

'No, no, the other Flòraidh,' Eilidh said, becoming more agitated.

'What was she meaning about the other Flòraidh?' Feona asked on the drive home, when she had collected him from the ferry after he had delivered his sister back to the asylum.

'She gets mixed up,' he said. He couldn't tell her that their daughter was named after a ghost.

It's so sad about Eilidh,' Feona sighed, 'though I suppose she's better off where she is.'

'If we could buy the croft and do it up she could stay in the mobile home,' Seumas suggested.

'It wouldn't work,' Feona said as she overtook a vehicle. 'Incidentally, Seumas, it seems a bit unfair you bringing your sister home, but not welcoming Mummy here.'

'My sister didn't make trouble.'

'Neither did Mummy. I keep telling you, it was my father. I told you already, Mummy's coming here on Thursday.'

'I won't be in,' he said as the Land Rover turned down the track, his daughter bouncing on his knee.

On the balmy Thursday evening he stood on *Blàr Cathaich*, the hill where the blackcocks fought till they were bloodied, even blinded. He watched Feona's mother making her way through the bogs in her checked body-warmer and matching hat like a man's, a haversack over one shoulder.

He went to meet Alice in the layby, and they went down to the ruins of the settlement. She was wearing a flimsy summer dress which she lifted over her head and threw over the precarious wall.

'What's wrong?' Seumas asked when he was sitting beside her on the fallen lintel, smoking, at peace as he listened to the birds on the moor, the insubstantial window on the hazy sea.

'We should run away,' Alice told him, moving restlessly among the ruins. 'I'm sick of this place. I want out of it, to do something with my life before it's too late. I'd like to be a mature student and study something.'

'What about Tommy and the girls?'

'They've been coping for years. And it's time you were away from her. She's not the woman for you. It's a betrayal of your Gaelic heritage.'

'I'm a father,' Seumas reminded her. 'I couldn't give my daughter up.' He stood up. 'It's got to stop, Alice. It's wrong. I won't be coming here again.'

'So she's got her claws into you,' Alice said bitterly. 'You'll regret it,' she added, gathering up her cardigan and handbag. 'I'll tell you this, though: you'll be back here looking for me before long.'

The next Sunday was one of the hottest days Seumas had ever known. Feona was walking naked in the shallows, carrying the naked baby.

'There's Leumadair!' he called.

The fin was coming inshore.

'Hold Flòraidh; I want to do something,' Feona told him, running up to the mobile home. When she emerged with a pair of flippers and a snorkel she entered the sea. He stood with the baby, watching the black air tube bobbing. Her head broke surface and she pushed up her goggles.

'I've examined its lower stomach. A male dolphin has two slits: one slit contains the penis and the other the anus. Female dolphins have only one slit, which contains the vagina as well as the anus. Leumadair's a male. I needed to know that for my thesis.'

'What difference does it make?' Seumas asked uneasily.

'It makes a lot of difference. Bring Flòraidh in to meet him.'

Seumas waded in and Feona took the baby's hand, holding it against Leumadair's back, though he was nervous because it was a wild animal, the male dolphin's eye watching him.

'I'm going to swim with him,' she told him.

She sat on the dolphin, sliding her naked body up and down his back.

'You'll hurt him.'

'Nonsense, he likes human contact. Why do you think he's been coming to your boat for all those months?'

Feona was rolling naked with the animal in the green water, his beak nuzzling her breasts.

'Don't let him do that!' he shouted.

Why not?'

As the woman and the animal were rolling again Seumas noticed something protruding from Leumadair, as if a blade was stuck in his belly.

'What's that?' he pointed.

'It's his penis! 'He's got an erection!'

Seumas felt faint as he stood in the sea with the baby, his mind churning with the thought that the creature could have penetrated her as they were playing.

'Come out now!' he ordered Feona.

He was in a strange state like a sleepwalker as they went up into the stifling heat of the mobile home. He took off his clothes while Feona laid the naked baby in her cot. She pulled him down on to the bed, rolling on top of him, pumping him into her.

He woke in the moonlight and left the mobile home, unable to sleep because of restlessness. He went into the old house and lit the lamp, having a strong feeling of the presence of the old man and màthair, as if he were a boy again, waiting for MacCallum. He took màthair's lined writing pad out of the drawer, starting to print out the Gaelic inscription for his parents' gravestone. It was amazing how easily writing Gaelic came back to him, as if the schoolmaster's fluent hand was guiding his from beyond the grave.

When he was satisfied that his grammar was correct he put the inscription into an envelope, addressing it to the stonemason, and taking it back to the mobile home with him. But he still couldn't sleep, and heard the distressed call of the *learga dhubh* on the solitary lochan on the moor as the drought dried up the water supply near her nest. The bird would die rather than leave her eggs.

The next morning the postman brought a letter over the hill, informing him that the estate had decided not to oppose his application to buy the croft, and that a fair price was being fixed in accordance with crofting law. He showed the letter to Feona.

'I'm certain Mummy's had a hand in it,' she surmised. 'So there's nothing to worry about now. You're making money from the fish Leumadair's helping you to catch, and I've got Granny's legacy. We can buy the house and get it done up for the winter. We can apply for an improvement grant. I think we should use the same architect my parents employed for the old schoolhouse.'

When her mother came that afternoon with gifts for the baby Seumas hugged her.

Next morning Seumas couldn't find Leumadair on the way out. The Brigadier's boat was following him with the owner himself at the big wheel, in his gold-braided nautical cap, pushing the chromium levers for more power. The twin screws were churning up the sea as the boat came alongside Seumas's launch.

Then Leumadair leapt, spectacularly, before he flopped over, entering the sea again, only to rise again, this time on Seumas's starboard side. The other boat was approaching to let the passengers get pictures.

'You're too close!' Seumas was shouting to the Brigadier.

Its bow was swinging round, forcing him to yield, but he didn't want to yield. He was turning the wheel to force the other boat out to sea, when he caught Leumadair's anxious eye as he sped forward to get clear of the two bows. Seumas slowed down, letting the other boat go on ahead.   When the dolphin leapt he turned the bow for his home bay.

Màthair always knew when someone was going to call, a gift she had brought from her island, and which had been in her family for generations. Her mother had announced one night in December at the supper table: 'Your father will be home tomorrow for Christmas.'

'Did you have a letter, mammy?' one of the seven children asked excitedly.

'No, Effie, I didn't. But I know he'll walk through that door tomorrow. His kilt will be in tatters because he's been in a long battle in France, but he's survived, not like the thousands of other poor souls who are in their graves over there, when they belong here.'

The next afternoon the Seaforth Highlander was seen coming over the hill in his holed kilt, and he tumbled out on to the table the contents of his haversack, wooden toys that his comrades, some of them now under crude crosses on the Somme, had carved in the trenches.

Seumas sensed, not that someone was going to come across the moor, but that an exceptional shoal of fish would be driven into the shallows by Leumadair within the hour, so he took out the net and went down to the shore. He filled six buckets from the sea trout flapping against his wellingtons, and as he carried the catch that hadn't even required him to cast his nest, he saw the fin ten yards from the shore, and it came to him that the dolphin was like Dìleas, driving shoals instead of flocks.

'My God, man, it's like the loaves and fishes in the Bible,' Donnie said as Seumas carried in the four packed fish boxes. 'I don't know if we'll have room in the freezer for all of them. You'll never guess who was in for dinner last night: Miss Maclaren.'

'She must be some age,' Seumas said.

'She's worn very well. She retired to Skye, where she came from, and was visiting friends. She said to me: I'm not surprised to find you the proprietor of the hotel, Donnie, I always thought you were smart. She told me something about MacCallum I never knew. He was a Captain in the army and won the Military Cross at El Alamein for bravery. He never mentioned it in school, but he must have been tough. That's why he gave me such a belting the day I had a feel at Heather Macgregor – not that she minded.'

Seumas didn't tell his best friend that MacCallum had been a frequent visitor to their house, and that he had gifted him the mouth organ which he had been given by a captured German soldier in North Africa. But he didn't know that the schoolmaster had won the Military Cross, and it was doubtful if the old man had known because MacCallum was a modest man, not only about his knowledge of Gaelic, but also about his achievement in getting to university from his poor background on Mull.

As he was leaving the harbour in the launch Seumas saw the Brigadier's boat waiting for its next passengers in an hour's time.

He opened the throttle full, and, rounding Rubha nan Ròn, saw Leumadair ahead, waiting for him. He slowed down and shut off the engine. He leaned over, touching the creature's head. The dolphin was watching him, anticipation as well as affection in its unclouded eye.

'Time for you to move on for your own good, friend,' Seumas told him in Gaelic, leaning over to stroke the glistening back.

The dolphin plunged, shooting up twenty yards ahead, and Seumas had to open the throttle to its maximum to keep up with him. Behind he could hear the approaching roar of the Brigadier's boat as the dolphin was bucking and plunging ahead.

Seumas knew that if he followed Leumadair much further, he would be out of fuel. Then he noticed a grey shape accompanying him on starboard. It couldn't be Leumadair, because he was well out of the water ahead. Seumas turned to port, to see another dolphin pacing the launch. Now there were two more on either side. Was one of them a female? As he slowed down the pod of dolphins were leaping out to sea, perhaps to turn westwards, towards the fabled land of *Tìr nan Òg*, Gaelic paradise of the ever-young.

He pressed the button on the tape recorder he carried in the launch. There were tears in his eyes as the song rang out over the sea.

> *'Fhir a' bhàta na hò ro èile,*
> *Fhir a' bhàta na hò ro èile;*
> *Fhir a' bhàta na hò ro èile,*
> *Mo shoraidh slàn leat 's gach àit' an tèid thu.'*

> Boatman, ho ro eile,
> Boatman, ho ro eile;
> Boatman, ho ro eile,
> Farewell, and may you keep well in every place you go.

On his way back he passed the Brigadier's boat, giving him two fingers.

Feona was sitting on a tartan rug on the shingle with the baby beside her when he came into the bay.

'I've finished my thesis!' she called. 'I've dedicated it to you. Is there something wrong?'

'Leumadair's away with other dolphins.'

'I'm sorry, but that's the way it should be, Seumas. Dolphins are like people: they need each other's company.'

He went into the house and sat in the old man's chair by the grate full of ashes. Had he driven Leumadair away for his own safety, or had the wise creature decided that it was time to go, knowing through their aquatic calls that there were other male dolphins, and perhaps females also, waiting out at sea for him to join them? The largest catch of Seumas's life which Leumadair had driven inshore must have been his final gift. Even if there weren't any more catches to give him a living, Feona had money to buy the croft and to keep them going. He had read about oyster farming and would try that in the bay. If that didn't work he would find something else to support his wife and daughter.

He picked up the pipe that the old man had been smoking before he went out to the *taigh-beag* for the last time. He removed the punctured metal cap from the pipe, then sprang the blade of the old man's clasp knife and began to ream the carbon from the narrow bowl. The tobacco in the golden foil was brittle as he stuffed it into the bowl and struck a light on the grate that màthair had kept alight all those years.

'I know how sad you are about Leumadair,' Feona said, standing on the step in the sunlight with the baby in her arms.

He had a flame in the bowl of the pipe now, and put the metal cap back on, resting his head against the back of the chair, sweet smoke in his mouth, the lamp with its fragile mantle on the table where MacCallum had sat with him, teaching him to write Gaelic. He felt that he was fit now to fill the old man's chair.

'I was speaking to Donnie this morning,' he told Feona. 'He says there are houses for the handicapped going up in the town. I'm going to try and get one for Eilidh and I'm going to start teaching you Gaelic so that you won't feel left out when the wee girl starts speaking it. Mr. MacCallum taught me to read and write Gaelic because he said that it could be useful to me one day. Maybe I could teach it at night school in the town.'

'I'll be your first pupil, darling.'

www.ingramcontent.com/pod-product-compliance
Lightning Source LLC
Chambersburg PA
CBHW051553030726
47592CB00001B/262